Marbot

Marbot

A BIOGRAPHY

Wolfgang Hildesheimer

TRANSLATED FROM THE GERMAN BY
Patricia Crampton

J. M. Dent & Sons Ltd
London & Melbourne

First published in Great Britain 1983 by J. M. Dent & Sons Ltd

English translation copyright © 1983 Patricia Crampton

Originally published in German, copyright © 1981 by
Suhrkamp Verlag, Frankfurt am Main, under the title *Marbot*

Printed in Great Britain by Biddles Ltd, Guildford, Surrey
for J. M. Dent & Sons Ltd
Aldine House, 33 Welbeck Street, London W1M 8LX

British Library Cataloguing in Publication Data

Hildesheimer, Wolfgang
  Marbot.
  I.Title
  833'.914[F]   PT2617.1354
  ISBN 0-460-04576-8

Acknowledgments

The author would like to thank the following for their help with this book:

Silvia; Walter Jens; Christiaan Hart-Nibbrig; Peter Horst Neumann.

Also Bepe Bevilacqua; Elisabeth Bott-Simmen; Inge Hacker; Christopher Holme; Ludger Honnefelder; Christoph Jörg; Rüdiger Klessmann; Ann Leiser; Evi Levin; Walter Levin; Felix v. Mendelssohn; Herman Meyer; Julian Oxford; Fritz Raddatz; Klaus Reichert; Frans van Rossum; Gisela van Rossum; Ursula Vogt; Gert Westphal.

The translator would like to thank Sue Boddington, for her tireless pursuit of rare reference books, and Paul Falla, for the generosity of his erudition.

For Silvia

"If I am to lend credence to the myth, your Excellency," said the 24 year-old Sir Andrew Marbot to Goethe, who had been enquiring as to the origin of his surname, "my family came from Périgord and arrived in England in the train of the Norman Conquest." "Well," said Goethe, "one cannot of course believe the letter of the myth, since it is true only in a higher sense. It is not myths that shape tradition, but tradition that incessantly reshapes myths. But what is it, my young friend, that inclines you to the belief that this is myth? The explanation seems to me very credible." "I distrust all tradition, your Excellency," said Marbot, "whether probable or not. To me the true alone is true, the probable no more than make-believe." "Not bad, my young friend," said Goethe, with evident amusement, and turning to Privy Councillor Schultz, who was present when this exchange took place on 4th July 1825, "it seems to me that we are in the presence not merely of a doubter, but of a rebel."

It was this same Prussian Privy Councillor who recorded the conversation in a letter to his wife. Goethe, he wrote, had displayed a lively interest in this tall, dark-haired young Englishman, who by the way spoke perfect German, and had questioned him further:

"Which member of the family, he wish'd to know, had first been ennobled? An ancestor, the young man explained, had placed a hundred infantrymen at James I's disposal in the Irish war, for which the King had created him baronet. 'Is that also myth?' asked Goethe. 'No, your Excellency, that is history.' 'An honourable history!' said Goethe. 'Well, your Excellency,' the Englishman retorted, 'the title was worth more to him than his fellow Catholics in Ireland.' 'You are a scoffer,' said Goethe, now, as it seem'd to me, a little vexed, and I judg'd that the subject no long interested him."

Thus Councillor Schultz

But the subject seemed to have lost its attraction, if indeed it had ever had any, for Marbot too. "The Marbot Myth", as he called it, had never engaged his speculations, he had never tried to do justice to his father's family. It is no doubt true that the family had come from France at the time of the Norman Conquest and this version of its ennoblement is probably equally true. It may, of course, be seen as a dubious transaction, a failure of loyalty to a religious community, but there is another way of looking at it: the few Catholic landowners in England deemed it expedient to display un- qualified conformity, in order to redeem the reputation of a minority, many of whom may well have been sympathizers with the Irish cause. That would be the historian's reading; Marbot was not at all interested in interpreting his family history.

Although it was certainly not customary for two visitors to address each other in Goethe's presence, Schultz, as he writes, was unable to restrain himself

"from asking the young Englishman where he might have learn'd his German. He turned to me, almost as if he had been expecting the question and said: 'I learn'd it from my tutor, who speaks several lan- guages, and to whom I owe all that I can do, if not all that I know.' This sounded to me as full of purpose

2

and rare fervour as if he had intended to imply by it that he owed nothing to his parents. But to ask more would have been to profane the place we were in."

We cannot judge whether this final comment was intended to be ironic, but probably not: Goethe and the effect of his personality provoked none but serious comment. But we are astonished by Marbot's sudden, almost violent communicativeness, since we know him as somewhat taciturn, if not reticent. On the other hand, we find it difficult to imagine that Schultz invented this spasm of eloquence, especially since what he said corresponds precisely with the truth as we know it. We accordingly accept, albeit with some hesitation, the episode as it has been handed down to us.

"...owed his parents nothing"? What Marbot owed to his mother we shall discover, since it is the subject of this book. It was true that he owed his father little but the fact of his existence, if we overlook the antagonism to him which set in motion that psychological apparatus which in no small degree determined his reactions and his thinking. It can certainly not have been easy to live a life of the intellect in the remoteness of Northumberland, where the family had resided since the sixteenth century at least, even if any member of the family had felt the inclination to do so. But there is no evidence of any such inclination, except for a quite well-endowed library, probably assembled by Andrew's grandfather Sir Anthony Marbot, who had travelled in France and Italy. Andrew, no doubt unfairly biased in his reluctance to spare a good word for his paternal family, insisted that throughout his childhood the Bible in the library had lain open at Matthew 24:45-51, the parable of the faithful and unfaithful servants, that this was the only open book he had even seen in his father's vicinity and that the only evidence that his father read at all was that he often quoted from a book entitled *The Complete Hunter*

3

(a translation of Hans Friedrich von Flemming's book *Der vollkommene teutsche Jäger und Fischer*, first published in 1709). This too must have been a considerable exaggeration. Andrew rejected his father, Sir Francis, at an early age, as an authority, as a source of commands and prohibitions, and unconsciously as a rival in his mother's favour, which he in fact was not, but as which the boy inevitably saw him. Andrew's remarks to Councillor Schultz must therefore be seen as a disguised outburst of deferred emotion, misplaced, perhaps, and scarcely in harmony with his general bearing, yet totally consistent as the symptom of a troubled relationship.

Marbot did not report on this first part of the conversation with Goethe. In a letter to Father Gerard van Rossum, that same highly-esteemed former tutor, he wrote in detail about the affable, if somewhat patronizing way in which he had been received, but his account begins at the point where Councillor Schultz stops, indicating that Goethe had changed the subject. In fact, the poet had asked Andrew to read to him from the English version of *Faust*, Part I, which had just been sent to him by his translator, Francis Leveson Gower. Marbot acceded, if reluctantly, to his request. He writes to van Rossum (in German):

> "After all, I had not come in order to discuss the possibilities of disseminating the works of this great man in my own country, but in order to partake of his greatness. He did in fact seem to me greater than his works, or at least those of them that I know. He has the inner radiance of a man in whom the forces of nature are concentrated at their noblest and whom they have selected above all other mortals to mediate between themselves and men. He is more aware than we are, although he may perhaps misinterpret many phenomena. He is wrong in much, but

4

he is not contradicted, for there is much that appears in a new light when he says it. He is a work of art, but perhaps one may wonder whether a work of art produces works of art? And are we capable of judging, without measuring them against the man who created them? His condescension is perfectly natural, he knows his own greatness, but if such a man were modest we would regard it as an intolerable error of judgment, as downright affectation. One of the notable signs of his greatness is that he never speaks of himself. He speaks about all things, is in all things, and when he speaks of all things he is speaking of himself."

Letters in this vein, generally addressed to Father Gerard or to his mother, are evidence of the profound insight into people which engrossed Marbot, an extraordinarily subtle judgment, the criteria for which he acquired in increasing measure and which, as far as we know, had not existed before him. Here, then, is a young man of twenty-four, sketching the portrait of a great figure whom he has only just met. No one else has said anything of the kind about the effect Goethe produced. Admittedly at this period Andrew was already quite used to consorting with important people He had argued with Schopenhauer in Florence, been involved in and severely critical of Byron's life in Pisa, visited William Blake a number of times in London and sat at table with Wordsworth at Redmond Manor. He had taught himself to weigh people up, especially those who were highly gifted creatively, to analyse their outward behaviour and to examine it for symptoms of their inner life, because that was the essential part of the task he had set himself. His judgment was not free from error—how could it have been!—and yet we find it most often confirmed, since it was based on a deeply-rooted talent for perception, a rare receptive flexibility, and not least on the capacity for

5

experience of a spirit which, being itself agitated, observed every agitation, every excitement, indeed, as we shall see, every flicker in the mind of his interlocutor. So even at the time of his visit to Goethe, Marbot was a recorder who could not be dazzled, whose judgment was not swayed by appearances, and no illusory glitter had ever blurred the brightness of his intellect.

Marbot also wrote to his mother about the visit to Goethe, in English of course, and, bearing in mind the distance between his immediate experience and her potential reliving of that experience, almost didactically. Goethe was not as familiar to her as to the priest, who had indeed read *Egmont* and *Faust*, Part I, with his pupil.

> "...he asked me to read aloud to him. I did so and felt myself observed by a judge as infallible as God, and as inhuman."

So the comments on Goethe's attitude are more critical and implacable here, with an odd trace of rejection about them. Here Andrew is not trying to be objective but to describe the reactions of his own psyche to someone who knew him better than anyone else.

> "...Goethe nourishes a flame in his bosom which seems to incend him strongly but leaves the visitor cold, if not chilly."

But his main criticism is reserved for Goethe's understanding of art.

> "Goethe knows what art should be like but not what it is. He therefore seldom finds his ideal conceptions realized, but were he to find them, it would be a lesser art."

This almost sounds as if Marbot were absolutely sure of his own infallibility, yet if we read him in context, this impression gives way to that of a profound and imperturbable conviction, which, I venture to say, is reproduced in the reader. From his notes:

"The reason why Goethe's appreciation of art is so fallible is that it is founded on a mistaken approach. When he writes or speaks of pictures he is referring more often than not to engravings *after* the paintings, in other words, to works made by another and naturally inferior artist, though with the greatest possible accuracy and empathy [probably the first time the word was ever used] from the works of the painter in question. These confer some idea of the compostion, which they follow with minute accuracy—although the generally reduced format of the print must produce a misleading effect in the quality of the dimensions, *for every painting has a size which corresponds to its conception and loses by its alteration*—yet they give no idea of the colour to which every painting owes its inner life, nor of the handling of the brush, the artist's signature, in which his soul and its relationship to the subject of the picture are revealed. The interpretation of a painting has as little and as much to do with the interpretation of its subject as the character in a play with that of the dramatist who invented him; the relationship is constantly changing. But if we compare an original engraving with the engraving after a painting, we have the difference between a human being and an effigy, if not exactly a corpse."

Here we have Marbot in his element, and his story is the story of that element: the work of art as the dictate of the unconscious impulses of its creator. He tried, as none before and few after him have tried, to feel his way towards these impulses, without, of course, any certainty which could supply proof that he had succeeded, and yet with a methodical system

7

for which he had first to forge the instruments, always mindful of possible failure, but with increasing and convincing self-confidence. "Après le génie, ce qu'il y a de plus semblable à lui, c'est la puissance de la connaître et de l'admirer." (The nearest thing to genius itself is the gift of recognizing and admiring it.) This astonishing statement by Madame de Staël might have been inspired by Marbot.

His slim oeuvre only appears to earn that decided assessment of almost infallible *arbiter artium*, which Frederic Hadley-Chase claimed for him in his biography *Sir Andrew Marbot* (1888). A far wider range of his writings will shortly be available—it is probably no longer feasible to present the complete works—and their reader will observe that they are unfinished, notes of stages in the process of discovering what it is that moves and actuates the creative genius, its pressures and repressions. He had no thought of transcending the bounds of empirical deduction here. His aim was less that of a scientific approach than of its preliminary stage of normative cognition, the outline of a universal typology. Marbot was constantly trying to devise objective yardsticks, although he knew the attempt was vain. "The word taste belongs to the dining-room, it is out of place in the appreciation of art."

If we then contemplate Marbot's life—or, more circumspectly, those aspects which are known to us—a picture emerges of a subjective self-sufficiency, and its objective consequences, such as one rarely sees: the case of a categorical nay-sayer in Schopenhauer's sense, in whom art alone commanded a Yea within the Nay, and who worked all his life at that response.

Goethe himself seems to have been singularly impressed by this encounter. Even when Councillor Schultz visited him six years later in July 1831, when he was eighty-one, he

8

spoke of the "curious, quiet resolution of the mysterious young Englishman that day. There was almost something like defiance in him." Goethe did not know that the young Englishmen was by then dead. He had also wanted to have him, like all his memorable guests, drawn by Johann Joseph Schmeller, which never in fact happened. Probably Marbot had refused, with "quiet resolution", because he mistrusted the artistic sense of the man whom he otherwise, however ambivalently, revered, and hence also his choice of artist.

Goethe's comment to Johann Heinrich Meyer (1826),"...this young man had already dug too deeply into his inner being to be able to build a happy future on it", is prophetic, especially when we remember that it concerned a man of twenty-four who was to live for only a few more years, because he did not wish to live any longer. And still more uncanny, especially in context, is Goethe's comment to Eckermann in December 1825, after a strenuous summer, crammed with visits:

"...After all, one does not want to be hollow and commonplace, but to say something seemly and appropriate. Now, however, I am gradually becoming free and feel inclined for conversation once again. One which gave me particular pleasure was my conversation with that young Englishman. What a singular person! He spoke as earnestly as if he were weighing every word, and yet, if one observes him speaking, one feels that he does not mean it quite so seriously, indeed that he does not take himself so very seriously. He seemed to me incapable of enthusiasm about anything. No naivety, though it well becomes a young man. A quiet audacity, a resolution to realize himself, even if that realization consists in idleness."

These words may remind one of Büchner's Leonce, of

9

whom Lena says after their first meeting: "He was so old under his blond locks. Spring on his cheeks and winter in his heart. That is sad." In fact at first sight there is a hint in Marbot of Leonce, in the comeliness of his melancholy, the ironic reserve with which he bore himself. But the fact was that Marbot never trifled with his sombre disposition, it was never a matter for self-indulgence or play-acting. Also, as a genuine melancholic, he would never have applied the word "melancholy" to himself.

Marbot must certainly have appeared to Goethe—and presumably to most of those he met—as an idler. To that there is only one answer: almost everyone of his social class—and not only in England—was an idler. The primary function of a gentleman was that, not being obliged to practise a profession, he could live according to his inclinations. Marbot did this too, strictly speaking, but he followed his inclinations with dedication and consistency because they were directed towards producing a result. Yet he would never have been able or willing to explain his "special field". His discipline had not existed before himself, he had constructed it, and as time was to show, not only for himself but also for the psychoanalytical branch of aesthetics. Criticism in his sense did not yet exist, and a criticism whose premise was an enquiry into the purpose of human life existed only in Schopenhauer, whom Marbot read only in his last years. His negative answer to the world was his expression of the constantly accumulating sum of his personal experience.

It is not the aim of this biography to give a moral assessment of Marbot's negative answer to the world; its aim is to seek out the motives which gave rise to that answer and the psychological situation which made it possible, or, if you like, necessary. We can scarcely refuse to admire this strange phenomenon—if I may speak of "us" as reasonably experienced readers and spectators of art. He himself, always the potential accused, referred to the idler within him. He wrote in 1826 in a letter to his mother from Urbino:

"I am privileged, and I know it. My life consists of attempts to conceal this fact from myself, but the attempt is vain. A man who has to work is cut from a different cloth and an artist the more so, for he works from an impulse external to his will and his control. If I were one of these, then I would be truly privileged and all idleness would be foreign to me..."

He saw himself clearly. That means that he saw others clearly too. After reading no more than a single sentence from his notes, Goethe—and everyone else—would have ceased to surmise that he was idle.

The supreme purpose of Marbot's life is contained in his suicide. It was the only right action for him. He left the world when he considered that the register of his receptivity and potentialities was exhausted, and foresaw a future full of necessary repetition: the gift of creation had been painfully denied him and for that very reason he was forced to regard his attempt to comprehend it in others as doomed. He regarded as applicable to himself something that Delacroix later wrote in his diary:

"Most books about art are written by poeple who are not artists; hence all the mistaken ideas..."

Not that at the end Marbot regarded his ideas as wrong—they were not—but they were no more than ideas about a sphere whose ultimate recesses were closed to him. He had come as close to the soul of creativity as a non-creative person can, but without achieving his desire to possess himself of that soul and thus give a purpose to his life. He had described artistic activity as a "vital pastime", as

"...a more or less foredoomed attempt to delude

11

oneself into forgetting the senselessness of life. We thirst after this delusion and are only too ready to submerge ourselves in its enjoyment by identifying ourselves with those who bestow it on us."

As we have seen, the "Marbot myth" did not pass into history until the time of the Irish wars and even then only at a modest, local level; it remained, as it were, privy to the county. London was a long way off and for Catholics who were forbidden connections with the court of the day, further still; they had, in the literal sense of the word, no business there. And Catholics the Marbots remained, astonishingly stalwart in their faith. It was their pride that they had always defied persecution, regardless of life and property. This at least is probably a myth: Andrew's version suggests that in the north of England they had in fact been fairly safe from persecution after the Jacobite risings were over; this assertion can scarcely be disputed.

Marbot Hall, built by the first baronet, Sir Thomas Marbot, born in 1568, to celebrate and demonstrate his elevation to the baronetage, and extended by the second baronet, Sir Robert, in order to display this rank in fitting manner, is still standing—the property of the National Trust —as converted by Sir Roger Pratt in 1650: a stately manor, something between an English country house and a mansion, in the continental style, distantly yet distinctly reminiscent of Palladio; not grand—the Marbots never lived beyond their means—but at the upper end of what was proper to their station of life. In Andrew's youth the house had plenty of room for the members of the family, ultimately five in number, about three times as many servants, mostly male, and a handful of house-guests, whose personal servants probably shared rooms with the domestic staff, in the customary way. The chaplain lived outside the manor, next to the chapel, the steward had his own house, coachman, groom and stableboy lived over the stables, the gardener in his cottage across the park. An autonomous household—the nearest village was nine miles away—a miniature state, in fact.

I am well aware that to record matters of secondary importance in such detail would be more appropriate to some figure other than an art connoisseur whose output was slender and of whom few people know very much. I offer the reader two reasons. Firstly, the decisive part of the Marbot drama— the active part—took place here, in Marbot Hall; the dramatis personae, Marbot and his mother, are the sole—and solitary— actors, but they were not alone on their stage, although they may have wished they were. The servants were there, the non-speaking parts, with whose potential and hostile participation as antagonists the two chief actors undoubtedly had to reckon, in the event of either choosing to speak. As things turned out, however, they apparently not only remained silent, but, as far as the action of the drama is concerned, deaf and blind as well. Two of them certainly were not so in reality, however: Lady Catherine's personal maid, Susan Williams, and, in so far as one can call him a servant, the steward, William Crompton. With their extreme devotion—and we are dealing with extremes—to their mistress, they played out their silent roles consistently, thus becoming the contrapuntal actors in the drama. The others remain in the background, but this background had to be indicated.

The second reason for all this detail is a didactic one, although of course it comes too late here to set a precedent. I want to emphasize an element which I have missed in most biographies, and not only in biographies but in diaries and travel journals: the description of everyday affairs, of matters unworthy of high-flown speech, or assumed to be already known and not worth communicating at the time, but whose importance as a contribution to the historical picture increases as the years and above all the centuries go by. The daily round, as action illustrated by concrete things: the props for days of work and days of travel; the physical preparations for day and night, the care of the body which is always passed over in favour of the care of souls—for instance, who washed when, if at all?—the games of leisure hours, the food and wine at meals, the premises and conveniences, the furnishings; the countless unmentioned characters without whom those who are mentioned would have been unable to appear in their roles as leading actors, as commentators and partners of the diarist.

At the start of his *Italian Journey* Goethe reports from Torbole on 12 September 1786 that the windows of his inn were sealed with oil-paper instead of glass: adding to our picture of peripheral civilizing development. He relates that the doors have no keys: revealing the state of trust and its justification in that time and place. The innkeeper assured him that nothing would happen to him, even if everything he had with him were made of diamonds. He would scarcely have lied, since he would have had to back up the claim. And the third point Goethe thought worth remarking on:

"...a most necessary convenience is lacking, so that here one comes quite close to the state of nature. When I asked the serving-boy for a certain place, he pointed to the courtyard. 'Qui abasso può servirsi!' 'Dove?' I asked. 'Da per tutto, dove vuol!' he answered cheerfully."

This is the only episode of its kind in the *Italian Journey* and after this promising titbit we find nothing to match it; the traveller must surely have come close to the "state of nature" several times thereafter. We miss these details in all the travel diaries of every age. We have to embark on a laborious search for information on the vegetative side of life; without it we lack the physical underpinning for the psychology. Is there anyone, on a guided tour of some castle or stately home of the past, who has not wanted to peep behind the scenes before which events fit for the drawing-room and hence for the history books took place? Not only into the rooms where the domestic servants kicked their heels when they were not needed, but also into those secret places which served the personal arrangements and requirements of their masters! The cultural establishment is exercising the desire for prettification which we find in the biographies, but which is only pretended; it is actually prudery performing a disservice to posterity. It means that even prosaic matters become a kind of history of ideas, a subject for speculation, just where a particular and important area could have been opened up.

The life of Andrew Marbot is certainly not going to be used as a pretext for discussing the history of civilization. It is simply that I feel an indication of method is called for, where the model biography could, so to speak, expand the picture of its subject with practical details.

II

Marbot Hall lies in the north of Northumberland, between Otterburn and Falstone, a few miles south of the Scottish border, among sheep pastures which stretch to the horizon in all directions in soft, almost regular waves, broken up into rhythmic rows, some of them criss-crossed by tree borders, mostly sycamore and elm, or by tree-fringed streams or perhaps simply by low, wooden boundary fences, to be jumped by a rider, but not by sheep. Here and there the lines of trees spread out, take in a few beeches and oaks and form a straggling copse, a green space through which the wind blows,

15

in which every raindrop echoes and the mists perform grey shadow-plays. And sheep everywhere, as if scooped from a plentiful store and sprinkled generously across the broad fields, in flocks or groups or singly; one glance round the landscape takes in thousands of animals; they inch forward, grazing, in all directions, staring into the distance now and then as they crunch and chew, as though for reassurance, or they settle under the trees or in the shadow of the copses: an idyllic view, as if from a northern myth, lacking only the piping shepherd leaning against a tree. In the distance, towards the skyline, the woolly bodies turn into white accents between the light green and the dark and grey-green patches of pasturage, sparse to all appearances, but making the livestock fat. It is a landscape of absolute tranquillity, a horizontal without vertical exclamation marks, in which even the park surrounding Marbot Hall seems from a distance to be nothing more than a chance, if quite extensive concentration of the general stock of trees and it is only on coming closer that one sees that it is enriched by yew trees, birches, horse chestnuts and white poplars. The park does in fact appear more natural than planned, since only the immediate vicinity of the buildings displays systematic compression into a deliberately designed garden. Evidently the Marbot menfolk went into action only at the point where nature, no longer tamed into manorial decorum, became usable in its raw state, to the livestock as fodder and to the hunt as enjoyment. The park grounds were no more than an agreeable framework and a social requirement.

In his later years Andrew Marbot never deliberately sought out the spaciousness of that landscape, but neither did he ever completely escape from it. It remained the unconscious contrapuntal accompaniment to those scenic prospects of acknowledged grandeur which he saw on his travels, at least those on which he commented. In contrast to the Romantics, who confronted the rugged mountain ranges as a challenge to their imaginative powers and made them into an atmospheric ideal—the monument of nature, revealing man's nothingness to himself—Andrew regarded the mountains as "wrinkles in the skin of the ageing earth", with astonishment, yes, and a certain respect for the tectonic arbitrariness of creation, in which, however, he never felt at home. Forewarned to some extend by Goethe, Byron or Wordsworth, he felt himself faced with having to test his sentiments, listen with an inward ear, so to speak, to find out whether the receptive soul would speak out in the presence of this beauty so abundantly documented by others. The results of the test were not completely negative, but were still tinged with scepticism. "What can be the state," he wrote to Gerard van Rossum in 1825,

> "of those who, faced with these towering masses and strata, this petrified primeval catastrophe, fall into euphoric mood, indeed into a state of creative bliss? How can I accept that a panorama crowned with snow-capped peaks must be regarded as objectively beautiful, when it impedes the freedom of my view and positively compels my thoughts to return within myself instead of roving abroad?"

Here then is the unconscious attachment to the open spaces of Northumberland. However, these thoughts appear a little unconsidered. Perhaps they are affected by emotion, possibly caused by the reduced state in which the illness from which he had only just recovered at the time of writing, in 1825, had left him. The landscape theme recurs frequently in his notes, always as an attempt to objectivize, seeking to eliminate the observing self, and generally measured against and exemplified by the creative artist.

> "Landscape arises in the soul of him in whom it releases emotions. He to whom it means nothing has no image of it. It has no beauty in itself but is rather

17

the object of the subjective will for beauty; of the longing of him who feels it as an ideal, for a life lived within that ideal, or of the pain engendered by the feeling of unattainability. But the artist who seeks to enthral such emotions in his painting must fail, because the objective value of the subject is extinguished by its representation, the landscape becomes a stage setting for the drama of his desire, which he may perhaps even be symbolizing in human figures. ...But the true artist, who settles down in a landscape in order to capture it, first analyses the objects of which it is composed, including the sky above them, so that a picture forms within him which also includes the invisible, which he then reduces to its two dimensions with the subjectivity peculiar to him, that which makes him what he is."

This note seems to have been made in Rome in 1826, after he had met the young Corot at Frascati—Corot, who, as Marbot says elsewhere, could paint the air. The first part of the quotation, on the other hand, is directed, as so often, against the Romantics in Rome, whose "soulscapes" he despised. One cannot help regretting that he did not know Caspar David Friedrich. We could trust Andrew to have tried to argue him out of figures as the intermediaries of experience, but above all as the lapidary symbols of self-communion which make us create ourselves. Yet there is no doubt that he would have admired Friedrich's pure landscapes.

In his manner of observing, Marbot is always the interpreter, advocate and not infrequently the herald of the artist, and it seems almost impossible that he should not himself have made some attempt at painting, although productivity and analytical talent are seldom found together in the arts. Certainly his urge for perfection allowed him no dabbling, no dilettantism. He saw enough of that in the houses he visited, where at least one member of the family, generally a female, painted watercolours. He undoubtedly saw himself, from the earliest days of his artistic awareness, in the role of the critical onlooker and observer, and so he remained. Of course, he became more than that.

So we know of no painting, no drawing or sketch from his hand. If there ever was one, then he must have carefully and inconspicuously destroyed it, no correspondent refers to any such work. In other words, he had perceived at an early stage that he lacked creativity, and the longer he was concerned with painting, the more pictures he knew and admired, the more painfully he felt his own imperfection. In the depths of his heart he probably regarded it as a blemish not to belong to the chosen ones to whom the phenomena of nature reveal themselves in a special and elemental way. He was privileged, and yet it was not granted to him to do what he would have liked to do; to practise what seemed to him by far the most desirable of all activities. So he never contemplated without discontent the masterpieces that he glorified. We must therefore see his life to some extent as a permanent act of repression, and his suicide—not only, but largely—as the consequence of an inevitable and definitive perception of the truth.

The field of work on which he decided—or rather, on which the decision took place within him—was the result of that repression, as it probably is for many a critic who owes his craft to the creativity of others, without whom he would be poorly off. But of course Marbot was more than merely a critic. Though it was said of him—and as we shall see, Goethe was not the only one to say it—that he was incapable of enthusiasm, the judgment was based on appearances and on his oral utterances. In contrast to most of his contemporaries, Marbot knew how to control his emotions and to process his experience forthwith, that is to entrust it to his intellect.

19

Nevertheless, there is no doubt that the works of art he chose as his subject moved him profoundly, not as evidence of the stages of development of their creators but as autonomous realms: in them he saw himself neither as conqueror nor as guide, but as a groping intruder winning knowledge and understanding from them. He perfected the method of doing so at an early age. Even as a child, learning by heart, one might say, the collection of his grandfather Lord Claverton in Redmond Manor, he was exploring pictures at leisure and with dedication, though naturally at first more concerned with the content than the form.

Redmond Manor, some seventy miles from Marbot Hall, to the north of Appleby in Cumbria, formerly Westmoreland, is now privately owned by an Arab. Robert, third Viscount Claverton, born in 1754, had been British Envoy at the Court of Dresden from 1781 to 1783 and British Minister Resident at Venice from 1784 until the extinction of the Republic in 1797. He was a cultivated, cosmopolitan epicurean, an expansive and sensual aesthete. In 1790, in Rome and in complete secrecy, he was converted, together with his wife and only daughter, to Catholicism. Catholics were debarred from the diplomatic profession as from all other forms of public service in England. Lord Claverton was therefore unable to profess his faith publicly and practise it freely until in 1797 he retired to his estate of Redmond Manor in order to live henceforth according to his inclinations.

We are not in a position to judge whether his conversion was based on a genuine change in his beliefs. It is possible that Claverton loved religion more for the sake of its earthly manifestations and displays; ceremonial and decorum were in tune with his lifestyle, so he felt himself singularly drawn to the Catholic rite. This tendency to a cosmopolitanism which, while symbolized in aestheticism, is nonetheless only show, is still with us today. Thoroughly conservative monsignori and abbots have chapels decorated by contemporary painters, preferably non-Catholics, producing a fine semblance of all-embracing generosity; a kind of universal indulgence emanates from these commissions, like incense. But we do not mean to do Lord Claverton an injustice, for after all he was consistent in his confession of faith and actively practised his religion till the end of his life.

His only child, Lady Catherine, born in 1781, probably in Dresden, thus spent a considerable and formative part of her youth in Italy. She spoke and wrote Italian and was better versed in the ways of the world, better read and more receptive than Sir Francis Marbot, whom she married in 1799.

Why she married him is one of those questions which marriages past and present so often tempt one to ask. We are often—I am often—faced with the enigma: what did he see in her or she in him?! The obvious answer in Marbot's case would be that Catholics marry Catholics, her father may have insisted on a Catholic son-in-law; daughters did not marry, they were given in marriage. Claverton, a liberal only in externals, was no exception to this rule; converts are seldom liberal. The well-to-do Sir Francis may perhaps have seemed particularly eligible, although formally speaking the marriage probably bore the slight taint of mésalliance: a baronet was not a Peer of the Realm. But Claverton must have weighed up the pros and cons.

Sir Francis was not a man of education, but neither did he expose himself to situations in which he would have felt the lack of it. His forefathers had been educated by the Jesuits of St Omer, but Sir Francis, whose year of birth, 1773, coincides with the temporary dissolution of the Jesuit Order, was brought up at home and never left England, which he would doubtless not have regarded as a deprivation either. Probably like all the Marbots before him, he was a man of the outdoor life, whose intellectual demands were restricted to the things which served his physical well-being, but otherwise, in a blustering, forceful style, he was a hearty indulger in elementary pleasures, of personable appearance, a man who stayed young and liked to see himself as the very paragon of eternal youthfulness. In a letter to De Quincey, Andrew calls him "hearty, boisterous, wide outside, narrow inside", but as we have said, Andrew was biased. Like his eight identifiable male ancestors, Sir Francis was distinguished for nothing except perhaps his talent for success in such areas as cattle raising and agriculture, and naturally for his versatility in gentlemanly pursuits such as snipe shooting, deer hunting, fox hunting, trout fishing, salmon fishing and other delights, which, though they may not further a career, are inconceivable without the material success of one's progenitors.

Yet one is inclined to suspect that Lord Claverton had other motives in his choice of a son-in-law; none of them so altruistic as to take the wishes of his daughter into account, of course, although he loved her and remained tenderly attached to her all his life, indeed it may have been for that very reason: he wanted to keep her near him. The day's journey from Marbot Hall to Redmond was far enough.

We cannot, however, completely rule out the possibility that Sir Francis was Lady Catherine's own choice. He was a handsome figure with a certain manly presence, his complacency could be interpreted as security and his noisy good cheer as open-handed liberality. He was straightforward and probably good-humoured. Perhaps these are not the qualities to make a man attractive to a spoilt and intellectually demanding daughter, but we can make no more assumptions about this possibility. Andrew himself perceived no merits in his father, to him he never seemed other than the Philistine that he really was.

22

It is even possible to suppose that Lord Claverton secretly despised his unintellectual son-in-law and regretted having encouraged the choice. He was all the more ready to take his grandson Andrew under his wing and it is easy to surmise that he intervened actively in the boy's education, with the intention of shaping him according to his ideal image. When Andrew was twelve he gave him a copy of *Il Cortegiano*, that classical manual of instruction whose author, Baldassare Castiglione, the Mantuan aristocrat at the Court of Urbino, was supposed to be considered and can actually still be considered today as the very pattern of a gentleman: a man of moderation and dignity and intellectual discipline, a stranger to all things Dionysian. Andrew read the book with enjoyment and profit too; it was probably one reason for later making his home in Urbino, since he felt that he knew the place already: a déjà-vu as the model for an ideal.

The company the Clavertons frequented was dictated less by social rank than by cultural quality. Of course the ritual entertainments were given or received on appropriate occasions, or they met at Redmond or on one of the neighbouring estates for fox hunting or holidays with more distant relations, but for himself the viscount preferred a different society from the hunting and fishing guests he met at the home of his son-in-law, who in any case lived off the beaten track. Lord Claverton's only frequent guest of equal rank to himself was Lord Burghersh, the future Earl of Westmorland, who was Minister Resident in Florence and later Ambassador to Berlin and Vienna and spent his summers at his ancestral estate of Apthorpe House, not far from Redmond Manor. A man of culture and a lover of the arts, he wrote some remarkable memoirs and composed three symphonies and seven operas as well as cantatas, madrigals and canzonettas.

The table talk here was therefore different from that at

Marbot Hall, and it was here that Andrew received his first impressions of the world in which he was one day to be at home. William Turner spent a few days at Redmond on his journey to Scotland in 1818 (not, as Hadley-Chase assumes, on his journey through northern England in 1816), and made a few watercolour studies in the park and the neighbouring countryside, which, besides their topographical accuracy, show the beginnings of his later atmospheric effects; he must have filled a few sketch blocks as well, since he was always in creative action. Henry Raeburn spent a few weeks at Redmond Manor in the early autumn of 1814, having been commissioned by his host to paint the now famous portrait of his daughter, Lady Catherine. Raeburn had already painted Sir Francis at the beginning of the century, during a hunting trip in Scotland. Also among the regular house-guests was the Scottish physicist Sir David Brewster, one of those cranky inventors to whom even the most practical device calls for improvement and who in 1817 astonished the company assembled there with a wonderful and curious invention: the kaleidoscope.

It was this invention that prompted Andrew Marbot's later observations on symmetry, one of those self-contained texts in his notebooks which may have been intended as the starting point for separate essays.

"...This kaleidoscope is satisfying because it enables the user to make pictures of constantly changing symmetrical design, thus realizing certain conceptions of aesthetic beauty; for in symmetry—that is, in equilibrium about a centre— he believes himself raised to a high degree of perfection and hence recognizable as an image of the ideal.

For beauty is apprehended by most men above all where it is unexpected and therefore occasions surprise, hence principally in the accidents of organic nature, whose phenomena the kaleidoscope reflects, apparently fortuitously in its turn, but actually in an ingeniously artificial way: a crystal spectaculum, which affords us childlike and undemanding pleasure. Here too, it is not nature but its imitation that is beautiful."

Observations on symmetry in the creative arts, especially in architecture, then follow, including some on Palladio, the apparently ideal model, whose perfection seems so unresisting as to invite its own overthrow. He, and above all his successors, had often made things too easy for themselves, for instance an inadequate design might be rounded out by duplicating it symmetrically into no more than ostensibly harmonious proportions, a superficial attractiveness, so that the lack of creative force should not come to light, since the effect had been made pleasing to the eye. And Marbot concludes:

"Since beauty by no means lies solely in the perfection of the result, but also in the work performed—not only, that is, in what exists, but also in what is becoming and the visible testimony to that becoming—it lies also in the work of overcoming the primary condition of productive and above all creative change, and hence in the creation of asymmetrical forms, the proportions of which arrange themselves in a new and compelling entelechy."

Other guests at Redmond Manor were the mathematician Mary Somerville, presumably with her husband, of whom I know only that he was her second, and a doctor; Thomas De Quincey, without his wife—again I do not know whether he left her at home in Ambleside of his own accord, or whether she was not invited. Perhaps De Quincey was asked simply in his capacity as editor of the *Westmorland Gazette*, or perhaps

Claverton was not so unprejudiced as to invite the daughter of a small landowner. It was, after all, on account of this woman that Wordsworth had terminated his association with De Quincey, especially since he had previously hoped that De Quincey would marry his sister Dorothy, whom De Quincey certainly valued, or affected to value, for certain intellectual qualities, but whom he was known to find extremely unattractive. Wordsworth too came once or twice to Redmond for a meal, also without his wife, whom he obviously did not regard as presentable, but with that same sister Dorothy, whom Andrew maliciously described to his mother as "a second-hand Wordsworth, a second-rate mind, a second-choice beauty", while he had nothing else whatever to say of Wordsworth, whom he must nevertheless have read. Coleridge, too, while living in Keswick, was probably invited to Redmond Manor more than once, and he also oddly enough, goes unmentioned by Andrew, though we know the latter admired his works. There is no doubt that painters meant more to him, however, "for in painting we encounter the work of art and can contemplate it, while in literature and music it passes before us." (To van Rossum.) He was most impressed by Turner,

> "with whom none of our contemporaries can compare. The phenomena of nature speak to him in their own tongue, which he alone understands and reproduces untranslated, so that not many understand him."

It was in Venice that Lord Claverton had begun to collect paintings—Venetian Masters, of course. He was the first private owner of Giovanni Bellini's *Portrait of the Doge Leonardo Loredano* (now in the National Gallery, London). He possessed two Canalettos (now the property of the Duke of Sutherland), a Guardi, and Titian's *Diana and Actaeon*

26

(National Gallery of Scotland, Edinburgh). He also owned the painting that was to play such a decisive role in Andrew's development, Tintoretto's *Origin of the Milky Way* (National Gallery, London). It was a handsome collection, lending Venetian colour to the hall and staircase of Redmond Manor. Engravings, by Giambattista and Domenico Tiepolo among others, hung in the library, and in that same library, encouraged by his grandfather, Andrew was already, at the age of nine, reading Alberti and Vasari. Of the latter he said afterwards that he could only be read by a nine-year-old, because his was "a children's guide, not so much to the history of art as to legends about artists", and we are bound to agree with him.

Every summer Lady Catherine spent three months with her parents at Redmond Manor, accompanied by nurse, groom, and the children, first Andrew, then Matthew and finally Jane, with their nurse and nursery-maid. Sir Francis stayed at home or went salmon fishing with friends in Scotland. He was evidently not missed at Redmond. In the autumn he would come over for a short time to hunt, probably the one activity that he and his father-in-law pursued in common, and certainly the one topic of conversation they could share.

Another welcome guest from Marbot Hall was Father Gerard van Rossum, the chaplain, who spent a few days at Redmond now and then. Lord and Lady Claverton had a special fondness for him. It was he who, as a young priest in Rome in 1790, had received the Claverton family into the Catholic church. Born in 1766 at Zwolle in the north of Holland, he had studied at the colleges of Cologne, Innsbruck and Rome, which became secular seminaries upon the dissolution of the Order, but nevertheless secretly retained their Jesuit spirit. Gerrit van Rossum was also a Jesuit at heart, and as soon as the ban was lifted in 1814 he became Father Gerard van Rossum, S.J. His education had been thorough in worldly as well as spiritual matters; he spoke Italian and German perfectly and was shrewd, tolerant and discreet. Claverton had said of him to Sir Francis: "If he were not a priest, and if I were ten years older, by God, I would have adopted this fellow as my son and heir."

When Claverton left Italy in 1797 he invited van Rossum to accompany him to England as the family chaplain—he had no Catholic tenants—librarian and secretary. Van Rossum accepted and it must have caused quite a stir when the family returned for good to Redmond Manor with a Catholic priest in attendance. For of course even in the neighbourhood no one had known anything about the conversion; now it was at last safe to make it public. In 1799, when Lady Catherine married Sir Francis, Claverton relinquished his secretary and companion to his daughter and son-in-law to enable Father Gerard to practise his true calling, since the Marbots had always had Catholic tenants. Thus van Rossum became chaplain and confessor to the family and spiritual guide to the tenants, but above all—which was undoubtedly what Claverton had really intended—tutor to the young couple's future children. The dual function of the priest as chaplain and tutor was then, especially before the great Jesuit schools were founded, quite customary among the Catholic country gentry. From 1800 onwards van Rossum lived at Marbot Hall, becoming tutor and mentor to the first-born son of the house, born on 4 April 1801 and christened Andrew Gregory Thomas on 11 April. In 1814 the thirteen-year-old Andrew was given a choice between attending the Jesuit school at Stonyhurst and continuing his studies at home, but rightly had no wish to leave his teacher. The younger son, John Matthew, born in 1804, went to Stonyhurst in 1814, no doubt to Andrew's benefit, for he now had his tutor entirely to himself.

Van Rossum was in fact a rare boon as a teacher. While profoundly attached to his faith and bound by its rules, he did not insist on his pupil showing that unconditional trust in God which he expected of the other members of the family and the tenants. He allowed him the freedom of many doubts, in the confidence that his pupil possessed the discrimination ultimately to choose the way of God. But van Rossum had more to communicate than the articles of faith. He was wise enough not to seek his God, or to construct Him in a didactic sense, in those areas where He preferred to remain hidden, withhold Himself or even refuse Himself to His worshippers. God was omnipresent, of course, but for this true man of God that did not mean that He must necessarily reveal Himself in the content of every work of art, literature or music. Still less was this to be expected in the natural sciences, although God was naturally hidden in every least particle of nature, only to reveal Himself unexpectedly when the path of research had strayed too far away from Him or the researcher was actually disavowing Him. To van Rossum all true knowledge was beyond the realm of value, to be recognized or rejected only by the knower or the learner, according to their inherent ethical laws. So Father Gerard began at an early stage to credit Andrew with the moral force to judge for himself. Andrew "justified this confidence, even when he fell into error, for that too was always in him the result of conscientious deliberation". We owe these comments to the thorough and extremely valuable notes of Father Gerard's nephew, Adriaan van Rossum (1798-1884), to whom the priest gave a detailed report of his life in England after he finally left that country. (Adriaan, incidentally, was the father of the Curia Cardinal Willem van Rossum.)

Father Gerard must indeed have been an unusual intellectual communicator, who studied and produced the necessary material, not for learning or teaching purposes but first and foremost for his own information and to extend his own awareness. Of course Andrew was also an unusual pupil, to whom languages and, proceeding from linguistic logic, the whole of culture and the arts in particular revealed their comparative connections almost automatically. Imaginative and potentially creative, he was capable of reliving everything he had seen and read vividly and realistically within himself, without separating matter and form. He was therefore able not only to experience in nature the reaction of his own psyche, but to pursue the impulses moving all those whose accounts of their experiences of nature he read in books or saw in paintings. So he grew up, with a constantly expanding repertory of reactive systems. He had no more than the usual five senses, as van Rossum wrote to his nephew, but they were developed to a higher degree of perfection than in other people.

Their course of reading was decided not only by the teacher but also by the preferences of the pupil, for here too Andrew was always looking at the human side of the author, which often spurred him to decided and not always fair criticism. Horace, for instance, appeared to him too superficial, "he does not allow himself to be touched by unpleasant things and avoids any resistance"—that is, he was objecting to what Hofmannsthal has called Horace's "sagely quizzical, never agitated spirit". Their reading of Dante actually had to be interrupted because Andrew refused with astonishing stubbornness to accept the premises which had impelled the poet into his implacable consignment of evil-doers to hell: although still a believer at that time, Andrew rejected faith as the supreme criterion of judgment and condemnation, and perhaps Father Gerard tacitly agreed with him since man, and therefore saint too are imperfect, God alone being perfect. So he apparently did not hold it against his charge that he should see in St Augustine—whom they were reading at his grand-

30

father's behest—a man whose chief claim to fame lay in his perfect use of the pluperfect tense. It was at his own wish that Andrew read with his teacher Lessing's *Laokoon* (on the English translation of which by De Quincey he was to make critical comments when it was published in 1826). It was at the priest's wish, on the other hand, that they read the *Cherubin-ischer Wandersmann* of Angelus Silesius, whom Father Gerard venerated and from which Andrew learned to quote by heart. Of the works of Sophocles they read—extraordinary omen!—*Oedipus Tyrannus*. The meaning that this tragedy was to take on for Andrew, indeed was perhaps gradually assuming as he read it, could not of course be suspected by the Father. Characteristically, on the first page of the systematic notes begun by Marbot in London in 1820, at the very bottom of the page, like a secret message to himself, in minute lettering, as if intended to remain invisible for ever, there appear the lines:

σὺ δ'εἰς τὰ μητρὸς μὴ φοβοῦ νυμφεύματα·
πολλοὶ γὰρ ἤδη κἂν ὀνείρασιν βροτῶν
μητρὶ ξυνηυνάσθησαν.

(You should not fear your mother's
     marriage bed!
So many mortal men have, in their dreams,
Slept with their mother!)

Lord Claverton liked to speak Italian with his grandson. From De Quincey, whose learning was such that he was capable of writing letters of complaint in Greek (although he never sent them off), we know of a brief Greek correspondence with Andrew, which was certainly conducted more for amusement than for any particular cause. With Father Gerard he generally spoke German. It is possible that the priest never achieved in English the extreme perfection of his mastery of German and Italian. At all events, Andrew read English literature on his own, probably directed by his grandfather to

31

this or that author and quite certainly to John Donne. At an early age and with immense pleasure, if not without difficulty, he read Chaucer and probably Pope and Milton, but above all he read Shakespeare, first and last.

Andrew read Shakespeare, if possible, in some favoured nook or "in a tree or in its shade", as he wrote to De Quincey, "and generally aloud, for I desired to hear the melody, the cadences and fermate." He slipped into the characters of his choice and tested the measure of his rejection against those who stood for the principle of negation while trying to be fair to them. An early annotation, not yet included in the systematic notes but kept with them, and probably written in 1819 after a theatrical season in Edinburgh, reads:

"Shakespeare's earthly form, if it ever really existed, perhaps as that actor he is supposed to have been, must have contained within itself many divine forms, dominated by the one great figure of their creator, who allotted the themes and to whom the other embodiments had to conform. From him we not only learn what it means—for good or ill—to bear a human destiny; we also learn to regard this bearer of destiny as a riddle, to convince ourselves of the insolubility of this riddle and to mistrust those deceivers who claim to be able to solve it. But we do not learn to resign ourselves to the riddle. Yet Shakespeare has so much comfort for us that we forget the question of the solution. ... Resignation is something we may learn from some philosophers, but we do not learn wherefore. For even from them we do not learn precisely what is this life to which we are intended to resign ourselves. From Shakespeare we do learn it:

'Life's but a walking shadow, a poor player,
That struts and frets his hour upon the stage,

And then is heard no more; it is a tale
Told by an idiot, full of sound and fury,
Signifying nothing."'

Here, then, we have him expounding one of his themes—the real Andrew Marbot, not simply the melancholic, ridden by a negative awareness of life, but also the sceptic and negator of life, led by his reason, which commands him to seek some support for his negation from the great men in the history of civilization. It was to Shakespeare that he was to return throughout his life, Shakespeare was his compendium, his incentive and consolation, his touchstone and his corrective in the assessment of human experience, not only with others, but also with himself. He is alleged to have told Crabb Robinson that he could really have done without any other poet.

And yet he was by no means uncritical, even of Shakespeare. This same speech by Macbeth after the death of Lady Macbeth—Marbot must have seen the play in Edinburgh in 1818 or 1819—goaded him to a protest against both logic and substance, in the form of a paraphrase in which Macbeth does not figure as the subject but is treated as the object. The criticism is complete and clear. Shakespeare's text reads:
She should have died hereafter;
There would have been a time for such a word.
Tomorrow, and tomorrow, and tomorrow,
Creeps in this petty pace from day to day
To the last syllable of recorded time;
And all our yesterdays have lighted fools
The way to dusty death. Out, out, brief candle!
Life's but a walking shadow, a poor player,
That struts and frets his hour upon the stage,
And then is heard no more; it is a tale
Told by an idiot, full of sound and fury,
Signifying nothing.

33

Marbot's paraphrase:

> When, Macbeth, should she then have died?
> Hereafter? Why? The time for such a word
> Was just this moment, and thou knowest it.
> Had she lived on, 'twere soon to be thy widow.
> If life is nothing but an idiot's tale—
> And here I do concur—why this ambition,
> Which taught thee nothing but the taste of fears?
> Thy wisdom comes too late, retards the play,
> But not thy bitter end. Thou hast not given
> A hint of deeper insight, while thou wert
> In furious action. Thine enemies therefore
> Will never know the one they slew was he,
> Macbeth, philosopher.

Although almost insatiable in his assimilation of intellectual nourishment, Marbot was not only that. He was no stay-at-home, no bookworm. His mind did not work cumulatively, but selectively and extremely critically from the very first. Every desire for knowledge immediately gave birth to another, and he threw out all ballast. Nothing was further from his mind than the idea of turning his knowledge to account. "The pressure to apply knowledge hinders its achievement," his grandfather had inscribed in the volume of Castiglione he had given him. The proposition is false, of course, but quite proper to an aristocratic aesthete such as Lord Claverton, whose views and style were still a legacy of the eighteenth century. Van Rossum, on the other hand, took a different view. He was accustomed to test the truth of all reading matter by its applicability to life, but this of course meant the life of a practising Catholic for whom his faith was the highest of all values and standards, though not the only possible one of them. But Andrew read differently, he read, as we can gather from the Shakespeare paraphrase, with a view to correction, trying to grasp the potential of the psyche in which a work originated, in order then to make the comparison with reality and to grasp the author's sense of reality, which meant, as we shall see, that his judgment was sometimes unjust and premature.

He tried to engage in human relationships, he cultivated his curiosity and wanted to understand "what makes people live and stay alive". He associated with tenants and farmers in the neighbourhood of Marbot Hall and Redmond Manor, but always picked his contacts with care, probably in accordance with an unconscious plan into which his immediate family, apart from his mother, did not fit. For instance he scarcely noticed even his brother and sister, John Matthew, born in 1804 and Jane Elizabeth, born in 1806, or at least he never mentioned them as far as we know. Whether an unconscious element of jealousy came into this, an anxiety over his mother's undivided favour, it is difficult to judge. To his father, at all events, he remained in silent opposition, no doubt never expressed to him personally; he had no desire to acknowledge him and his circle, neither his relations and friends, nor the house-guests at Marbot Hall, mostly landed gentry from the same county, their interests identical with his father's, the hunting and other parties,

"booming, bragging and carousing, with their talk of game and fish, grazing and cattle, that is, the useful part of nature, whereas only her useless part appealed to me, her ruthless self-interest, the multiple forms of her untamed and untamable self-realization, or of the creature which expresses herself not at all to men. Here, where neither precept nor prohibition rules, I felt myself understood, for no one took account of me." (To De Quincey)

This is Marbot the Romantic—almost the zealot—a side which he seldom reveals when speaking of himself; it is

35

generally the rationalist who speaks, the self-denier and sceptic. Marbot refused to give himself above all when tradition and propriety prescribed duties which, having examined them thoroughly, he did not accept. He was strongly aware of his own intentions and desires and was prepared to compromise only when his mother and his relationship with her prompted it as the expedient solution to an internal or external conflict. Although probably a good horseman, he did not ride in company, still less go out hunting, which he regarded as unworthy and barbarous. He rode alone. He refused to learn the flute because music as practised in his circle seemed to him a senseless waste of time which could never lead to perfection, and perfection was his goal from the very first.

So Andrew passed his childhood and youth, his life and experience encompassed by Marbot Hall and its environs as far as Edinburgh, and by Redmond Manor as far as the Lake District. Edinburgh, "this black beauty under a grey cover" —so it was black even then—was a small, manageable London, fashionable, but less dominated by the modish customs of the Georgian era. The dandies here were of a provincial variety, but Edinburgh was more receptive to music and the arts than London, and Andrew owed much of his early inspiration to Edinburgh.

Marbot Hall represented nature to him, Redmond Manor culture, despite the fact that the more obviously beautiful landscapes were also nearer there. Andrew often rode in the Lake District when he was visiting De Quincey at Ambleside, yet this was not "his" landscape; even at that time he had probably been prejudiced against it by the descriptions of its bards—"that romantic topography", as he later called it.

At all events, Andrew did not leave these timeless, unworldly surroundings for the first nineteen years of his life. Apparently he himself was not conscious of any desire to leave.

Without suggesting that he was a little prig—which is anyway quite unthinkable in his case—I believe that in those early years his mind was absorbed in the creation of a world of his own and he did not want to confront it with reality until it was manifest. He suspected that anyone who lacks an inner world will misinterpret the outer one, in so far as he apprehends it at all as a reality to be faced. One may of course wonder whether Marbot himself ever really faced that outer world.

So until he set out on the Grand Tour in 1820 Andrew had not left his native land. He spent over two-thirds of his life "at home", resembling in this way his contemporary, Leopardi, who left his own home still later and who had rather less freedom of movement there, since it was not the home of his choice. So there were certain externals which the two had in common: each had sufficient time and leisure in his years at home to build up an inner world of his own, though the two worlds were very different. Leopardi's world was that of an ideal past beside which the present paled, whereas Marbot made no distinction in his between real and ideal; imagination and reality, dream and acute wakefulness were intermingled. In contrast to Leopardi, he did not see himself as an innovator in an objectionable present but exploited that present, finding in it every bit of the past at his disposal, requiring only his selection. One thing in which the two must have resembled each other was their rejection of the conditions imposed on human beings, and therefore of life. Yet, as we shall see, the sources of this rejection were quite different.

Also common to both was their adverse relationship with their fathers, although the causes are of a totally different nature. Neither was understood by his father, but Leopardi had to suffer under his, which he neither dared admit to himself nor ever admitted to another, while Marbot did not suffer under his; he took little account of him and not only admitted it to himself but also hinted at it to others. It was as if he were

37

called upon to justify himself and were shifting his guilt to the injured party. Councillor Schultz's interpretation was probably right.

At the age of six Andrew was already studying the paintings at Redmond Manor closely and absorbing every detail of them: as thematic elements, of course, not for their stylistic features. His phenomenal memory later enabled him to describe this impressionable period of life. In his notebooks he comments:

> "The programme of the imaginative child's life is guided by pictures into the way of realization, whereby the child is naturally absorbing the content of what is depicted rather than the quality of the depiction. In these paintings he sees naked or strangely clothed adults—and often children, too, with whom the gazing child identifies himself more especially—with expressive countenances filled with meaning, causing or enduring, or embroiled in events which the child does not understand but which he soon begins to expect of life. Disenchantment and disappointment begin when he realizes that these events, and with them the subject matter of art, do not correspond to life but are rather the result of wishful thinking by the artists—those privileged people who are capable of expressing such perception and thus ridding themselves of the wish, whereas it remains fixed in the child's imagination as something unfulfilled."

The child, first and foremost, is Marbot himself. And as far as the wish for the artist's experience is concerned, he continued to be that child for the rest of his life.

Naturally Andrew asked his grandparents or his mother, and probably servants as well, or anyone else who happened to be present, to explain the meaning of the picture under which he was standing at the time. The replies can seldom have been satisfactory, and his grandfather was probably the only person who had adequate explanations ready.

Tintoretto's *Origin of the Milky Way* was particularly difficult for the child Andrew to understand. The subject: Jupiter[1] is holding his bastard son Hercules, whose mother Alcmene was, as we know, a mortal, to the breast of his sleeping wife Juno, as if to legitimize him with her milk if not actually to foist the child on her. But the child sucks so heartily that the milk squirts out in two streams. The lower stream sprays across a meadow and turns into lilies there, though this lower section has been cut off and was already missing when Claverton acquired the painting.[2] The other stream shoots skywards, giving birth to stars: the Milky Way. The theme, not particularly obvious even to grown-ups, is naturally difficult to explain to a child and in recording the experience in his notes Andrew admits to not having understood very much of it, especially since, with his almost inexhaustible thirst for knowledge, he demanded an explanation of every detail: the function of the peacocks, the bow and arrows, the birds of prey and the unusual nets, and why the angels needed wings, while Jupiter and Juno managed without them and could still hover

1. I am loth to use the Latinized names of Greek gods, but I cannot change the names by which the creators of the paintings knew their mythological characters. Marbot in fact despised the Latin names. "Rubens ... painted an acceptable Bacchus, but would not have been capable of a Dionysos..." (1828, to Carl von Rumohr).
2. They are lilies in the explanatory text offered by the National Gallery in London. A drawing by the Master's son, Domenico Tintoretto, after his father's painting (Galleria dell'Accademia, Venice) and after this a parchment painting by Jacob Hoefnagel (Staatliche Museen, Berlin-West) show a female nude lying among the lilies, evidently Alcmene, whom some amateur more attached to femininity than to value and authenticity probably severed from the painting for himself.

in the sky. He also wanted to know why, in all its puzzling disorder, the painting was beautiful. As to the question in whose eyes the child was supposed to be legitimized, when after all Jupiter as the Lord of Heaven must also be the supreme judge, this probably did not occur to him until later, when he had fully grasped the function of marriage in fiction and reality, both human and divine.

After his grandfather had tried to explain the subject of the painting to him in so far as he understood it, and no doubt avoiding anything improper, but had evidently not succeeded to Andrew's satisfaction, he one day asked his mother, then twenty-five years old, to explain it again, and above all, since she was visibly of the same sex as Juno in the painting, to show to him the corresponding parts of her body which made their appearance with such surprising frankness in Juno. His mother refused this request, but not at all indignantly; she laughed and took the child in her arms so that he was able to discover "this mysterious territory" for himself, "not with his eyes, but feeling with his body".

"...his first conscious memory, and the most wonderful. Here he was, in beauty softly embedded, feeling with all his senses a previously unknown territory which he was to explore and conquer later."

This observation, probably made in 1820, when he had just begun his notes, the second of its kind after the Sophocles quotation, is the start of a kind of secret diary, kept sporadically and often only in the form of keywords, in which Marbot makes an attempt at detachment by putting himself into the third person singular, as if his intention were to make fiction of his experience. The supposition that he was planning an autobiographical novel of psychological development is obvious. Nevertheless, since he did not write it and since there is no external proof of such a project, it must remain conjecture.

These secret notes, spontaneous inspirations or scraps of memory, always bearing the stamp of the extraordinary intensity of total recall, appear in tiny, often hastily scribbled characters like an interjection at the bottom of the pages of his practical memoranda; as if the reader were not only to forget them at once but even to doubt his own memory of them. The reader was naturally only Marbot, confronting himself as the potential hero of a novel, in order to distance himself from the recurrent source of his dismay.

At all events, the entry quoted above is definite evidence of his later incestuous relationship with his mother, but not some self-accusatory or justificatory document. It is more likely that Andrew is nostalgically recalling the past to his own eyes and senses, an acute and overpowering memory aided by objective observations which in context pursue his general theme:

> "...The moment of the first experience of art does not come until one day when, looking at a picture, we no longer think of the event depicted but of the painter who has made it happen, because it is happening to him. Unfortunately this moment is no longer remembered later, like many another moment which determines some portion of our fate and which can no longer be remembered, even if it is perceived at all during the event itself..."

This was an insight not vouchsafed to many in Marbot's day. It is certain that the five-year-old child did not experience such a moment when contemplating the painting by Tintoretto, for at that time it was naturally the subject and not the manner that concerned him. Here, then, is a textbook demonstration of the mother-son relationship, perceived doubly, in the conduct of the mother and the reaction of the child. Of course the painting was ideally suited to the role of release mechanism and as the object of the demonstration. Naturally its function was not casual; the Oedipus complex is not triggered off on the occasion most favourable to it, but is formed early in the unconscious as the result of the child's relationship to one of his parents. In our case it was the typical unconscious desire to possess his mother and destroy his father, as being the rival and at the same time the supreme authority. We have said that Andrew despised his father. In reality the child no doubt reacted to his father with latent hatred which may have been intensified by this scene—his mother's explanation of the painting and her reaction to Andrew's demand. Andrew may well have asked himself who this father (in the picture) was, pushing the son towards the mother and yet able to take him away again at any time, and how it was that the son was with his father and not his mother. And he probably suspected that the "mysterious territory" was open, not to him, but to his father.

Analysis of the Oedipus complex was still a long way off, but the thing itself was not new. In *Le Neveu de Rameau* Diderot writes:

"...If the little savage were left to himself and...if he
combined with the undeveloped intellect of a child
in the cradle the violent passions of a man of thirty,
he would wring his father's neck and lie with his
mother."

This brilliant hypothesis seems made for Marbot's case, and in retrospect he must have recognized the truth of it. There is considerable evidence that he attempted later on to investigate his childish feelings, wishes and desires. Above all, there is the remark he made to Henry Crabb Robinson, with whom Andrew, though twenty-five years the younger, formed a close friendship during his two visits to London.

Crabb Robinson, the conscientious diarist, most discreet friend of many important contemporaries and one of the best listeners of his time, reports a conversation in the course of

42

which Marbot told him that his father had never been important to him, but that at a certain point in his life he had hated him. Marbot was certainly not the man to confide or pour out his heart, so that this statement carries particular weight. Of course he did not have in mind the moment of physical nearness between mother and child but the physical nearness of two lovers, the event which was to mark his life: the consummation of incest thirteen years later.

At all events the Tintoretto experience was not only decisive but cathartic, not in the ethical sense, of course, but in its significance as a satisfying purification from childish error and—who knows?—secret fears. In his mother's arms, although a conundrum had not yet been solved for the child, it had been translated from the world of imagery into tangible reality. Andrew did not write of this experience until he was twenty, as a memory, in fact, of something which had happened fourteen years earlier. Far away from his mother, so that she was unable to fill in his memories, he set down what had probably always stayed in his mind since the event itself. This is the only explanation of the clear—and of course committed—vividness of the account in which—or so it seems—he is retelling the experience to himself. Not suddenly produced in the light of a déjà-vu, but constantly relived in all its significance, the event grew into a retrospective wish-fulfilment dream of innocence early lost, the absence of the beloved partner intensifying it to still more piercing effect and deeper pain. As we have already said, there are indications that Marbot planned to put this "secret diary" to use later on, in order to "write himself free" as the opportunity arose. Admittedly, this supposition is contradicted not only by the rarity of these entries but also by his relatively early manifested decision against life and the increasing clarity with which he envisaged his death.

The second, and last, documented experience of his early youth did not take place until eleven years later. In 1817 Andrew met Thomas De Quincey, who was a frequent and favourite guest at Redmond Manor. We can only conjecture what qualities made the sixteen-year-old boy take to him. Though his constitution was weak—in fact Crabb Robinson compared his physique to Leopardi's!—De Quincey's person was altogether pleasing, inspired by a gentle magic, indeed he even had something of the involuntary charmer about him, suggesting a delicate other-worldliness; prone, not without a certain relish, to ill-health and using it to avoid the harsher forms of existence. He was gentle and articulate, a good and reliable story-teller, and as such he made a powerful impression on children. He was also exceedingly well read, possessed a considerable library and an astonishing memory which enabled him to quote from it at will. Andrew, who went for long rides from Redmond Manor, in the early years with a groom, several times rode over to Grasmere in the Lake District to visit the then newly-married couple. It is perfectly possible that the singular attraction which De Quincey, sixteen years older, exerted over Andrew stemmed from a secret, a many-layered enigma which suffused, indeed almost dominated his life, turning him into a—never self-confessed— outsider. For this was the very time, around 1818, when Andrew too began to detect the outsider in himself, certainly not without deep and growing distress.

In 1818 De Quincey's opium excesses had reached their culminating point, which could not of course be hidden from the younger man. And in fact, in September of that year, during one of Andrew's visits, De Quincey was in an excessively euphoric state which made an overwhelming and lasting impression on the seventeen-year-old. Naturally Andrew had no clear idea how to classify that impression at the time, but he recorded it with extreme accuracy:

44

"...he spoke without intermission, but very distinctly and coherently, with a calm enthusiasm which mounted now and again to an evocation beginning with some exclamation such as 'Oh' or 'Ah'. In fact he made liberal use of the vocative. His voice was always a little raised, as if at the next moment he might start singing. He quoted Shakespeare and Wordsworth and it was as if he were calling to them from his own darkness. It seemed to me as if he were delighting himself in his sinister soliloquy. Now and again he would go to the door and cry 'Margaret dear!' or 'My dear Peggy!', as if he wanted his wife to have some share in this monologue, but she did not come; perhaps she was unwilling to witness this drama, which must have been sinister enough to her too, in the company of a stranger. The spectacle made me uneasy, and yet it was a scene which only a man of education and intellect could have played, even though that intellect was deranged."

Even this deep and ambiguous impression fitted into place with Andrew as soon as his reason had grasped it. He recorded it in 1827 in the light of his observations on the artist as a man outside society.

"It seems difficult to count De Quincey among the artists, since his talent was analytical rather than creative, but with a vision quite peculiar to himself, which sometimes made him unjust and one-sided; but his own particular eloquence generally made the listener forget this subjectivity. Perhaps he was a fine artist after all. At all events he was a solitary, not because he took opium, for surely more people do so than we know, but because in the sober state he seemed ridden by his guilt respecting it; he wanted always to defend himself. He was weak and had not

45

the strength to overcome this apparent guilt in himself. And because he saw and accepted it as such it was also seen and accepted by others. People said that he acted against nature, but who, I wonder, is to decide what nature is, besides nature herself? For most people, nature in this case signifies the majority. Inasmuch as De Quincey felt that he must defend himself, he subscribed to that opinion."

Marbot then takes De Quincey to task, not on account of his excesses, but on account of the petty attempts to hush them up which he thought unworthy of such a man. It amuses him that De Quincey and Coleridge, who was also emotionally unstable, accused each other of opium addiction and that each in his own way nevertheless tried to make his peace with heaven and earth by behaving in a God-fearing and conservative manner in order to clear their account with society. They had at times displayed an almost insufferably conformist virtuousness and sometimes actually felt that as secret sinners they must be like sycophants at the beck and call of their contemporaries.

Perhaps he went too far in these assertions. We do not know. Both De Quincey and Coleridge certainly showed traces of this kind of behaviour, but Marbot's statements show a curious degree of commitment, almost as if he were defending himself. The reasons are obvious. When Andrew wrote the above words he was naturally well aware that his own case must, if it were known, seem more despicable to society than an addiction indulged in by many and which could possibly be exorcized, whereas what he had done could not be undone. What is strange here is that he transposes his subject into the past, as if into a time long distant. Coleridge survived Marbot by four years, De Quincey by almost thirty.

Naturally it was no part of Andrew's intention to take exception to abnormal tendencies or even simply to deplore them—he knew only too well that it was not for him to criticize. He was stern only in condemning those faults which he himself never committed, such as that of "ridiculous moralism" as he called it. So he makes fun of De Quincey's disparaging remarks concerning the virtues and talents of others, for instance Goethe, whose want of patriotism and religious feeling he deplored—apparently in a letter to Marbot himself. Later, in *Reminiscences of the Lake Poets*, De Quincey made his criticism of Goethe public: he compares him with Coleridge and finds him

"...profoundly inferior in strength and breadth of intellect...Both are now gone—Goethe and Coleridge: both are honoured by those who knew them, and by multitudes who did not. But the honours of Coleridge are perennial, and will annually grow more verdant; whilst from those of Goethe every generation will see something fall away until posterity will wonder at the subverted idol, whose basis, being hollow and unsound, will leave the worship of their fathers an enigma to their descendants."

Marbot would probably have found this abstruse paean of misjudgement as astonishing as we find it ludicrous.

Apparently De Quincey, in the state of euphoria in which Andrew found him on that visit, offered him opium too, but Andrew refused, probably for reasons of good sense but certainly also fearing this unknown and sinister life support, but the offer alone gave him a glimpse of an abyss, so that, probably for the first time, he became aware of moral peril. It is certain that in a sober state De Quincey would never have gone so far; far from wishing to corrupt, his sense of responsibility was of the kind that knowledge of their own instability often evokes in those who suffer from the consciousness that they are destroying themselves. For self-destruction was also

47

contrary to his religious principles, which may not have been very deeply rooted but were qualified by convention and tradition, as they were for most Englishmen at that time, from whom he was at pains not to differ too obviously. From time to time he was successful in his endeavours.

In reality, despite sometimes very large doses of opium, De Quincey did not destroy himself. He died in 1859 at the age of 74, a gaunt, eccentric old gentleman, an odd, friendly yet spectral figure, who despite severe reverses, had held on, not entirely without suffering some moral damage himself. The life of a journalist imposed on him by material poverty had compelled him into a number of indiscretions and made him guilty of some striking demonstrations of disloyalty. This had meant the loss of his friends, at least those who were not dead already. Yet he seems to have got over this too.

And it was De Quincey who in 1834 was the first to give a warm welcome to the publication of Marbot's writings, observing at the same time that the text must have been refined and trimmed. "I knew the author. He is no longer alive," as he wrote in *Blackwood's Magazine*, "but we can be sure that he would not have approved the book in this form." He was right and his comment (unlike his comment on Goethe) is evidence of his subtle perceptiveness. He was not fully aware of the circumstances of this publication. We shall be returning to these. Marbot and De Quincey probably did not meet again after 1820. Apart from the brief correspondence in Greek we know of only two letters from each to the other, of which only Marbot's have survived. They show that a casual correspondence was kept up, probably until not long before Andrew's death.

In 1820, aged nineteen, Andrew embarked on his Grand Tour. The first stop was, of course, London.

Lord and Lady Claverton maintained a spacious town house in Curzon Street, to which they moved every year at the end of April, generally accompanied by their daughter, Lady Catherine, returning to Westmorland at the beginning of July. The Marbots, on the other hand, had never owned a town house. Sir Francis did not like the town very much, nor, in all probability, had his ancestors. He would have cut no figure in social life, and knew it; probably he did not even want to. That is not to his discredit, although it was seen differently in those days; at that time he was the prototype of the unpolished provincial gentry, that popular butt of all the caricaturists, dandies and their flunkeys.

Between 1810 and 1820 the Regency was at its height, the dandies held sway in London. After Beau Brummell left England, having fallen from grace at court in 1816, the Prince himself was the focus of social life. He set the tone and the rest danced to his tune. London was a man's world and only a favoured few ladies were allowed to play a part in it, as arrangers, planners and commentators. The strategic centre was the club. This was where fates were decided: who was to be "in" and who "out"!?

Claverton did not court "Prinny", and he himself was beyond the age at which fashion and the fashionable were cultivated as an end in themselves. For him London was still a centre of culture and over and above that, the place where he met families he liked, whom distance prevented him from seeing for the rest of the year.

In 1820 Andrew was of their party for the first time. He had at first intended to leave London for the Continent in June but changed his plans. We know what held him back: his mother. For it was here in London, in the Clavertons' town house in Curzon Street, in one of the two upper rooms that it happened, the abomination took place. That which had been pent up through the years now erupted in full force, bringing at last the fulfilment of a burning mutual desire than which scarcely anything more illicit and sinful can be imagined: the consummation of incest, the appalling fate which it had been not possible to resist, and which perhaps neither of the two partners wanted to resist; thus they both became victim and perpetrator in one.

The imminent parting was undoubtedly a contributory cause of the awakening of their desire for physical union from that stage of latency which, presumably only because of unpropitious external circumstances, had not as yet been transformed into actual consummation. It is unlikely that Andrew and Lady Catherine would have worked out a plan some time before, confided it to each other and waited for the right moment to put it into effect. It came to them suddenly and violently when, on one night among many, they became aware that no obstacle of place, time or persons stood in the way of their deed. Conditions at Marbot Hall and Redmond Manor would not have been conducive to illicit intercourse; Sir Francis, Father Gerard, the servants, house-guests and not least the brother and sister—quite enough spies and interferers, whom each of the two might have silently wished away, but whose hampering presence they would certainly not have lamented to each other. There was no mutual agreement to take advantage of the first opportunity, the word was not yet spoken, its significance not yet understood. Incest is not planned in concert: it happens, if it happens—or so I think—as the unpremeditated effect of a power which is stronger than its victims. Andrew's letter to his mother from Paris at the end of July of that year adds certainty to this conviction: "How little did we know then what was in store for us in London! Did we wish for it or did we not?" This question may have been discussed between the two lovers later on and it would be enlightening to know how it was answered. "We did not wish it, but the wish formed in us", would probably have been the answer, but we do not know if the two of them could possibly then have distinguished Id from Ego.

50

I picture it thus: night-time after a party at Claverton House, the last guests leaving the hall, echoes of conversation; outside, the coaches drive away, drowsy footmen extinguish the lights in halls and corridors. Lord and Lady Claverton have already withdrawn, Andrew and Lady Catherine are mounting the stairs, he gives her his arm, she presses it to her side, their separation is imminent, they whisper together sadly about the parting—which is to be deferred that very night; suddenly each imagines that parting and is terrified, the usual good-night kiss becomes unusual and turns into a hot mingling of breath, an embrace in which their hands touch forbidden things. It is too late to stop now, Lady Catherine breathes a half-suppliant, half-swooning "No", like a last despairing effort at self-command, but by then the word no longer means No, the cry goes unheard, the real world is submerged, with all the claims of decency and reason; all caution is blotted out, who draws whom into the bedroom is uncertain, the unnameable deed takes place—and a new dimension is abruptly awakened in Andrew's consciousness, an emotional centre has come to life which guides and governs him from then on; without giving him a lasting and universal vision, it nonetheless makes him look in all his future encounters for hidden or suppressed forces beneath the surface. "Sinning yourself,/you seek the sin in others", August von Platen jotted down for him in a perceptive moment in 1829: not altogether the truth, but not too far removed from it. For the beauty which strikes us in a work of art—so Marbot's emergent theory ran—is only on the surface; it and what lies beneath it obey different rules. A man's achievement is one thing; the motive and psychology from which it springs, another. On the one hand, the illuminating effects, on the other, the dark origins. Thus it was that his own experience became the spur to dig deeper, below the level that manifests only what is conscious in man. From then on, he

51

would investigate the directions and misdirections of men's behaviour, seeing in their works the effect of those conditions of life which had been bearable or unbearable, burdened or unburdened with guilt for their creator; tracking down the taboo, its source within the human soul and its justification in art.

But in the first place both Andrew and his mother must have been preoccupied with the intellectual and spiritual assimilation of their offence, a different, but parallel process to the no less difficult task of measuring the consequences. Both were profoundly conscious of the enormity of their behaviour, yet they must have realized that that night was not to be the last of its kind, although they may have meant it to be; they knew that they were too weak for the final renunciation, and they were.

The Clavertons' house was not one of London's fashionable meeting-places. The spirit of the age was regarded as a fleeting thing, and no one tried to adjust or conform to it. Andrew, like Claverton, had nothing in common with Prinny and probably never gave him a thought. The society in which Claverton moved was sounder, probably older and as it were more timeless than the transitory tonesetters, the ephemera of a decadent mood in cultural history. Its morals were probably not as lax, either, but we cannot be sure of this: that period did not insist on a moral life, even less on moralism; Victorian prudery was still a long way off.

Andrew cut a good figure in London, even if he did not hide, or take the trouble to hide, the fact that the salon was not his spiritual home.

Lady Charlotte Bury, a distant relative of the Clavertons, noted in her diary:

"...a tall, silent young man with fine eyes, fine hands and good manners, although he was unable to conceal the fact that for the most part the conversation at table did not interest him. He has two things to learn: how to show interest and how to conceal the lack of it."

Marbot probably learned neither, because he probably did not trouble himself overmuch to learn them. But it is also true that party talk bored him and that in later life he avoided it whenever possible. No doubt his taciturnity and reserve originated to some extent in his preoccupation with himself and his "case". He was listening inwardly, listening to the tumult in his soul, which could not be drowned by conversation of any kind.

We may assume that in the houses to which he was invited Andrew was more interested in the paintings than in the other guests, and that his hosts were prepared to show him their collections in private as well. Andrew made some momentous discoveries in the course of these visits. Fourteen great portraits by Rembrandt alone, besides a large number of etchings, which have long since returned to public ownership in Holland, were to be seen in private houses in London at that time. In addition to four important Rembrandts, including the *Self-Portrait* of 1666, Lord Colbourne, who left his collection to the National Gallery, owned the entire triptych of the *Crucifixion* by Gérard David, of which only the central panel is still in London (National Gallery), and Vermeer's *Girl Reading a Letter* (now in the Gemäldegalerie, Dresden). Andrew naturally saw many works by Van Dyck and especially Rubens (he could scarcely have missed him!) but he also became acquainted with Van Eyck and Memling.

And so, having previously been raised exclusively on the Venetians, he made some discoveries of vital importance to him. Characteristically, he began there and then on the systematic notes which he kept up from now on, sporadically perhaps, but with the clear intention of recording his exper-

53

ience of works of art for assessment at a later date. He had three leather-bound quarto volumes of eighty pages each made for himself, which in his case was indicative less of a pretentious whim than of the collector's zeal and a habit of industry. Had he been a little older—or so we may assume—he would at least have done without the leather, and probably chosen a handier size.

His first, undated entry reads:

"Great painting tells no stories; it reveals a deeper
truth that escapes other media. It expresses the result
of a cognition that words cannot replace. If they can,
it is not a great painting."

A remarkable observation for a nineteen-year-old in those days, if a little over-hasty. Once on his journey, he would soon realize that art can convey a cognition allegorically while telling a story as well. If Andrew had had the chance to publish his notes himself, he would very probably have deleted that comment.

His special field of study was the self-portrait, because he felt that here the artist's cognitive will, expressive power and gift for observation were exclusively concentrated upon himself. Here, moreover, he was at the furthest remove from commissioned work—"for probably there was no patron ever said to an artist: 'I want to hang your likeness in my library' "; he was alone with himself and believed he was depicting himself, but was in reality depicting the image he had of himself,

"since the wish to discover and understand oneself is
different from the wish to depict oneself. The way
one sees oneself is different from the way one wishes
to be seen; and the way one is, is yet a third thing."

Such statements are already beginning to throw light on the initial stages of Andrew's self-analysis and his choice of the means to perform it. The question: "Who was this artist?"

must lead to the question: "Who am I?" We shall never be able to find out which self-portraits he used to pursue his researches, other than those by Rembrandt, Reynolds and Gainsborough, and he probably underestimated the last two.

One of the earliest notes:

"The truth of a work of art is subjective, for it is the truth of the artist, not of his subject...The great artist is he who is capable of convincing us of his subjective truth in such a way that we begin to see the subject with his eyes, that it assumes a fresh structure of appearance for us, and thereby a metaphysical quality. But the artist who seeks only to depict the metaphysical semblance before capturing the subject in all the dimensions of its corporeality, is, however honest he may be, a bungler and a dabbler."

Marbot later expanded and demonstrated the first statement through Turner's paintings, which he so greatly admired. It has been suggested that the second is refuted by modern art, but only because without an example it is not completely clear what Marbot had in mind. However, as the context shows, he was in fact referring to William Blake.

Marbot met Blake at a dinner given by Lady Caroline Lamb in the middle of May 1820. Among the other guests was Sir Thomas Lawrence, just returned from Italy and elected President of the Royal Academy. As we learn from Lady Charlotte Bury's diary, he was the table partner "of the lovely and graceful, though no longer young, Lady Catherine Marbot, Claverton's daughter".

"Once again she was accompanied by her son, handsome and enigmatic, who, however, was listening with the utmost attention to a humble little artist by the name of Blake."

55

Apparently Marbot had found in Blake someone capable of fascinating him in conversation, although probably less because his views on art were illuminating than because they were eccentric. How Blake came to be at such a party we do not know, but Lady Caroline had always delighted to satisfy her eccentric whims, which even Byron in his time had thought out of place.

Blake was then thirty-six years old. Marbot visited him in his newly-leased house in Fountain Court and there met Henry Crabb Robinson, with whom he became friendly in the course of the succeeding weeks. Robinson, not creative himself but an admirer of the creative, a sensitive, quiet man of moderation and sense, was loyal and dependable in his friendships. He had known Blake for some time, had occasionally bought a drawing from the penurious artist and had a patient and forgiving sympathy for the visionary, and therefore tiring, enthusiast. Marbot also felt a liking for that unusual man, but could not summon up any patience with him, nor did he wish to. He was afflicted with an almost emotional, stubborn imperiousness, which of course also possessed Blake, only in him it came from quite the opposite side. It is to Robinson that we owe the record of the conversation, if we can call it that, for it was one-sided. Blake's tirades and sermons rambled on aimlessly, they were monologues, which Robinson naturally was not hearing either for the first or for the last time. Thus Andrew now learned to his astonishment that oil painting corrupts the artist, that the Venetians were all bunglers in their use of colour and Rembrandt and Rubens no better—"falsifiers" all. From art he proceeded to nature. Nature, said Blake, also not for the first time, was the work of the devil, and so man was by nature evil; the whole earth, which was not round as they asserted, but flat, was a morass of sinfulness and depravity. Marbot noted: "An honest, God-

56

inspired madman, a genius of misbelief. "A decided opinion, to be sure, but just as close to objective truth as the theory he propounded after this visit, that Blake's artistic abilities were not equal to the overwhelming power of his visions. "For", Marbot writes in his notes:

"the mightier the visions of an artist, the less he is able to realize them in his art, in so far as the vision is not composed by the painter's will itself, that is, on a visual basis. In Mr Blake, however, they are built upon religious delusions, which, like every form of illusion, resist artistic reproduction. A mystic should never paint."

Here then is the first note of another persistent theme: the relationship of quality of experience to that of its treatment—of will to skill.

"He draws badly and diagrammatically, revealing every muscle; anatomy is everywhere visible, which though it may show the surgeon where the organs are located, will not show the beholder the seat of the soul. With him celestial or cosmic rays are turned into planks of wood, air into bodies, light into mass. His figures enact a melodrama, but even in such roles they fail to convince, for they are stiff as puppets...Divine inspiration is not enough to make an artist. Everything is formless to him because he is incapable of thinking in the dimensions of this world. He is incapable of thinking at all, nor does he wish to do so. Mr Robinson is right when he says of Blake: 'He hates reason more than anything, perhaps for fear that reason might expose the fallacy of his dreams'."

And to van Rossum Andrew writes:
"Blake says that education is a sin and we human beings should all persist in divine ignorance. He

really did say 'divine ignorance'. When I asked him what he meant by it he looked at me as if I were the devil. Perhaps to him I am. He is disordered in his thinking but wordily effusive in his speech. Yet he is kind and friendly. He says he wants no earthly fame but only spiritual glory and he is completely honest in this. He is always honest, even when he says that the dead speak to him, for to him knowledge and belief are identical. He seems almost too innocent for this world. He appears to take scarcely any nourishment, indeed not to live in this world at all. Therefore he does not see the dirt in his own dwelling, nor the squalor that surrounds him."

This would suggest that Marbot's first visit to the studio must have been rather a disillusioning experience to the nineteen-year-old. But he seems to have seen it as a first step in a course of instruction and it is characteristic of him to have remained matter-of-fact and objective in his judgment, weighing positive against negative, even if the final verdict was negative. Hasty or not, he had arguments to justify it. Many of his compatriots have resented Marbot's criticism of Blake, since for most of them he stands above earthly criteria, as a harbinger of the hereafter. Hadley-Chase—in traditional biographical style—speaks of Andrew's judgment as a "folly of youth".

The letter to van Rossum continues:
"I have been wondering whether cognition and imagination not only contradict each other but exclude each other. Or whether cognition without imagination is impossible. I hope to get to the root of this, although perhaps I have no idea what cognition is. Is it the act of knowing, or its result?"

The question is justified, yet the connection between Marbot's description of Blake and these reflections is not altogether clear. There was probably an association of ideas here, Blake being the concrete stimulus to an abstract train of thought arising from the occasion. Andrew goes on:

"It is not my primary wish to know the great men of the present world but the world itself, which produces great and small, good and bad, beautiful and ugly, without evaluation, so that it seems to turn us all into fortuitous figures."

This sounds rather like a clever schoolboy, and not quite in tune. Moreover, van Rossum must surely have disapproved of this remark, since his God did not permit accident. Had Andrew thought this out? In any case he goes on:

"If I none the less exert myself to be admitted to some of the great artists, it is above all because I hope to discover whether their greatness is an additional quality, a further dimension, which we ordinary mortals [the phrase was not yet a cliché] lack, or if the quality which raises them above us also affect the other aspects of their humanity, that is, those which impart themselves to others—in other words, whether they are in all other respects as we. For I could imagine that where the creative element in man spreads and grows, human qualities become atrophied."

Marbot's intention is clear. Whether at the end of his researches he found confirmation of his surmises, we do not know. There is much to suggest he later realized that with the artist one cannot speak of a qualitative difference but of a displacement; but he had not yet reached this point.

From this letter written to van Rossum in early May 1820 we also know that Andrew had intended to leave for the Continent at the beginning of June. He had apparently not yet postponed the journey, which must mean that the fateful night still lay ahead; further evidence that the consummation, or its date, had not been planned in Marbot Hall, but that the last precipitation of events towards their inevitable conclusion took place in London. We can set the date in the middle of May because by the end of May the postponement was already fixed; we know this from Crabb Robinson, who notes Andrew's decision under the date of 22 May in his diary, without mentioning any reason. Significantly, however, this note contains Andrew's momentous avowal of a spasm of hatred for his father. Robinson notes it without comment, perhaps disapprovingly, because if we are right about him, he regarded communications of that nature as immoral, or at least contrary to propriety.

For Andrew and Lady Catherine a new life had begun, which soon moved away from the climax of fulfilment and increasingly demanded that its consequences be controlled and ordered. Their eyes had been opened, they saw behind them the deed and before them a menacing, unchartable panorama of future possibilities and impossibilities. Both were only too aware of the urgent need for a separation, so as to allow their violation against the laws of ethics to recede at least to its former latent state. A period of abstention, time to think, which after all, as it turned out, became nothing more than a waiting period, for the smouldering fire within them was constantly rekindled by reminders and recollections, by letters, the tone of which, however reserved, nevertheless throbbed with all their experience, all their longing and desire appearing between the words—a resounding silence, as though both partners, having been mortally frightened, had withdrawn in order to assimilate this beginning and to assess the fearful danger of continuing. The duration of the journey would perforce mean an interlude: a time for remorse, but no longer an opportunity to turn back. For just as one murder makes a man a murderer, so the one commission of the sin made these two lovers sinners; they knew it, although Andrew struggled against the knowledge all his life.

As far as I know there is no similar case in psychopathology. Consummated incest between mother and son is rare, and on the intellectual and social level of this case it has to my knowledge never been described; admittedly there may have been "unreported cases". At all events we know of no laws to cover such a relationship. Lady Catherine and Andrew were truly not amoral figures in an ethical sense, and yet we have to admit that there was some instability. A never-extinguished susceptibility to the charms of the forbidden made them—taken in the strict sense in which I hesitate to take it, for I myself am not assessing their predicament—into pathological "cases". Many of us may have had an early experience of a potential involvement of this nature, but it is not called to memory, and fades as consciousness grows.

The Oedipus complex ultimately disintegrates, or, as Freud puts it: "becomes latent". But in this case it did not. Manifest Oedipal tendencies pervaded and dominated Marbot's life, never to leave him in peace again.

III

The diary which had been kept in sporadic and casual fashion after Andrew moved to London began to take on system and structure. It was here that he began to make purposeful entries and at the same time to work on what became the task of his lifetime. I do not venture to call it a "life's work", as I am not certain if it was planned as such. We shall never know with absolute certainty whether the notes were intended for subsequent publication. The argument that he would other-

61

wise not have made them favours the probability; on the other hand, he left them uncompleted and without any instructions when he took his own life.

What does seem certain to us today is that he did not want to have the notes published in the form in which they were first published by John Murray in 1834 under the title *Art and Life*. Gerald Ross appears as the editor. The book aroused some attention in artistic circles, but those few concerned whom Marbot had known, including Turner and Crabb Robinson, observed that the texts were too arbitrarily strung together and suspected some unauthorized manipulation. De Quincey, whom I have already quoted and who was then forty-nine and living in Edinburgh, wrote in *Blackwood's Magazine*: "An illuminating work, full of general truth and insight into the artist's soul." But, said De Quincey, the author was no doubt the posthumous victim of his editor, so that "this noble and highly vivid prose" was too frequently interrupted by inconsequential ideas. The reader would stumble over abrupt joins, obviously caused by omissions. By this means the ideas were often reduced to aphorisms and the "deductive scheme" quite lost. Here was wonderful, firm flesh, lacking only the skeleton to hold it together.

De Quincey's review reflects the opinion of a perceptive critic who was not himself intellectually concerned with the subject matter but who had become acquainted with it through its author, whom he had known as a young man when the trains of thought which led to these notes were not yet fixed but were already moving clearly and inexorably towards their theme. His was in fact the very first review, which had its effect on other critics: they all praised the work, while questioning the authority and objectivity of the editor.

In 1839 Marbot's work appeared in Germany under the title *Die Kunst und das Leben*. Here it was Carl Friedrich von Rumohr—a friend of the adult Marbot—who cast doubt on the authenticity of the text. Rumohr, himself the possessor of a fine sense of taste, who as Marbot had done, and probably under his influence though only secondarily, was seeking insight into the artistic mentality, observed that this book "exhibits a spirit as noble as its study, but limps at least on one leg because it has been injured". Not only must the individual sections of text have been written at widely separated times, giving rise to thematic repetitions (which apparently escaped De Quincey and others), but the observations were obviously addressed to various individuals and were not intended to take effect at a distance unknown to their author. Here Rumohr is probably at fault, perhaps because he was remembering conversations with Marbot and recognized in the book opinions which Marbot had expressed to him; moreover—as we must assume that they spoke German to each other—these ideas were probably formulated better, because spontaneously, by Marbot himself than in the German translation by Heinrich Wilhelm Schulz (not to be confused with the Prussian Staatsrat Schultz, whom Marbot had met with Goethe). The translation is stiff, academic and inflexible. The undertone of suppressed irony which so often surfaces in the original, always appearing to call the writer's own judgment in question, escaped Schulz's skill; it is in any case a difficult tone to translate.

As we know, the criticism and scepticism turned out to be justified. Nowadays we are aware of what Hadley-Chase already suspected but was unable to prove for certain:[3] that the editor, "Gerald Ross", was none other than Father Gerard van

---

3. Here the comparison with a parallel, though still more extreme case cannot be avoided: Pascal's *Pensées sur la religion* appeared in 1670, eight years after his death, in a distorted version which provided no indication of the order and sequence of the individual sections of text. Even now no final conclusions have been reached about it, and yet this obscurity is not prejudicial to the significance of the work.

Rossum, who had made an attempt to bring all the material he could lay his hands on, the notes and letters to him and others, into context; an enterprise as audacious as it was naive, especially for a man less familiar with the subject than its author.

The fact that Marbot's work has nevertheless gained steadily in importance and was the first to show the way towards psychoanalytically-oriented aesthetics, is a testimony to the material, which has survived its unseemly treatment. Even now, this manipulated patchwork has lost nothing of its meaning; on the contrary, some of Marbot's theories can now be authenticated, some of his attributions, in so far as we may assume a constant in the science of art, have proved correct—it would be a mistake to speak of certainty of proof in this area. At all events, the book is in a sense unreplaceable, there is nothing of comparable nature or·worth. The false light in which it puts its author, by appearing to feign infallibility, has never ceased to illuminate an aspect of the material under discussion not previously available to the viewer, because he did not have the equipment for it, and most biographers—in my opinion—do not have it yet.

The blame for this lopsided, over-simplified view lies with van Rossum, to whom the material was much more alien than it was to De Quincey; for, at least until these papers were published, which must have opened up new vistas to him as well, the priest regarded aesthetics as infinitely inferior to ethics. All the same, to resent his editorship would be both inappropriate and unjust, since for him it was a venture undertaken on behalf of his dead friend and pupil. As a priest, and a Jesuit at that, he should not have come into the public eye as editor of a worldly, indeed very worldly work. We do not know if he consulted some superior in the Order in this matter of conscience, but I think any such placet is improbable; even as an educator he had had a conception of his responsibility. In any case he had been the recipient of most of the letters which he had, or believed he had, woven into the text of the non-epistolary notes.

At the end of 1830, when Marbot had to be presumed dead, Anna Maria Baiardi, the companion of his years in Urbino, sent to his mother in England the collected notes—those same three leather-bound quarto volumes, closely written on one side, and a further quarto book of thirty-two pages, written on both sides—and all the other writings and letters she could find. It is not to be supposed that Anna Maria had tried to read them. Not only was she too discreet; she understood neither English nor German and would certainly not have allowed anyone else to translate for her from the personal papers of the man she had loved and so sadly lost. Lady Catherine, on the other hand, read all that she could read; she would have been a sanctimonious monster had she not done so. She crossed out the intimate—and really revealing—entries written in tiny letters, because she naturally recognized herself at once under the disguise, and gave the books to van Rossum to read. Realizing their importance he decided, with Lady Catherine's eager consent, to make them into a book with the aid of pertinent and explanatory material from the letters to himself. These, one might say, were the limits of his responsibility, yet Lady Catherine went just as far as he did in her conviction. She left to the priest—and hence to her confessor!—the factual portions of the letters in her possession, after destroying the intimate passages and making illegible, as she believed, the incriminating transitions from the personal to the abstract and vice versa. There is no doubt that these portions of the letters—passages of an apparently particularly penetrating nature, as if the writer were drawing the beloved into the centre of the picture—made the book more explosive, which of course neither editor nor reader noticed. It also appeared that Andrew assumed that his mother took a marked interest in his research; this was presumably confirmed by his experience.

It was this material, then, that van Rossum arranged according to subject, not entirely without skill, but without being aware of the precise dosage of the substance to be administered. From the notes which make up the greater part of the book, as well as from the letters, especially those to Andrew's mother, he once again sternly deleted anything which might have been regarded as a personal allusion, rightly, no doubt, from his point of view. For at that time Andrew's younger brother John Matthew was about to embark on a political career, and, although it is not probable that he was close to van Rossum as a man, the priest would naturally have wanted to avoid anything in the book which might have been detrimental to him. Above all, however, by eliminating everything personal he certainly wanted to make it appear that his friend and pupil had displayed that objectivity of view which, he no doubt felt, would elevate the contents of the volume to the level of pure intellectual worth, unclouded by human desires. No guilt then attaches to van Rossum here either. On the contrary, it is to his credit that he attributed to his former pupil that high level of judgment which Andrew never claimed to have reached and which is in reality unattainable. However that may be, the reconstruction of a world of ideas is impeded here by that very mystification to which we owe its preservation. For without Father Gerard van Rossum we would know nothing of Andrew Marbot.

The Father's ideas for the future use of the material entrusted to him, after the publication of the volume, can no longer be discovered. He was old by then and his time was running out. Since he regarded the passages blotted out in ink by Lady Catherine as definitively illegible, and the passages simply deleted by himself were not incriminating, he seems to have left it to chance that the entire literary legacy should fall into the hands of a posterity which at that time of course had scarcely any interest in it. Van Rossum died in 1847 at the age of eighty-one at a Jesuit house in Rome, and it can be assumed that in the care of souls, which he had undertaken late in life, but voluntarily and gladly, he had forgotten—not, of course, his former life, but—the possession of its documentation. The legacy passed to his brother, who was living in Amsterdam; the brother's nephew, Adriaan van Rossum, preserved it, though without arranging it, since he did not think himself either entitled or qualified to do so, and yet, either in tacit acceptance of a testamentary, though never stipulated wish of the Father, or from his own understanding of concealment of sin, he extracted the fragments of the letters to Andrew's mother and placed them under separate cover. They were seen by no one, in fact there was probably no one who had any idea of their existence, until Frans van Rossum, the last descendant and heir to all the family papers, including these documents, put them at the present author's disposal and thus made it possible for me to write this book. How research, which was in fact only in its early stages, explained the origins of those passages in *Art and Life* which had been extracted from the letters to Lady Catherine and the originals of which were therefore unknown, remains obscure. Hadley-Chase thought they were verbal communications to van Rossum—a relatively consistent explanation and the most probable, other than the truth itself.

Apart from the approval of the few people who had known Marbot, we know little about the reaction to the book on publication. Only a handful of authorities, of whom there were relatively even fewer then than there are today, were capable of artistic appreciation, but those few, as De Quincey records, read the book and discussed it keenly. But the time was far from ripe for psychoanalytically-oriented aesthetics, so, apart from that handful of critics, we have scarcely any evidence of contemporary reactions. Turner praised the book in his academic lectures in 1836, when he apparently said that Marbot painted the soul of the artist as no artist had ever been able to paint it (although it should be remarked that no such attempt has ever occurred to most artists). Later Ruskin and Pater referred repeatedly to the book, quoting and discussing it, but never converted it into a theoretical instrument for their own use, since it did not actually touch on the aesthetic areas with which they were concerned. In Germany the name of Marbot became known at least to those who attended Herman Grimm's Berlin lectures in the winter semester of 1874, in which he discussed Marbot and Rumohr as two outstanding experts on late Romantic painting.

Obviously Marbot's field—the artist's psychology and its decisive influence on his choice of material, the content of the painting, its composition and execution—must have appeared strange, if not positively outlandish to contemporary and indeed all nineteenth-century aestheticians, and not only to them but to the artists themselves. Marbot's celebrated utterance on Turner explains this reaction:

"Many an artist would be terrified if he could interpret the motives which lead to his painting. But he would be still more terrified if he could interpret the image of his inner self which leads to his motives."

Turner repeated this remark gleefully and often, perhaps because he knew that no one could make this truth apply to him.

At all events, Marbot was never appreciated at his true worth. Admittedly, the late nineteenth century saw his work as an interesting, but far too eccentric contribution to the reception of art, its merit lying more in its uniqueness than its validity. For instance, the—otherwise estimable—American art historian Frederic Hadley-Chase claims in his monograph that what is to be admired above all in Marbot is his "creative imagination"; he clothed his figures in the "flowing mantle of Romanticism, which does not, however, suit everyone". And Edward Renshaw, in his book *English Art Criticism of the Nineteenth Century* (1904), calls Marbot an amateur of genius, who tried to combine the history of art with psychology. Both stress the eccentric element in Marbot, not as a defect, but as a quality which entitled him to be included in the ranks of those odd people whom England no doubt rightly regards as peculiarly characteristic of itself. But the fact was that Marbot did not belong to this type, so that thanks to inaccurate biography his image fell under a false light, in so far as there was any light at all. No doubt he was an eccentric, but more probably a man who lived at a profound, solitary and secret level; not a man to calculate the effect of his behaviour and court public reaction, neither a dandy nor a pretentious oddity. He did not cultivate his "differentness", never tried to adapt, not even to the minority of outsiders. Yet he did not ostentatiously withhold himself.

It is really of little use to delve into the existing material about him, unless preoccupation with the response to his work and influence is an end in itself. There was evidently scarcely one of his interpreters who was capable of swallowing his unacademic and only apparently unmethodical appreciation of art. That is why there has never been a critical edition of his work, which in any case would have been highly unsatisfactory, since the texts which supply the ultimate revelation of the relationship of life to work have been missing. They are the sole key to an understanding of Marbot the man.

Marbot's Grand Tour lasted for two years. Such a long period is unusual and it can be assumed that the journey was made in the interests of a weaning process, of an attempt by Andrew, and by Lady Cahterine, who remained behind, to practise renunciation. It is quite possible that he would have prolonged his travels even further had he not been recalled to England by the death of his father in the autumn of 1822. It is even possible that Father Gerard would have ordained a permanent separation, if Lady Catherine had made up her mind, which she did not, to confess her sin as soon as it was committed. In that case Andrew, had he lived, would not have returned home until after his mother's death.

The separation was undoubtedly easier for him to bear than for her. He was able to distract his mind with intellectual pursuits and, had his psychological make-up in the circumstances permitted, he would have been able to find an erotic substitute. Perhaps he did; we do not know. But if so, it is questionable if he would then have returned to his mother's arms. Before the return he had taken part in the Venice Carnival. Such a personable young gentleman, one would think, would have found it difficult to avoid an amorous adventure there unless he took special pains to prevent it. But in that case, why attend the Carnival at all?

In his notes, once again written small at the bottom of a page, there is the tell-tale jotting—though we do not know what secret it reveals: "One whose innocence was raped by an angel loses by every further experience." Did he then prefer to do without the "further experience" in order not to blot out the exquisite image of the angel? Or did he accept the loss in an attempt to expunge that image from his soul for ever? Probably the latter, since he would scarcely have spoken of the experience had he not had it. Or is it a warning to himself? We do not know. But the comment forces us to think of Lady Catherine, reading it and trying to make it illegible with violent strokes of the pen. She must have suspected, and her reason must have approved, his attempt to find a substitute. His failure might well have pleased her. She probably never learned that he had failed, but perhaps she suspected it.

Marbot travelled without due style, without servants or friend, with little baggage; he never rode in his own coach, not even later, on his second journey, until he settled down at Urbino, where he kept one servant and a coach and coachman. There are very few dated entries relating to his first journey, no details of the intermediate stops, no indications of the where or the how. Even those letters which have been preserved generally, if not always, omit the personal. We suppose that his sense of what was worth communicating did not allow him to record his physical disposition or indisposition or to squander his energies on commonplaces about trivial events—we are the losers, of course, because even apparently inessential detail would have interested us. And yet, here and there—appearing suddenly like will-o'-the-wisps calculated to parody the aesthetic, depersonalized argument, to highlight the inconvenient bodily nature and thereby as it were efface himself—there are jottings such as this one:

"After supper in the inn at a mountain village whose name my memory was rightly disinclined to record, I passed a night of violent stomach pains which moved the lower part of my body like waves, so that the upper part was obliged willy-nilly to translate the feelings into thought. I observed that pain renders one homeless. Suddenly one no longer has any idea where one belongs; at all events not to the world of those who have no pain. A great longing pervades one for a life in which one has no longer any pain, and in which there is not the least fear of pain. In this situation the recognition takes shape that man is alone with himself. Seeking examples in art, one finds none. Such a recognition does indeed exist in literature, but it gives examples which will not occur to the understanding of the person thus isolated at the moment, for they remain hypothetical. The aching heart imparts itself to the other heart, but the aching body does not do so to the other's body."

As the reader will discover, Marbot turned the opportunity for such incidental witticisms against contemporary literature into something like a system, with the purpose of demonstrating how unimportant it was to him.

From the beginning Marbot was intent on objectivizing his ego, on not betraying his inmost feelings, his true mood or his state at a particular moment. But from the few entries which refer to him personally, or from the letters, the melancholic is darkly glimpsed. "Why," he wrote to van Rossum,

"when I see beauty, do I always feel I am seeing it
not for the first but for the last time? Is this sensation
part of the essence of beauty, or is it part of me? Do
others feel it as I do?"

Characteristically he seems never to have asked anyone, and he probably in fact knew scarcely anyone he would have wanted to ask.

"By others I mean, of course, those who are capable
of feeling anything at all besides their bodily needs
and the satisfaction of them, in so far as such people
exist."

Here his melancholy takes on a tinge of misanthropy, yet it would not be possible to say that Marbot was hostile to people; on the contrary, he deplored their lot and their resignation to it, he sympathized, indeed often suffered with them.

So it would not have occurred to him to make an inventory of his days; he was no diarist. His notes are not cumulative and are seldom in the past tense; most—not all—of them are confirmatory observations of what had been revealed to him, but not personal records of the act of discovery. He did not write "I feel it to be so", but "it is so", leaving it to the reader, in so far as he is addressed, to add: "for me, Marbot". He needed no aids to memory; his visual memory in particular most have been extraordinary. Pictures stamped themselves on his mind, one above another, layer by layer, and all of them remained permanently present in all their detail and subtlety; the stocks of whole museums were stored in him. And his mental experience was not very different. "A thought which escapes the mind never does so without good reason", as he wrote to his mother. So he had also pondered the processes of forgetting and suppressing, even the process of reflection itself, with its path determined by the unconscious. In this too he anticipated psychoanalysis.

We know that he often interrupted his journeying for days in order

> "to share in the apparent peace of Nature, that silent and mighty power, to whom we are a matter of wondrous indifference. Many poets have asserted that she hates us, but to me this seems a monstrous over-estimation of human beings. Still more have claimed that she loves us, and this in turn is religion. Blake says she is the work of the devil. This means that he at least concedes her the power of successful temptation."

Marbot was constantly grappling with the concept of "nature", until he decided, and he may have been one of the first to do so, to use it exclusively for the sensorily accessible opposite of the man-made or manipulated—that is "culture". So what he meant here was not only "untamed self-realization", not only the grandiose or idyllic, and not only those landscape backgrounds in pictures of which he has given an unsurpassed interpretation, but also the conspicuously inconspicuous, the unportrayable, or at least not yet portrayed, which "awakens longings for nothing determinate, unless it is to live backwards, gradually sloughing all experience"—and here we should probably add: in order to return to his mother's womb at last. For, according to Marbot: "Longing is retroverted curiosity."

From some notes of the later years we learn which landscapes he may have had in mind. First of all there is the scene of his childhood and youth, Northumberland, that "horizontal composition with vanishing vertical accents"; then the regions which, while not reminding him of his home, represented in their inconspicuous fascination the counter-pole of the splendour glorified by others, such as the Po valley, which he must have known from mountain source to mouth.

"The Po, a powerful, imperious stream which demands homage like a strict yet unjust father, floods from time to time and without the least meteorological pretext causes farmsteads to disappear with men and animals. It is untamable, though never unbridled, it does not fling itself against its banks but covers them and takes them to itself—but when at rest it makes of these very banks flights of chambers, separated off by trees and bushes, which the mind explores at leisure while the soul is in repose. For these billowing waters suppress the inward uproar and transmit a feeling of eternal or at least of ever-returning peace." (To his mother.)

Yet another romantic utterance: nature subdues the unquiet soul; almost a commonplace and yet not so, since it is perfectly easy for us to re-experience the soothing effect of those "billowing waters". So we see him lingering there in the soft light filtered by rows of poplars; he has made his way through clumps of wild blackberries; now he is sitting in the sand, on a surface fretted by reeds, above flooded land, perhaps looking across at a fisherman on whose passive occupation, peaceful and radiating peace, his thoughts have fastened. Perhaps he himself would like to be that fisherman, whereas the fisherman, if he notices Marbot at all, thinks how much he would like to be that idler Marbot—something that Marbot, if he even guessed at such an idea, would not wish on him. Here our hero rests, in an all-obliterating leisure, surrounded by a panorama of stillness and eternal melancholy, which to less discerning travellers—and all but he were probably that—was nothing but a thirsty stretch between Alps and Apennines.

Marbot to his mother:

"...sitting like a Biblical figure in the shade of a pinetree in some churchyard—or like some simple fisherman by the broad banks of a mighty river, I seem to regain my equilibrium and my innocence."

We have jumped too far ahead. Marbot is not yet by the Po, but in Paris, where he stayed until the middle of October 1820. The Louvre, which Napoleon, with the proud gesture of the conqueror, had filled with the fruits of victory, was in its first, not yet perfect bloom. Baron Denon, half artist and half general manager, who had received the emperor's order, had tried in about 1800 to set up a chronologically arranged universal museum, an ambitious undertaking in which he had partly succeeded. There were real signs of the ideal museum, which was subsequently to turn into an over-sized warehouse. In those days it was not yet labyrinthine as it is today, but within the viewer's grasp, sparsely filled and, in the painting department at least, well arranged. Napoleon's booty included a few German masterpieces: portraits by Holbein—including one of Anne of Cleves—Dürer's self-portrait of 1491 and the head of a woman in a round frame, over the dating of which the scholars argue, as is their wont. If we are right in our interpretation of the chronological order of Marbot's notebooks, he would have jotted down the title without

75

making any attempt at interpretation. His critical commentaries on early German art could scarcely have been founded on the few paintings which he saw at the Louvre or later in Nuremberg.

The one painting he discusses in detail during his first stay in Paris is Watteau's *Gilles*. Once again we recognize from the impression which this particular picture made on him his method of selection, the preferences and priorities which he introduced into his system for the sake of his theory; the description of the individual removed from his surroundings who unwillingly reveals his inmost being, hence an experience which moves him far more deeply than external events, than Bible, myth or history, although it will be the sublime exception here. On *Gilles* he notes:

"Gilles is the clown absolute, his very essence, both as earthly embodiment and as his everlasting monument—for the picture is truly monumental. At the same time, however, it is the self-portrait of a painter donning the garment of the fool bestowed on him by fashion, and so demonstrating his inability to make himself at home in that world. Such a person probably existed here, and Watteau painted him more than once, and his like probably still exists today...There he stands, the helpless jester, as though others had put him away here, like a Jumping Jack at rest. We do not know which way he is looking: at the floor, from shame at the variant of humanity that he embodies? Or at the viewer, from whom he dares not expect understanding? Or into his own soul, in the vain hope of finding approbation within? Or at God, with a plea for release? At all events he is out of place in this world, he does not know what to do, standing there in his short trousers, he does not know how to hold his arms with their over-long sleeves, at whose elbows the material folds and bunches; and this is to our gain, for the silken costume is wonderfully painted, the outer garb becomes a symbol of the inner state, for he who elicits compassion has a value that is divine. Sixteen buttons see to it that this heart does not tear itself out and take flight into the background landscape, which he might like, had he not turned his back on it; or into the air, that luminous sky which surrounds the upper part of the figure, darkening at the outlines by a subtle difference to make the white more lustrous. There he stands, the solitary soul, quite weightless, almost as if he were dangling there on strings, utterly ridiculous and yet imbued with a secret dignity, with which he accepts his ridiculousness. The figures behind him seem to take no notice of him, characteristically, they are interested in a donkey which becomes, as it were, if only for a short time, their substitute victim."

Here then is Marbot's programme, clearly broached: isolation as the theme, the choice of a human symbol as pictured object, and identity between the artist and the model thus chosen.

There were some painters' studios in which he was then confronted with the current trends, and in particular, of course, with Classicism, moribund but not yet dead. Its chief exponent, Jacques-Louis David, was at that time in Brussels, but Marbot saw some of his paintings in private houses, including that of Denon himself, whose guest he often was. We know as little of the connection with Denon, then thirty-seven years old, as we do of Marbot's introduction to François Gérard, whom he visited several times in his studio. It is remarkable how rapidly Andrew felt at home in the art world and how naturally he moved about in it, though he was not yet twenty and had spent almost all his life until then in country surroundings. Gérard would certainly not have conveyed to Marbot that feeling of greatness which he expected of the ideal painter, but what he did give him for the first time was the atmosphere of a genuine studio, the scent of turpentine, the profusion of podiums and pedestals in front of heavy velvet curtains; a place, moreover, full of pupils whom he watched as they painted portraits or figures and on whom he conducted behavioural studies which, as we shall see, were later to stand him in good stead. The question inevitably arises: would he have liked to be one of these pupils? The answer would probably be: in principle yes, though probably not in Gérard's studio. The style did not appeal to him, the extravagance, the structure of the scenery seemed to him unnatural. In a letter to Crabb Robinson he writes: "Gérard and David together do not amount to a single Gérard David." We may excuse the aspiring art critic for his lack of appreciation for the admittedly relative qualities of the two first-named, especially since, if we take this estimate literally, he was right.

In Paris too he stayed longer than he had planned. We do not know what held him there, nor even whom he frequented. We cannot see him as a friend of Denon or Gérard, even if we overlook the difference in age. Delacroix and Géricault were still young and unknown, although the latter died only four years later, whereas the former was later to become Marbot's friend, despite some artistic reservations. So the only man of whose acquaintance with Marbot we have proof is the German connoisseur Sulpiz Boisserée, who was spending two months in Paris at the time. They met in Gérard's studio. Boisserée notes on 14 October 1820:
"A handsome young man, dark-haired, though an

Englishman. Speaks little French. (—We are surprised that he spoke any!—) But perfect German. Making the tour to Italy. He is reserved and rather overbearing. We left about eleven, walking a little of the way together. Were followed by two wenches: 'Nous sommes aimables et complaisantes.' What morality!"

Andrew describes their meeting in that very letter written—in German!—to Crabb Robinson:

"The first occasion to employ my German again after our conversations arose here in Paris. An art collector named Boisserée—and I was thinking my knowledge of French would not be sufficient for such a man—turned out to be a German, and in correspondence with Goethe. An honest, courteous man, but neither inspired nor inspiring. He said German painting was the finest. If that is so, I have something to look forward to, for what I have seen until now seemed to me clumsy and uncultivated[?]. He accompanied me when we left Gérard's studio and we were followed by two cocottes, which [!] moved him to indignation over the depravity of morals. A virtuous man, without a doubt."

So much for that meeting, which seems to have been their only one. It does not appear to have awakened sympathy or mutual interest on either side. Andrew's verdict on Boisserée, brief and comprehensive, sounds like the confirmation of a suspicion: honest, yes, obviously morally austere, but for a collector, who does not deal in art but senses its inner worth and exposes it, he remains strangely narrow and tediously mute. Perhaps he was unwilling or unable to communicate, perhaps it was a principle with him to be sparing in his utterances, though there is many a prosaic entry in his diary to refute that possibility, for instance the information that he had bought himself a hat.

The next stopping place we know of is Padua, but it can be assumed that even on this journey Andrew made a stop at Vicenza, which at that time and earlier would not have been omitted by any German or English traveller, since buildings by Palladio were part of the cultural programme. Admittedly Marbot makes no mention of the visit itself, but in the fragment on *Symmetry* already referred to he describes some Palladian buildings in passing: not only the Rotonda, that obligatory showpiece of Classicism, but in particular, and repeatedly, the Teatro Olimpico, "for which one should really write symmetrical plays, lest the grouping of the actors should disturb the harmonious proportions of the background". Hadley-Chase is not the only one to have taken this comment seriously!

We do not know what route he followed from Paris, but in all probability, like most Engliah travellers, he would have either taken the road by Mont Cenis or gone through Geneva and the Great St Bernard down to the Po valley. As we know, he commented in letters on mountain ranges and deep valleys, but these were all written on his second journey. On this first journey he wanted to reach the "home of all art", and hence his own potential home, as quickly as possible and not squander the fires of expectation on bypaths.

He describes Padua as "a dirty comfortless hole". Measured by his precise mode of expression this appears to be unexpectedly sweeping, but perhaps at the time it too was not far from the truth. August von Platen had the same impression, but I would ascribe still less objectivity to him, since his writing fed on emotion, whereas Marbot's tried to achieve objectivity with clarity.

Marbot had read Vasari on Giotto, but since the painter appears there mainly as the resourceful hero of anecdote, Marbot had probably rejected Giotto or taken scarcely any notice of him, particularly since no one in his own circle knew

Giotto's work. Coleridge, in his essay of 1818 on *The General Character of the Gothic Mind in the Middle Ages*, had indeed mentioned him, but it is not likely that he had discussed him with the young Marbot at Redmond Manor, if they met there at all. In any case Coleridge, like all the others who did not hesitate to pass judgment on Giotto—including Goethe and Hegel—had never seen his work; their opinion was based on engravings. Oddly enough, Vasari makes only passing reference to Giotto's work and influence in Padua, so that Marbot had presumably never connected him with that city. We do not know who then suggested, or in fact revealed the frescoes in the Cappella degli Scrovegni to him. We are completely confident that (with the certainty of a sleep-walker) he found the very place which was to open up for him a great and previously unsuspected kind of vision. For until then he had never seen frescoes, and now here they were in a splendid and truly fabulous manifestation. I imagine that he was overwhelmed, but unfortunately, as was probably his usual habit, he later destroyed the evidence of his first impressions on the spot.

Hadley-Chase proposed the theory—Renshaw concurs and I myself would like to substantiate it here, in so far as subjective certainty permits such a judgment—that Marbot carried out this process of destruction systematically; that as soon as he felt he had reached finality in his judgment of a particular theme, whether it was the painter or the work, he consistently erased the records of the preliminary stages; as if he wanted to present himself and—who knows!—potential users, not with infallibility but with his subjective certainty, and to obliterate the traces of the learning process. There are of course several explanations of this kind of procedure. Hadley-Chase adduces Marbot's urge for perfection, which required him to rise as quickly as possible above the steps which led up to it. This is plausible, but one should also consider the fact that Marbot was a great discarder who, unable to subdue the past in

81

himself, at least destroyed its concrete substance, including that which would have brought him more glory than blame.

Then of course there are probably many notes of first or early impressions of which we have no knowledge, unless he recorded them in letters, differently formulated as a rule and presented less didactically. It is this procedure in particular which suggests the intention of future publication.

Thus he first wrote on Giotto in 1828:

"Of the life of Giotto di Bondone we know nothing but a few dates, and we shall certainly never discover anything more about him. Vasari, that assiduous originator of legends, recounts that as a boy herding sheep Giotto amused himself drawing his animals on stone, on the ground and in the sand. There one day Cimabue, en route from Florence to Vespignano on some business or other, stopped beside him and asked him if he would like to be his pupil. The boy Giotto, it appears, consented and followed him to Florence. This legend is as improbable as if Perugino had chanced to pass by a sheep-herding Raphael drawing on stone and invited him to accompany him. In fact it is still more improbable, for Raphael was Perugino's pupil, while Giotto was certainly not Cimabue's. [I was unable to discover Marbot's reasons for being certain of this.] ...Herding animals is a motif which has evidently lost nothing of its legendary charm since the days of antiquity. I think it is meant to symbolize the state of intellectual cultivation of the future genius— perhaps what Goethe calls the 'state of nature'— from which the will of the gods, or of God, raised him, by sending a gifted agent to release him...

In reality Giotto had no teacher. He painted because he painted, as the rose blooms because it blooms—only he painted as no one has painted or—who knows—dared to paint since pre-Christian times by making men of saints...In his vision of the world, identical with the vision conveyed to and imposed upon him by his faith, he remained a lifelong child, painting for children; for in the contemplation and interpretation of pictures his contemporaries were children, to whom this divine story-teller told fairy tales in the form of legends of saints and ecclesiastical history. As he depicted miracles, so his picture of them became itself a miracle, and not only that: in painting he experienced the miracle in himself, so that he depicted it, not only in those whom it befell or who brought it about, but also through his own intense experience and therefore with twofold force. Overwhelmed by the mysteries of the history of faith, he overwhelmed the beholder and does so still. His incomparable greatness lies therefore not only in the convincing, because convinced, forcefulness of his portrayal, but primarily in the power of his own experience of the divine, which he is communicating to us as he paints picture after picture on the wall, in truly disarming innocence, in obedience to a law which instructs him what and how to paint and which excludes the possibility of mistake or error, even of weakness. Here then the saints are for the first time not set apart as objects of adoration, but people captured at that ecstatic moment for which they have been living and which justifies their earthly existence to all eternity. And the unholy, tormentors and sinners, are portrayed in such a way that every beholder can picture to himself the measure of the punishment awaiting them in hell.

From the moment of their transgression, they too will never be the same. But, be they holy or unholy—never before or since has exaltation been portrayed in such perfect harmony of colour and composition... The sole element which remains enigmatic and which we cannot explain, which indeed betrays the Byzantine origin of his figures, are the eyes, which though they reflect a supreme experience, reveal neither its kind nor its quality. ...Giotto's eyes seem always weird and enigmatic, if not, indeed, sinister. No matter what the lower portion of the face seems to reveal, good or ill, guilt or innocence, ecstasy or indifference, the gaze of those piercing eyes directed at the source of the event does not tell us its nature..."

This is a sample of his thorough and detailed notes on Giotto, years after he had seen their subject, from memory, with the help of the jottings made on the spot. Only a single passage from a letter to Crabb Robinson in November 1822 expresses the direct impression of his visit to the Scrovegni Chapel in Padua:

"Our Mr Blake could have learned from Giotto how supernatural figures move. For this Master shows us angels, not as ideas congealed into matter, but as children of flesh and blood, with wings growing on them as naturally as on birds and with which they can fly, too; even when grief at the Crucifixion of Christ seems to be tearing their hearts in two, they hover, weeping, if not indeed howling and screaming, but nevertheless gathered in sublime grace about the Cross."

And later to his mother:

"With Giotto we once again become children, believers in the miraculous, and refuse to believe the

84

adult who tells us: it does not exist. We point to
Giotto and say: there it is!"
And *we* add: "...and so we regain our innocence."

Marbot did not go to Rome on this first journey. With
no imperative aim, following at will the mood engendered by
landscape or weather or climate, he ranged across Veneto and
the Marches, Umbria and Tuscany, not in pursuit of culture
but with a mounting thirst for paintings and their motifs, for
landscapes and seascapes, in search of evidence to support his
theory—and increasingly on the right track—a secret which he
was not to unfold until it revealed itself to him as cognition. In
the autumn of 1821 he wries to van Rossum:
"Paintings appear to me more and more as framed
enigmas, previously not only unsolved, but never
seen by anyone as enigmas at all. Perhaps even I shall
not solve them all, many of them are probably no
longer to be solved, but I believe that I am on the
scent of the nature of the enigma, namely the soul of
the artist, which has moved him to paint the
particular painting that he has painted and no other;
to paint it in the way he has painted it and not
otherwise. For everything is anchored in the soul:
theme, composition, colour, ductus, everything.
Quod sit demonstrandum."
This dictum appears rather complacent to us; on the
other hand it is an earnest of his profound commitment, indeed
his preoccupation with the object of study he had discovered
for himself. One might almost call it a sublimation enforced!

At Venice, his next stopping place, Marbot discovered
for himself Carpaccio, "that gifted story-teller". He stayed
there until the spring of 1821, that is throughout the Carnival.
We have no information as to his society or the intensity and

85

degree of his participation in it, since we do not know him as gallant or gossip, we have not seen him as a "joiner". To Lady Catherine he writes:

> "Strangely enough I enjoy making myself unrecognizable, although scarcely anyone knows me in any case. I, so to speak, feign unrecognizability to myself."

So "scarcely anyone" knew him, but not no one at all. Who did know him, and how had he made their acquaintance? Whenever he uses that "I", his words become on the one hand revealing, on the other hand enigmatic. At all events the sentence seems to imply two things—unconsciously: in reality I and my behaviour are totally unrecognizable to myself; consciously: if you and I were unrecognizable, known to no one, we could enjoy our love, in unmolested bliss, for the rest of our days.

In the spring of that year Marbot was in Urbino for the first time, on the scent of the *cortegiano*. Little is known of this visit, either, because it is not even documented by the way while mentioning a work of art, but only by Giancarlo Catani-Ligi, later his friend in Urbino, to whom he spoke of the visit four years later: he had spent three months there—had no idea what he had done, probably nothing, as was so often his way—there were places where simply to be there was an engrossing occupation. Many readers may, as I do, feel quite capable of imagining this condition of "being" fully in one place or another; I have indeed experienced it often myself. No doubt this satisfying occupation was one of the reasons why Marbot chose Urbino to live in, after perhaps considering and rejecting other possibilities.

We can go some way towards reconstructing where Andrew stayed until the winter of 1821 from the art appreciations in his later notebooks: Montefalco (the Gozzoli frescoes), Perugia, Assisi, Arezzo and Volterra; he probably chose the last less for its art then for its situation, the fantastic landscape in which he claimed to recognize ideal backgrounds for paintings. To van Rossum:

"This town seems to have been clapped on top of the mountain range by a painter desirous of creating the model of an apocalyptic scene for his backgrounds. I am living in the guest-room of a Franciscan monastery situated above a deep chasm, and in stormy weather I expect the wall which separates me from the precipice to be swallowed up, leaving me in the open. So you see I am learning what it means to live on the brink of an abyss."

The monastery in which he was probably staying has since in fact collapsed into the valley below.

In the winter of 1821-2 Marbot spent a month in Pisa with Byron and his circle. The purpose of the visit must certainly have been less to frequent the society of an admired poet than to investigate his creative motives. When he had written to van Rossum from London in 1820 applied equally to the decision leading to this visit: he intended to examine the relationship between the artist's creativity and his command over his own life.

Byron, sceptical at first and then curious about Marbot, invited him to one of his Wednesday dinner parties, thus submitting him to the scrutiny of other members of his circle. The result was evidently more positive than negative, and so communication was established. The poet was installed on the *piano nobile*—the first floor—of the Palazzo Lanfranchi, where he lived with a shifting entourage consisting, while Marbot was staying there, of Byron's beloved, Countess Teresa Guiccioli, her brother, Count Pietro Gamba, Tito the

87

factotum, Moretto the bulldog and four white geese in a cage. The ground floor was inhabited by Leigh Hunt with his Marianne and their children, as spoiled as they were grubby, in something approximating to the "natural state". The rest lived outside: Shelley, whom their neighbours called "l'Inglese melanconico", "listening to the solemn music of the pine tops", with his blond, windblown locks, reading Calderón aloud to everyone, whether they liked it or not; Trelawney, called "the Turk", a somewhat dubious but amusing figure who insisted on playing the pirate and was always organizing perilous excursions in virtually home-made sailing boats. The remainder of the cast fluctuated.

Byron must have looked pretty ridiculous to the inhabitants, with his short tartan jacket, blue velvet cap and overwide nankeen trousers—that was how he dressed when the group went out for pistol practice, mostly outside the town, to which Marbot was invited, although he himself refused to shoot. A hopeless, for ever insuperable disorder prevailed in the Palazzo Lanfranchi, not least because Byron—Marbot's opposite in more ways than this—never threw anything away, heaping everything up around himself, from scraps and sheets of paper and tickets to oars, planks, sails, keels and other nautical props. Moreover it was appallingly noisy, not only because of the four Hunt children but because of the animals Byron kept: from time to time he also had goats in the house, several parrots and a barn-owl—that at least was apparently inaudible.

In a letter to De Quincey Marbot describes the curious state of affairs in the Byron household:

"The house is agitated by perpetual chaos. No day resembles its predecessor. New figures are also constantly appearing, expected and unexpected, one never knows them all. To the permanent din of men seemingly composing their works but always declaiming are added cats, dogs, birds, goats, children, couples (of which each partner is half of a married couple whose other half is elsewhere). An eager and active immorality prevails, and when it dies down Mylord rekindles it; everyone seems to be living with another's wife and he himself lives with all, or at least boasts of doing so. This immorality does not trouble me, of course, but it has something over-vehement about it, as if all of them, but Byron in particular, wished to prove something to the world; but the world insists on going on as it is. I do not care for Byron, but I admit that he is able now and then to rouse himself to flashes of wit and great ideas. The supreme commandment is: nothing shall come to rest, πάντα ῥεῖ. It is an exotic household. Mylord with the foot of a faun to counterbalance the head of a god—this deformity is the root of all his doings, he must ever be proving himself anew. A club-footed Apollo! An Adonis, the foot alone misshapen, to avenge the beauty of the rest. His outward life is an everlasting active compensation for this blemish; he believes he must achieve more in order to make up for it. So at times he gives the impression that it is the goat's foot that prevents him from floating off into the empyrean. This blemish is none the less the most human thing in him, for his beauty is both wicked and malicious. He keeps a court jester, Trelawney by name, who behaves as if he had sprung from one of Mylord's books and was one of his heroes; a court rival called Shelley, who is a better poet than he, which he knows; and a mistress called Teresa Guiccioli who is as beautiful as she is silly, yet governs him. I believe that he does in reality despise women, if not everybody!"

Marbot seemingly did not revise his verdict on Teresa Guiccioli when six years later she became his own mistress for a brief but lively period. One would occasionally be inclined to observe that human warmth was not one of Marbot's qualities, but this would be a mistaken estimation, which can be refuted by closer observation of his sporadic love affairs. The evidence—which is admittedly little enough—proves that he was capable of a deep empathy with his partners; indeed, that for the duration of the relationship he tried to share their destiny. Certainly even these efforts were made on behalf of his psychological researches, yet he never did distinguish between pure experience of life and applied experience. His love for his mother must moreover have worked like a transmuted radiation on those women in whom he sought his mother—without of course ever finding her.

The letter, as we have seen, was addressed to De Quincey, and therein lies a certain diabolical deliberation, a desire for didactic demonstration. He knew that De Quincey was always trying to find an accommodation with society and conform to its rules in order to lay the spectre of what he probably thought of as his vice. Marbot had noted this at an early stage: the all too obvious striving for virtue, the tendency towards prudery and bigotry, which was compensatory, not natural. Marbot sought to counteract this sanctimoniousness by describing to De Quincey eccentric circles in which he himself mixed without expressing any criticism on grounds of principle. Whether De Quincey understood this and was irritated by it is uncertain. In any case Marbot knew that he could not have written such a letter to Crabb Robinson, for that bachelor was a steadfast and unswerving champion of decency, virtue and religious observance, a Protestant, church-goer and, like all his circle, a stern critic of Byron the man; in his prudery he was a forerunner of Victorianism. Of De Quincey, for instance, he said: "I neither like the man nor

90

respect him. I admire only the writer." He was always fair and that makes him estimable. When Byron died, he wrote:

"The death of Lord Byron, since announced, has probably interrupted the course of a fiction which would have been as useless to the more discerning critic and to the moral world as all the other works of the author. I do not join in the lamentations which will assail us for the next month from every quarter."

Marbot would certainly never have agreed to his friend's narrow-minded pronouncements. But he knew that Crabb Robinson's humanity transcended such trivial convictions, for it was deep and genuine; in contrast to De Quincey, he had nothing to hide. A letter of that nature would probably have offended and disappointed him and, in relation to Lord Byron, confirmed his opinion; Robinson was a lovable Philistine.

Incidentally Andrew's deliberately didactic letter to De Quincey came too late. He had not known that his friend had by then decided to take the bull by the horns and had succeeded in creating a positive sensation: the first edition of his *Confessions of an English Opium-Eater* had come out in 1821 and caused a general commotion, not only because of its confessional nature, but also because of the vivid pictures it conjured up of states of intoxication which made many an unstable reader resort at once to opium-taking. Andrew did not read the book until after 1822, at Marbot Hall, and at the sight of this prose, as controlled as it is suggestive, "this music of persuasion like the sound of sirens", he may have felt impelled to offer a tacit apology to its author. Nothing is known, however, of any subsequent meeting.

In Siena—"a city like a work of art"—he met Baron Carl von Rumohr, who had taken up residence here for a few weeks on his second Italian journey. In him Marbot to some extent discovered his model: Rumohr's self-chosen occupation and independent way of life corresponded to Andrew's idea of his own future, or that span of future he allowed himself. Still more: in Rumohr he was meeting a man who knew how to carry his status as a secret "outsider" with the bearing of a man of the world and of intellect. He did not carry it too heavily either, for as a sovereign despiser of petty convention he was uniquely at home in the world of the beautiful. This for him did not of course mean only art but also the cultivation of existence with many a self-imposed obligation—he was a convert to Catholicism—and corresponding indulgences—as we know, he kept an exemplary kitchen. In contrast to Marbot—who outdid him in some respects in his secret life as an outsider—Rumohr was no dilettante but a professional art historian, perhaps the first: one who has rightly been called the father of the scientific study of art. To Marbot, whose judgment was more intuitive than schematic, Rumohr's verdicts often appeared academic and uninspired. In one—oddly detailed—letter to van Rossum he writes:

"This German baron knows a great deal and has seen more than others, but like most people he too approaches paintings in a way which fails to further our understanding. For the historical classification and comparative analysis of style is not enough to explain the essence of the individual painting as a product of the mind. For instance, Rumohr is critical of the failure of some artists to do justice to this or that rule of composition or even to the material interpretation of a biblical or mythological event, whereas it is of course artists themselves who set standards. To Herr von Rumohr artists are dramatis personae of art history—as people are now beginning to call it; this art history is—as I see

92

it—no more than the constantly frustrated attempt to prescribe or describe roles for the artists in a drama. He has never concerned himself with the psychic necessity of the artist which causes a picture to be painted as it is and not otherwise. He does not first ask whether the artist has achieved what he should. He is none the less an excellent man, of superior intellect, thoughtful and serene; for him even daily life, eating, for instance, becomes as it were an art. Never have I been so aware of this activity as at the meals to which he has invited me. It is a ceremonial which begins with silent tasting and then, aided by brief comment, takes on independent life. He does not conceal the fact that eating absorbs a great part of his interest, indeed even while eating he talks of eating, and is both aroused and arousing. Not only does he take his cook with him on his travels, he also directs him what and how he is to cook. If I have a cook one day, as I begin to wish, I shall bind him apprentice to Baron von Rumohr."

Marbot did not actually do this, but a later note, probably from Urbino, where he had his own house with some land and a garden, indicates that from this visit onwards he took an interest in the art of cooking and instructed his cook personally, in so far as he had confidence in his own authority. He had also begun to ponder on eating as an essential component of a widely-conceived programme of life:

"Conversation on bodily well-being does not occur in the drawing-room, its vocabulary being regarded as indelicate. Meals are concocted in the kitchen; we partake of them with more or less relish and say no more about it. The kitchen premises have a language of their own. What Herr von Rumohr calls the science of the kitchen is not regarded as a subject.

93

The result is that our food is never mentally digested, since what the body is not allowed to communicate is also denied to the mind. And yet eating has a metaphysical dimension, to be discovered only by one who eats with full awareness and concentration. One might search long before finding anybody who is prepared to talk of eating while eating; of the great theme of nourishment, by which I naturally do not mean its destiny, but its origin. Of the absorption of art from nature, from growing things, and of course also from dead things. Of the life-supporting cruelty—for as flesh-eaters we are all barbarians—which allows us to look into the beautiful great eye of the peaceful cow in the meadow as if she were not ultimately to be our victim—though this will come after a long, quiet life which many a one would envy her. To follow the trace of what first finds fulfilment in our mouth, only to pass on into darkness, would lighten so much in this darkness. This is not by any means intended to justify the loquacity of my father, who would hold forth about hunting over five courses, while its spoils were being consumed, as if his listeners had not themselves been huntsmen...

The dignity and magic of the helpless and vulnerable adheres to the beast, even to the wild beasts of Africa, whose time will run out in a hundred or two hundred years. That which has four legs will sooner or later become the prey of that which has only two, and anyone who is troubled, as I am, by that fact should hold to the thought of those creatures who either have none, like the fish, or those whose skull is too small for a brain to make them conscious of their imperilled existence. The plump hen in the field I regard without pity (where I am concerned) and without a head (where it is concerned) in the pan (where Herr von Rumohr is concerned), larded with sprigs of that lilac-flowering rosemary bush which flourishes up there in the hilly fields in a luxuriance of shrubs whose fragrance is wafted to me on a gentle breeze, and when I discover these pine-needles exuding their aroma under the roasted skin of the bird so unloved in life, the landscape of the Marches appears before my eyes, taste and memory merge, spirit and flesh are one."

In a passage like this—admittedly the only one of its kind in the notes—we find the presence of Rumohr's influence far more strongly than on the subject of art criticism. The fact is that the baron made no secret of his preoccupation with eating, which he gladly confessed to every guest and the fruits of which the guest had, after all, to perceive to his own advantage, which greatly astonished his contemporaries; indeed one feels that none of them attached any importance to good food. "Rumohr's works on the art of cooking, often so interesting but rather unexpected in a man of such intellect", as Carl Gustav Carus said, were not well received by them. It was in fact Carus who in 1843 dissected Romohr's body and observed an enlarged lower abdomen, the "well-nourished physiognomy", no doubt brought about by a "comfortable, mainly sedentary way of life". The baron's spirit can happily stand up to this posthumous rebuke.

The young German painter Franz Horny, taken to Italy by Rumohr in 1818 and resident from then on in Olevano, where he was to die four years later at the age of twenty-six, visited his patron in Siena in April 1822 and met Marbot. In a letter to his parents he describes him as

95

"a distinguished young Englishman, who spoke impeccable German, in dazzling white, freshly starched linen, showing at throat, breast and wrists under his always dark costume. He wore a golden bracelet which drew my eyes again and again, and spoke lovingly to the house cat as if she had been a person."

We may assume that the bracelet was a farewell gift from Lady Catherine; also that many others who met Andrew regarded it as the bizarre property of an eccentric. It is not impossible that he was aiming at just such an assessment and that he occasionally liked to see himself playing the stranger. What is certain is that he attached importance to his outward appearance, in contrast to his host Rumohr, who seems to have neglected his own. "A big fat man with dirty linen", said Heinrich Laube, and an Italian nobleman called him a man who "looks like the keeper of an inn in which one would rather not eat". If this was really so it does not seem to have worried Marbot.

At all events Marbot was absolutely fair to Rumohr as a cook, but not as a connoisseur. Even if Rumohr's verdict did often miss the true worth of a work of art because his receptive register was limited, nevertheless, he succeeded in establishing criteria which are still valid, and he did so by an attempt at a methodology. "A work of art cannot be wholly enjoyed until such time as the circumstances and conditions under which it originated have been established..." Marbot would certainly have given whole-hearted support to this. Only for him the "circumstances and conditions" were less the object of an historical view than of psychological insight, and that was not Rumohr's intention. Rumohr did not—or not willingly—take the content of the painting for granted, at times he obstinately refused to regard a work as something commissioned; on the contrary, he wanted the theme to be judged as an object of the artist's choice. Marbot criticized him for that, and he was probably right. Yet Marbot certainly did find much to admire in the baron. As we can see from a letter he wrote to him in 1827:

> "...Perhaps when analysing a work of art one should not listen to the voice of emotion, indeed should completely exclude it. It must surely flow quite sufficiently into our judgment without our observing it. But I could not bear to think that in that case the person whom we desire to acquaint with it or to instruct would not discover whether I regarded the work as good or bad. It is therefore better on the whole to allow the emotions to speak, if not too loud or too passionately, in the hope that they are also communicated to others. For why should one speak of painting at all, if not to open the eyes of others to it?"

On this journey there is not a word about the Sienese painters, but the notebooks of 1828 and 1829 reveal quite clearly that Marbot was unable to work out a real understanding of them for himself, and knew it.

> "We shall never be able to learn to understand the painters before Giotto, especially the Sienese, who still saw neither sky nor skyline and therefore filled in their backgrounds with gold, for this dimension, which was lacking in their pictorial representation, was naturally also lacking in their cognitive ability. Their picture of the world was not false, rather they had none... To them creative art was a service to God and to the church. It was not for the representation of 'eternal ideas' (Schopenhauer), but for the glorification of Jesus Christ and the saints and hence

the confirmation of the faith, whose hostility to nature had infected their souls. This is not a criticism but the assertion of a fundamental alienness. However wonderfully Duccio may have mastered his compositions, still he and the other Sienese are illuminators, inspired by the moral function of art, yes, but not by its sensual will."

In other words the individuality of the Sienese was beyond his grasp—and that of anyone else at the time. Their "rigidity of style" obstructed his vision, his view of the artist's soul. He always needed the artist as the key to the work: "...my purpose", as he wrote to Rumohr, "is to be able, as it were, to picture the painter to myself." So for him the concept of "inconceivability" became a receptive category. To the present author it seems a pity that this has now vanished from the science of art and biography. Anyone might conceive anything now, it seems.

The weakness of Marbot's method may perhaps lie in this one-sided approach, resulting from a defective evaluation of the period under consideration. Marbot sought the "spirit" of a work of art far too exclusively in the painter's psyche, taking too little account of the stream of time, from which the artist not only could not withdraw but which he consciously lived, and which may indeed have come into being partly through the great exponents of the arts, since they have played an instrumental part in many changes. Yet Marbot never pronounced on an isolated work of art until he could buttress his judgment with comparisons. He never uttered a word about anything that he could not think through to the end, however much it preoccupied his mind. He was a pioneer in the evaluation of the individual, but he did now and again sacrifice other criteria in his effort to penetrate the psyche.

Marbot reached Florence at the end of August 1822 and

described it to his mother as "hot and oppressive, close and cruelly damp so that the very air seems to stick to our body, only the river-bed is dry". He lived in the house of the English Minister, the Earl of Westmorland, who had invited the grandson of his friend Claverton to stay. The Earl himself did not return from England until the end of September, so that Andrew had a cool and spacious palazzo on the Lungarno Corsini, a well-stocked library and the whole staff at his command, plus a small but select collection of paintings. To his grandfather he writes:

"I take my meals, when I am not invited out, facing a *St Augustine at his Studies* by Botticelli. As you know, I have never been able to abide this saint, for which you have always generously pardoned me and for which God will certainly pardon me too, for He is just, He too cannot abide him, this verbose zealot with a guilty conscience. Nor is this painting calculated to bring him closer to me, for in it he is completely lifeless, and if none the less I look across at him now and again as I take a sip of wine or chew some roast meat, it is only for the sake of a wonderful monochrome tondo behind him in the picture, representing a Madonna and Child, of which I must say that the Madonna looks too worldly by far for this saint, who admittedly has her at his back. Botticelli is in general a painter of the worldly, all his figures have something heathen and sinful about them, they are very beautiful and very uncheerful, and one never knows what they are thinking, as they are removed from the event in which they are to all appearances participating. None of the figures in the painting of *Primavera* in the Uffizi is thinking of the spring, none rejoices—I think the artist will have known why...He is none the less a wonderful painter, incomparable in the tenderness of his clear tints and in the sureness of his drawing, above all of the moving figures, ever poised and as I have said, sometimes impassive, yet in a curiously cool fashion, living. This *Primavera* does not let me go, yesterday I sat an hour in front of it. I believe that this event, utterly soundless as it is, takes place in an Elysian orchard in which all previous sinfulness has turned into innocence again..."

So this *Primavera* does not let him go. Or is it the theme of sinfulness turned into innocence that does not let him go? The frontal view of St Augustine which Andrew faced while eating now hangs in the Uffizi, to which Westmorland bequeathed the painting. It may have been a later work than the fresco in the Ognissanti Church, in which the saint is seen in profile in a lively, curiously dramatic pose, almost as if inspired by divine wrath; his glance and the expressiveness of his long hands have something artificial about them, if not even an element of mannerism. Of this painting Andrew writes in his notebooks:

"There he sits, this repugnant saint, quivering with fierce submissiveness and, perhaps, enmeshed in remorse, at the vanished sweetness of his youthful sins. The official version can be read in Vasari. This picture at least was not painted voluntarily, it was commissioned by a repentant sinner!"

There are copious notes on the Florentines, which it would be difficult to separate from their context without sacrificing coherence, and which I will therefore leave to the new edition of *Art and Life*. They were written in England between 1822 and 1825. Marbot makes comparisons here between the representatives of the Florentine School, in which he distinguishes openly and expressly between objective quality, as applied until then by the still young and tentative

100

science of art criticism, and his personal preferences, which he can eloquently justify. For instance, he depicts Benozzo Gozzoli as a great portraitist and a great landscape painter—"in his backgrounds the wanderer, striving to escape from all the superficial heraldic pomp of the Medici, is lost in a dream world fashioned on strictly tectonic lines, which neither knows nor desires to know anything at all about history and politics..."

—but an artist to whom his patrons, these same Medici, never accorded the freedom of self-realization. We shall return to this theme.

In October 1822 Marbot met Schopenhauer in Florence, probably with English acquaintances, for Schopenhauer frequented Englishmen here in particular, probably less from choice than by chance, a fact on which he himself has commented ironically. He wrote to his friend Osann of an "extremely agreeable young Englishmen of remarkable understanding. Above all he seems, despite his youth, to be one of those rare people who do not judge lightly but know how to account for their judgment."

Marbot writes to van Rossum:
"I met a strange and lively little German philosopher by the name of Schopenhauer, who claimed that I would understand the world better had I read his great work. He is not precisely a man one would love, but then that is not his object. He does not like women, he finds men more beautiful, indeed in theory he dislikes the whole of creation, he finds the world not only faulty but a failure; but he seems nevertheless to enjoy it and lives in great comfort. This morning we strolled together in the Boboli Gardens. Our conversation at first turned towards

101

art, and he asked me if I were an artist. No, said I, but I would like to be. Then I was right, said he, for artists were the only people who, perhaps without knowing it, understood the world, by means of disinterested contemplation. At first I did not perceive what he meant, but later I understood that the artist has no interest in appropriating his subject or the world in general, but only in its ideal depiction. Only the truly great artist, said he, could grasp the eternal ideas of creation. I replied, if creation appealed to him as the object of the arts, then he must assent to it after all. Thereupon he stood still and said with a laugh: 'No, my young friend (he is perhaps fifteen years older than I), it is not so simple as that. Read my work! Then we shall talk further.' I promised, and shall do it, for, funny as the little man may be, there is something strangely seditious about him."

Seven years later Marbot read Schopenhauer and, though he may not have understood the world any better—in so far as he had ever misunderstood it—he did find his own views confirmed in many ways, particularly, as Schopenhauer had predicted, in his view of the role and mission of the artist, the value of which he too had by then learned to doubt. In his last letter to van Rossum in the autumn of 1829, he wrote:

"The little man I met at that time in Florence is in reality a great man. I took him for an enlightened pessimist. But now I know, although I do not agree with everything he says, that he is the discoverer of the absolute truth about human beings and the prophet of a doctrine whose effects must henceforth be everlasting."

But Marbot must have met Schopenhauer at least once more while he was in Florence and been further initiated into his aesthetic theory, for the truly astonishing comment which follows was demonstrably recorded before 1828, and therefore before Marbot had read *The World as Will and Idea*:

"Music, the highest of the arts? I think we must distinguish carefully here between creator and listener. The creator eludes all non-musical and hence all earthly thoughts and feelings; in his Heaven he may be involved in everlasting ideas, embedded in them, so to speak, for as long as and whenever he likes. The listener, however, lives a precisely limited span before falling back into his wretched state as the music ends. Indeed, I would even maintain that it is transitoriness itself, the precisely and inexorably measured lapse of time, which bestows on us the bliss in which is contained grief at the all too brief duration of our perfect happiness.

Painting enjoys two advantages over music. It needs no mediator to intervene between creator and spectator and to interpret the work according to his own volition and ability. But above all, its enjoyment is not limited by time. Whereas a piece of music counts the lapse of time in notes and bars, no bounds of time are set on the contemplation of the picture.

This circumstance leads me to the idea that painting, too, might produce works which have no object beyond themselves. I can conceive of pictures which would not delight us by reproducing forms such as those we see and experience in life, thus feigning the dimensions of reality, but which would affect us directly through colours and surfaces and give rise to a kind of emotion that only pure intuition can generate. When a picture reflects the recognizable we may easily find ourselves desiring that recognizable thing. If, however, the picture conveys what is unknown and unknowable, we must then desire the picture itself, not in order to possess it, but as the lasting source of an illumination of the mind, the effect of which cannot be captured in words. The picture then appears to us as the representation of a hitherto unsuspected order, and as such it continues to operate in us. It does not represent ideas; it *is* the idea."

In this effusion by Marbot the Romantic, almost startling in its exuberance, we have a presentiment—admittedly idealized and idealistic—of abstract painting. What strikes us about it is the intensity of imaginative power applied to a territory on which no one had yet set foot, the exciting experience of art without the "work of art" as hitherto understood.

In this prodigious act of invention Marbot forgot to whom he owed the impulse for his thinking. It was not in fact his nature to withhold gratitude from those to whom he owed it. In a certain way these lines are typical of the methods of Schopenhauer's successors. For people of Marbot's intellectual stamp, Schopenhauer's philosophy was a practicable edifice of the mind, in which everyone could find accommodation according to his ability and intellectual capacities, in such a way that he forgot the builder.

We find no report in the notebooks of this meeting, which represented something like a turning point in Marbot's life, or at least a step towards a wider view of life.

On the page with the comment on Botticelli, at the very bottom, as usual, as an aide-mémoire, are the words: "Arthur Schopenhauer *Die Welt als Wille und Vorstelung* [*sic*] and *Über die vierfache Wurzel des Satzes vom zureichenden Grund—*

the latter to be read first."[4]

But under this annotation, in tiny letters, as if the note were intended to become illegible even to himself in the future, we find line 987 of *Oedipus Rex*:

καὶ μὴν μέγας γ᾽ὀφθαλμὸς οἱ πατρὸς τάφοι.

(So will thy father's grave become thine highest joy)

Left unaltered by his mother, who was unable to read it, but struck out, though not made illegible, by van Rossum, this truly shocking note, untouched by moral self-criticism, as it were like a spontaneous gasp of indrawn breath, refers to the news which reached Andrew, probably with some delay, in Florence: his father was dead. Sir Francis had been thrown from his horse while out hunting and had apparently succumbed at once to his injuries. Andrew, now Sir Andrew, set out at once by the quickest route to return home, route, to his mother's bosom, in a disturbingly true sense of the word.

IV

A rare, quite possibly unique case, nothing resembling which has ever been reported before, unfolds before us. We have here a man of the highest sensibility, of considerable intellect and controlled sexuality, whose libido never outgrew the love-object of the Oedipal phase, of earliest, unremembered childhood, although he never manifested any other symptom of infantilism, instability or any form of disturbance at all; and a woman of lively mind and perhaps unbridled imagination, in any case dominated by an intense emotional life, totally enthralled by her son, so that she was deterred neither by the

4. "The World as Will and Idea" and "On the Fourfold Root of the Principle of Suffficient Reason".

enormity of incest nor—at first—by religious precepts, nor by a sense of ethical responsibility.

The case is quite different from, let us say, that of the incest between Byron and his half-sister Augusta, even apart from the fact that the horror of a transgression against morality, ethics and custom does not attach to an erotic relationship between brother and sister in the same degree as to a mother-son relationship, where the secondary anomaly of a generation gap makes the act more astonishing and reprehensible. Brother and sister generally grow up together until a certain age, and are not separated until custom and decorum demand concealment of the difference of sex, directing attention to the very bodily parts whose visibility gives rise to society's commandment, and perhaps actually begetting the desire to violate the commandment by means of something so obvious and challenging. In retrospect brother and sister are aware that they complement each other, each seeing the other sex embodied in the companion of their childhood days. But incest between mother and son, already burdened by its brooding mythical antecedents, is from the romantic standpoint a fatal entanglement, promising a tragic penalty. To the analyst, however, it is no more than a psychoneurotically based extension of the Oedipus complex (which itself is probably inherent in everyone), an indication of the failure to resolve it in the latent stage. Byron and Augusta—I make no judgment, but it is clearly true—were amoral beings and therefore ruthless in offending against morality, which Kant called "the perceived dependence of private life on the common will". Nowadays we would use the word "conscious" instead of "perceived" and regard the concept of the "common will" as too vague; it almost seems to contain a pejorative component, like a kind of legalized vox populi. Byron always regarded it as his due and his privilege to set himself above commonly accepted rules of morality. In his unconscious, as Marbot saw and as we would confirm, this privilege became a burden because it kept him in a state of constant strenuous action, which, as Marbot very rightly observed, he used—successfully, it would appear—as a compensation for his physical deformity.

Of course Marbot did not have any such ambition. He was a consistent but at the same time completely natural individualist, not committed to convention, or tied to custom, but not driven by the desire to violate them. All his life he preserved his intellectual independence and hence his independence of action, without ever parading himself as a nonconformist. What he denied to others was not himself but information about himself. His uniqueness and his greatness lie largely in his unobtrusive and dignified elected solitude. He was certainly in secret rebellion against those externally imposed rules which denied him the possesion of the person dearest to him, but it was for the sake of that dearest one, in order to give his mother back her peace of mind—it was too late to preserve it—that he finally renounced the fulfilment of desires which would have meant acting openly against society. But he could not refrain from quarrelling with those rules; analytically speaking it also meant working out the conflict with himself. We could not have expected him to provide an exhaustive interpretation of his own anomaly, nor would it have alleviated the conflict.

In Brunswick, two months after the final separation (we are anticipating now) at the end of June 1825, he wrote a letter to Lady Catherine which—fortunately for us—he did not send but kept by him, perhaps intending to send it later. Instead, he sent her another letter, the surviving portions of which will be quoted in the appropriate place. The first, a kind of rough draft, reads:

"The word 'sin' still means nothing to me and I would
allow no one to use it of your actions and mine. The

107

word is a human invention, but no one has exactly circumscribed its meaning. Sin, so I believe, is an act which precipitates other, innocent people into unhappiness. Our act did not do that, for it touches no one but ourselves. No one has suffered through us, we have robbed no one of happiness. Neither of us would be able to live, had we done so. And for the feeling of guilt, the grounds for which neither you nor I can put into words, because although we feel, we do not know its laws, we are now punishing ourselves by eternal separation. Anything more severe, if such a thing exists for us, would be unjust and undeserved. If the God in whom you still believe is a good God, he will accept this."

So at that time Andrew no longer believed in God. The situation was therefore a little easier for him than for his mother, who remained a firm believer to the end of her life. On the grounds of social convention, which, as he knew, he could not sweep aside, he had acquiesced in the unalterability of the separation. Even if he was unconvinced in his heart of hearts, still he perceived that otherwise there would inevitably be misfortune for the family; not some mythical misfortune, not the vengeance of God, but social shame and isolation which, though they would have been a matter of indifference to him, his mother would have been unable to bear, for she was still dependent on society. Moreover there was the younger son, Matthew, who could not of course be allowed to become a forfeit to repentance or an object of retribution. For then Andrew's concept of sin would have been realized: misfortune for others, whether loved or not.

So the separation was settled from the very beginning, although the date of it was constantly deferred. For there is no doubt that these two years from the winter of 1822 to the spring of 1825 were the happiest for both partners, despite all the most strenuous precautions of secrecy. Probably Lady Catherine had never before experienced ultimate and supreme fulfilment in love. Andrew certainly had not either, for even if the carnival in Venice had really included an amorous adventure, it could not have matched this passionate relationship in which, as we see it, there was something of a Tristan element. Andrew was never again to know true happiness in love, but he found a substitute for it in his self-imposed task. Lady Catherine, on the other hand, had the sadder fate, for she found less compensation in intellectual pursuits, nor would she have had much opportunity for them. So she remained a captive to memory, locked to the end of her life in an agony of deprivation.

I have anticipated. The couple are still united and are making use of their time, always mindful of its limitation and aware of the risk of discovery. Part of their thoughts and actions had always to be devoted to the strategy of secret planning. To this was presumably added much inward humiliation: the ever-recurring recognition of their weakness, the ever-renewed resolve that the hours passed the night before must be the last, which they never were; and added to this, the growing feeling of sin on Lady Catherine's part, and on his, helplessness in the face of his own will and an inability to take the final decision.

These secrecies, this seizing of the opportune moment, the stolen looks, the game of hide-and-seek, deceits practised on unsuspecting households and guests at Marbot Hall or Redmond Manor, the inevitable lies—all this must have eaten away the happiness of those stealthy hours. The threat of discovery lurked everywhere, the anxious question: could this or that servant or guest have seen one of the two on the way to the other? There can be little doubt that one or other of the servants was taken into their confidence, and from a remark in a letter of Andrew's to which we shall return, we find that this is reasonably certain to have been Lady Catherine's personal maid, Susan Williams. While she must have been utterly devoted to her mistress, it is scarcely likely that she would have connived at even passive encouragement of the relationship, had not a strange act of identification been involved which made her blind to the outrage. Older than Lady Catherine, she too must have loved Andrew and have enacted in her imagination the consummation of a relationship with him. We can scarcely imagine the matter otherwise. But in this case we are bound to ask: did Lady Catherine sense this and rely on her maid's feelings as a pledge of secrecy? I think it is easier to suppose some such—perhaps tacit—arrangement than to believe that Lady Catherine might have bought Susan Williams' silence—or anyone else's silence—for money. Such a move would have debased the affair in a way which it would have been difficult for the couple, or even for us, to endure. Nevertheless, a degrading element was forever and everywhere present, urging them again and again to stop gambling with danger, and no doubt there were moments of despair because this element would not prevail. As long as they were together they could not keep their distance.

So was it delight in sensual love, with sin as an added stimulus? The sweetness of forbidden fruit? It can scarcely have been otherwise. For they themselves called their fulfilment "sinful bliss", even Andrew, who tried to banish the sense of sin by analysing it when its time was past. And however our own close analysis may envisage this relationship, there is still an element of the inexplicable in it which we seem unable to reach.

Lady Catherine's bedroom was on the west side of the Hall, overlooking the park. It was separated from the south-west corner only by the closet, to one side of which, behind a door giving on to the inside of the house, her maid slept. The question is, did she really sleep there during those two years? And if not, how would Lady Catherine have explained to her that she was not needed, unless the psychological situation was as we have imagined it? Would it have been possible for the events and the offence to take place in Andrew's bedroom, which had once been Sir Francis's bedroom, on the north-west side of the house? For Andrew had early and finally refused to have servants of his own, he never wanted anyone about him whose sole task was to carry out his wishes. But can we really see Lady Catherine stealing at night down the dark corridor, to vanish into Andrew's bedroom? Can we see it? Did someone else, an accomplice, see it?

These are secrets of the bedchamber, in the true sense of the word. But we can go no further here without uncovering them. I have never supported the view that the biographer should stop outside the bedroom door, for the erotic life of his hero belongs to him and provides essential—if not the most essential—information. Here again, it may be asked, does Marbot's significance, his rank in cultural history, justify the knowledge and recital of the most intimate details of his life? It should be obvious by now, however, that the answer will be in the affirmative, for without a knowledge of those details Marbot's writings would be—and have been!—robbed of the dimension of depth. The basis in his personal life and hence the experience of the work of art would be missing—the very element which enables the viewer to relive the experience by exposing a deeper layer in the artist or, to be more precise, by attempting to explore the artist's libido.

Precautions of secrecy, the possibility and impossibility of preserving it, prevention of discovery—this is a theme which engages me, and probably others too, so often when reading history or visiting historic places. Conspiracy or even

111

murder, the secret liaison—when, and above all where did that happen which officially should not have been? For there were always servants, everywhere, even at night, if not always visible; bells, and even whistles or rattles stirred them from sleep, in so far as they ever got to sleep at all. We have little idea where acts of illicit love took place, where Lady Caroline Lamb received her Byron, or her stepmother Lady Melbourne her various lovers, one of whom, probably the Prince of Wales, begot with her a future Prime Minister, and a Victorian one at that.

But even fictional love sets us riddles. The baron in Goethe's *Elected Affinities* leads his guest, the count, by night through a maze of halls and passageways because the count wants to chat—as he calls it—a little longer with his beloved, evidently accommodated in the women's apartments. Maids and valets must sleep soundly, or else they are housed elsewhere, up under the roof perhaps, where they have to share a narrow room, if not a bed, with one of the house servants. What talk must have gone on in those attic rooms! But it is more probable that at that time, before the Revolution, a servant counted as a non-person, who was quite simply denied a soul and from whom no more thought or sense was expected than from a piece of furniture; dumbness and dullness were the qualities required. In Marbot's day this had already changed.

The National Trust (which administers historic and outstanding buildings and places, and perfect examples of their period, and opens them to the public) mentions Sir Andrew in its guide to Marbot Hall as the most important member of the family and refers, though rather vaguely, to his book *Art and Life* as having

"caused quite a stir in the world of art, as he was the first to explore the workings of the artist's mind."

This, we can safely assume, will be the first time that

most visitors to Marbot Hall have ever heard of our hero. But none of the half-inquisitive, half-apathetic horde of visitors who willingly allow themselves to be propelled through the flights of rooms on the first floor knows that in one or other of the bright, spacious corner-rooms with the vertical, white casement windows and a view of sycamores, chestnuts and yews, an act took place, and was repeated, that would elude their imagination only a little less than the imputation of a similar sin of their own.

Marbot will probably not be very much better known after the new edition of his work is published. The philosophy of art is unlikely to become common property, but one can assume that fresh access to the understanding of art will bring the beholder closer to the person who made that access possible. This does not mean, of course, that on future guided tours of Marbot Hall the chamber of the sinful couple will be pointed out as the one in which that person gained his psychological preparation for his portrayal of the artist.

It has always been difficult for the world to live with its scandals, which is why historians and cultural historians have succeeded again and again in suppressing the anomalies of their heroes and victims. The man whose ideals are discipline, moderation and order banishes the more secret practices of his heroes or models from sight, unaware that he is repressing the disclosure and cognition of something he senses potentially in himself, and feels bound to oppose, instead of accepting it as part of the human lot, which distinguishes his hero as one of those complex beings whose qualities cannot simply be classified in the positive or negative categories which he regards as universally applicable. Biography too is beset by these "terribles simplificateurs", who draw lopsided and therefore false pictures, or take care that they are perpetuated in intensified form.

Nowadays we view Marbot Hall as an original and

therefore nostalgically beautiful piece of evidence of time past, we move from room to room and relive the tragic tale of love with some emotion, though we may lack some of the keys to the inner life of the two participants. We look out of the great windows at the trees swaying in the wind and hear them rustling—I would be tempted to say "whispering" if it were not for the associations of the word—we look at the objects in the rooms, all looking and standing just as they did a hundred and fifty or more years ago, witnesses therefore to those events which some of us might prefer not to be true, but which are true nevertheless, in so far as the past is still true at all.

On 22 April 1825 Marbot left his home for the second and last time. He must have been moved by the parting from Father Gerard, since he already knew what the Father would not learn until Lady Catherine's confession: that Andrew and he were not to meet again.

Before his departure Andrew paid a last visit to Redmond Manor. Whether he found it hard to take his final leave of the two scenes of his childhood and youth, the landscapes to which he owed some of the images in his mind, is an irrelevant question in view of the parting from his mother, which must have obliterated any lesser pain. This parting was delayed, however, since Lady Catherine, presumably by covert agreement, followed her son two days later so that just once more they might be united for a few days, no longer under the eyes of the staff at Marbot Hall, where suspicion must have been accumulating little by little, whereas Redmond Manor, where they had spent only a few summer months during those two years, still promised security and with it the last indulgence of a few night hours together. This union of the lovers, which they now knew was never to occur again, must of course have made the parting still harder, intensified the pain and heightened the sense of "never more" to the level of tragedy.

Lady Claverton, of whom we know curiously little, had

114

died the year before. At seventy-one, Lord Claverton was in failing health and needed nursing, so that Lady Catherine's visit to Redmond Manor seemed perfectly justifiable on practical grounds. It cannot have been difficult for Andrew to persuade his grandfather of the purpose and necessity of another journey to Italy. Although now master of great estates, the existence of which had to be accepted as unavoidable, he must have been able to represent himself confidently as a worker in the service of a form of knowledge whose pursuit obliged him to travel, since its field extended beyond Marbot Hall and its boundaries; after all, his grandfather himself had sown the seeds of Andrew's wider-ranging interests. Claverton must in fact have learned with some satisfaction that the subject of his own hobby was becoming the most important thing in his grandson's life. How the prolonged absence of their new master was explained to the tenants and staff of Marbot Hall we do not know. Perhaps on the grounds of health; the need for a better climate would surely have been more understandable than the appreciation of art, of which scarcely anyone in Northumberland would have been able to make anything at all. An eldest son has no business to live in Italy devoting himself to study; he should stay at home, actively in possession. Admittedly Byron had also left his—very much smaller—estates to be managed by others, but as he had not come into possession of them by direct inheritance, none of his few tenants had known him from childhood or looked to him as the future master. Marbot, on the other hand, was known to all his people, they had been expecting him, and it is possible that they regretted his departure.

The deed of renunciation which Andrew deposited with a notary in early May or early June—in London, since from Newcastle, the county town, such news would have spread immediately and sensationally—did not immediately become common knowledge, so that his arrangements could pass at first simply as preparations for another journey, on returning from

115

which he would finally take up the reins. Only his younger brother, John Matthew, was informed of the decision, though naturally not of the reason for it, which Andrew probably explained to him simply as a wish—capricious, perhaps, but irrevocable—to live in Italy, which was not in itself so unusual. John Matthew came to London from Cambridge, where he was reading for his BA, to sign the document which made him heir. Andrew received eight thousand pounds a year, a very considerable sum at that time, in exchange for Marbot Hall and all its revenues. The title he did not renounce in his brother's favour. He was probably acting pragmatically in this: he knew that on the Continent, and especially in Italy, doors, gateways and portals would open more readily to a "Sir" than to a mere "Mr". Anything but a snob himself, he expected the guardians and owners of the things he needed for his research to be snobs, and as the price was not a sacrifice but a natural right which lent him prestige, he paid it gladly. What he did leave to his younger brother was the title of Viscount, to which he would legitimately have succeeded on the death of his grandfather in 1826. In the circles he frequented and would continue to frequent in future he was already known as Andrew Marbot and as the future Sir Andrew, so he did not covet a change of name. So it was that after taking his degree in 1826 John Matthew occupied the estate of Redmond Manor and his seat in the House of Lords as the fourth Viscount Claverton. In the same year his sister Jane Elizabeth, then eighteen, returned from the convent of St Vincent de Paul in Brussels, where she had been educated, married a well-to-do Irish officer called O'Shea a year later and perished with him in an avalanche on Mont Cenis during their honeymoon in the autumn of the same year. No more is known about her.

Lady Catherine stayed at Redmond Manor until the autumn of 1825 with her father, whose health improved for a time. Then she returned to a bereaved Marbot Hall. It must have

116

been a grievous homecoming, and more than that, one heavy with misgiving, for now that the transgression had been carried to its utmost limits and was over, and there would be no more sin to confess, confess she did. The nature and extent of the sin must have hit Father Gerard hard, and not only that: it must have taxed his idea of the possibilities of susceptibility. He would have looked in vain for a precedent whereby to assess the penance. How he resolved the confession, spiritually and intellectually, is an open question; the conflict in the priest's soul during confession is something he will never allow an outsider to divine, since here, presumably, permissible and impermissible, what is repressed and what is yet to be repressed dwell in close proximity. Van Rossum's outward reaction to the penitent Lady Catherine is shown by a letter which will be quoted in context later on. It is more difficult to guess at his emotions. He was an excellent man in many ways, more than a priest alone, but he was not a god; there is much to suggest that he loved one of these two people, and perhaps both. As a priest aged twenty-five, he had first met Lady Catherine as a convert in Rome at the age of nine and they had been friends ever since. Even a priest is aware of budding charms, if only platonically, or in order to prove to himself that he has successfully mortified all fleshly desires. At the age of forty he was entrusted with five-year-old Andrew, who grew up under his eye and his protection, apparently into just the kind of young man a responsible tutor could wish for. Even a man for whom asceticism is a precept does not have to have excessively aberrant tendencies in order to see such a pupil as a love-object; a precious plant, largely of his own cultivation, for the sake of which he might well even love himself. And now these two beings, the boy and his mother, were united in a fatal passion. Now sixty, Father Gerard was certainly a stranger to envy and petty jealousy; he was above wanting to punish human failings. None the less, his office as priest and confessor had to be peformed. He could not have been expected to understand such an extreme fall from grace—even a non-cleric could scarcely have done so—but he met it with an effort at empathy which one might call superhuman, unless here too some unconscious process of identification was involved. In any case we know that once the sternness of the father confessor had played its part, he resigned himself to the irrevocable, the more so as it could not be repeated, and practised leniency. *Homo erat; humani nihil a se alienum putabat.*

"His dear compassion consoles, quietens and refreshes me," Lady Catherine wrote to Andrew, probably in September, but in any case some time after the confession. Proof that, if God had not, one of his intermediaries, admittedly among the gentlest and most considerate, had forgiven her. After this Father Gerard stayed on as her friend and support, until her premature death.

Another friend and confidant was the steward, Samuel Crompton, who was nearly seventy when Andrew left Marbot Hall, but still active and authoritative in the management of the estate. Always more devoted to his mistress than his master, he probably worshipped her all his life, and he was not the only one. Andrew's letter from Brunswick dated 30 July 1825 hints at this and also at the reliability of the nurse, Susan Williams:

"I am easy in the knowledge that Williams is loyally devoted to you and that Crompton will watch over and care for you and in so doing probably succeed in realizing a dream long cherished."

So Lady Catherine vanishes physically from Andrew's life. Psychically they not only remained close to each other but were so absorbed in one another that until their death no outsider could ever find a place as the object of strong emotions in their souls, which remained henceforth in constant, sometimes calm, sometimes agitated and always tragic communication. Barely two years after the death of her son, in 1832, Lady Catherine died, at the age of fifty-one. If we like to consider the case as the romantic drama of an act of God—or, as some people would probably prefer to maintain, of the devil—we could say that Lady Catherine died of a broken heart. Without wishing either to start a legend or to assent to it, one must admit that there is some truth in this version. For her will to live must have been long extinguished; without hope or confidence, and above all with nothing to live for, she withered away and died. The stated cause of death is unknown.

Andrew stayed on in London until the middle of June 1825, in the unreasonable and gradually fading hope that his mother would join him. Yet despite the loss, which was far more painful for her, she naturally never even considered such a reunion. His view was that a convention already breached in secret might now make it possible to violate the social taboo to the very end, to ignore the prohibition, to break completely with the society which supported it and to live far away from it together with his mother and beloved: an idea not only psychotic but hyper-romantic. No doubt if the deed had been detected, if the relationship had been revealed in all its outward shamefulness, then even on her side nothing would have stood in the way of such a step. Lost to the memory of the world, especially her world, they could have abandoned themselves to "sin", but only as souls ultimately depraved and eternally damned. But she would never have taken this step, she would sooner—however novelettish it may seem to us—have entered a nunnery, which she may in fact have considered and—who knows—might have done, had Father Gerard not stayed with her. But even if a situation had arisen in which she was no longer forced to regard the liaison with her son as a risk, it would still have been a grave mistake. For the auspices were really anything but favourable. At the time of her first night with Andrew Lady Catherine was almost twice his age. To be

119

sure, she was as intoxicated as he was by the fulfilment of forbidden love, and perhaps the forbidden was an unconscious attraction, and her emotional life was governed and engrossed by this passion; but she had not suppressed all her common sense by making plans or taking action. She must have been perfectly aware that her charms would fade with age, and it is indeed hard to imagine that Andrew would have lived until his death with a woman who would by then be nearly fifty. At the same time, it may be that that woman would have been able to prevent his death-wish taking effect.

For if we look at this event in the light of psychopathology—and in order to see it clearly we must do so again and again—we find a far more complex picture than the passive view generally adopted by biography even now, which, with no regard for more profound conclusions, leaves out the unconscious impulses of its heroes. This, then, is the picture of a unique case, in which the Oedipus complex is projected on to the real situation in which it arises as a complex, its pathogenic effects become manifest and it becomes the reality in which it is lived out. And perhaps, despite the fading charms of the love-object, sublimation of erotic desire would have been inhibited, perhaps the ageing would have become a stimulus and motive force in itself, had not separation put an end to this dangerous development. Henceforth only the memory of the physical relationship lived on in the imagination of both, as an omnipresent memory, only gradually abating in intensity. This at least remained to them until the end of their lives; a feeling of loss which was rekindled over and over again. So the tragic element counterbalances the pathologcal, indeed is reconciled with it—in so far as in this case we really make up our minds to apply the pathological aspect. If I, as a biographer, do so now, no moral judgment is implied.

It is evident from Lady Catherine's behaviour and her words that she had always been convinced of the necessity for a final separation. There was another, dominant element: the religious ban, ignored at first but very soon frighteningly manifest. In dark moments Lady Catherine may have foreseen the threat of excommunication. Though her reason had been perfectly able to grasp Andrew's arguments against the concept of sin, in her heart she was governed by the awareness of having committed a twofold sin: incest and adultery. Neither of these feelings ebbed away on the death of Sir Francis; on the contrary, the sense of sinfulness swelled into an evil dream in which she herself was responsible for her husband's death.

Andrew was probably made aware of several outbreaks of this guilt feeling, in the form of self-incrimination, not accusation, and it must have disturbed him profoundly, realizing as he did that delusions were immune to reason. Moreover, as long as Andrew was still with her, Lady Catherine had been unable to bring herself to confess this all-mastering sin, since it would have meant immediate renunciation. Hence in her own eyes she was drawing nearer hour by hour to her damnation, still further intensified by the awareness that she would later have to confess not only this sin but also its increasingly grave concealment, for which, if it persisted, absolution could scarcely be expected. The excessive liveliness of her imagination was not restricted to the enjoyment of love but also tended towards the dark, reverse side of its consequences; she believed that she deserved anathema.

Lady Catherine could not simply sweep her faith aside like Andrew, who had claimed freedom of thought from an early age and been allowed it by a perceptive tutor; and who now felt that on his journeys he had gathered considerable evidence against the necessity for unqualified belief. She, however, had grown up in the faith. After her early conversion she had spent much of her girlhood in Italy, and hence in an atmosphere of strict religious practice. Her religion had been conveyed to her, not as a rigorous compulsion but in the guise of happy trustfulness, colourful as the paintings of the

Venetian Masters. Piety was natural to her, she had never neglected her religious observances and now she saw herself in some fearful future time, after the painful process of the great confession, not only returning to the life of abstinence which she tried to see as desirable, but also forced into the permanent contemplation of past sinfulness: for virtue, she realized, can be practised but not restored.

Moreover, in her circle, quite apart from religion, it was not permissible—in other words, impossible—to deviate from social conventions and lead an individual life. If you made a mistake you had to toe the line again, and if you would not acknowledge the mistake you were ostracized and guilty of ruining your descendants far into the future. In Lady Catherine's case there is no indication that her younger son or daughter was very close to her, but what is certain is that their mother did not want to harm her children. The great nobles surrounding the court could permit themselves amorous escapades until well into the Victorian era, but the landed gentry, especially Catholics, were strictly bound by the moral code. Incest between mother and son, if the occurrence was recognized at all, would not have been forgiven by anyone.

We have looked at this affair from the psychopathological and ethical standpoints; there is also the romantic aspect, the yearning renunciation, the "never more", the voluptuousness of painful abandonment, the tragic role assumed with conscious suffering; the sacrifice to an inexorable fate, to which the abandoner yields, allowing it to rule henceforth without resistance or anger, but with bitter tears. If we wish to take the more frivolous view of this episode which we generally adopt towards the activities of the Romantics, their heroes and other figures—I myself at any rate am unable to take them quite seriously—then we must admit that Lady Catherine's role as heroine suited her well, that she played her part with bravura until her early death, which was the

Sir Andrew Marbot
Portrait by Eugene Delacroix (1827)
Paris, Bibliothèque Nationale

Lady Catherine Marbot
Portrait by Sir Henry Raeburn (1804)
Edinburgh, National Gallery of Scotland

Sir Francis Marbot
Portrait by Sir Henry Raeburn (1803)
London, Tate Gallery

Robert Viscount Claverton
Portrait by Anton Graff (1782)
Winterthur, Reinhart Collection

Thomas De Quincey
Portrait by J. Watson Gordon
London, National Portrait Gallery

Marbot Hall

Redmond Manor

Tintoretto
Origin of the Milky Way
London, National Gallery

William Blake
The Blasphemer (*c.* 1800)
London, Tate Gallery

Henry Crabb Robinson
Portrait by Johann Joseph Schmeller (1828)

Antoine Watteau
Gilles (1719)
Paris, Musée du Louvre

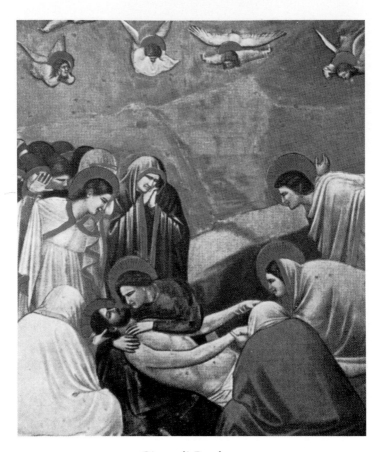

Giotto di Bondone
The Burial of Christ, detail
Fresco on the left side of the Scrovegni Chapel, Padua

Lord Byron
Portrait by an unknown artist
Newstead Abbey Collection

Botticelli
Primavera (1477–1478), detail

Benozzo Gozzoli
Self-portrait (1439)
Detail from fresco on the right side of the Medici Chapel, Florence

Jan van Eyck
The Arnolfini Marriage
London, National Gallery

Giorgione
Self-portrait
Braunschweig, Herzog Anton Ulrich-Museum

Ottilie von Goethe
Portrait by Heinrich Müller

Rembrandt
Nicolaes Bruyningh (1652)
Kassel, Staatliche Kunstsammlungen

Andrea Mantegna
Sala degli Sposi: Family of the Marchese Ludovico
Mantua, Duke's Palace

Anna Maria Baiardi
Etching by an unknown artist (1827)

Eugene Delacroix
Death of Sardanapalus (1827)
Paris, Musée du Louvre

Countess Teresa Guiccioli
Portrait by an unknown artist after E. C. Wood

Count Giacomo Leopardi
Portrait by an unknown artist

necessary ending to the drama. Andrew, on the other hand, improvised his own role, that of a secret rebel against an archaic law, which Romanticism did not recognize. Today he appears to us as the only man of his time capable of withstanding the established norms by thinking and acting independently without openly declaring his independence, since he knew that no one would understand him. But he could not withstand them on someone else's behalf: even he was incapable of offering resistance in the name of his beloved partner against his own better judgment, his conscience, and not least against his mentor, Gerard. By cutting himself off from his past he was also cutting himself off from all hope of happiness.

Until the middle of June 1825 Andrew lived alone in the Claverton town house with the staff, probably consisting only of the butler and his family. He had intended to maintain his incognito, to avoid contact with family friends, their evening routs and other diversions, but then realized that this would mean missing the chance of seeing the pictures in the houses where such entertainments were given, and for the last time at that, for he knew by now that he would never return to England. So he accepted a number of invitations, trading his presence against the inspection of his hosts' treasures. Many a table partner who might perhaps have cherished the hope of a closer relationship was courted because her husband or father was the possessor of Dutch Masters or some other kind of art collection. We have no precise details, since the notebooks mention only the quality of the work, and not how he came to see it. Once again he beheld Rembrandt, Vermeer and van Eyck, and for the first time—at the house of General Sir John Hay—van Eyck's *Arnolfini Wedding* (now in the National Gallery, London). Of this painting he wrote:

"A married couple pose for the painter in their bedroom. This in itself is remarkable, especially as the painter seems to be occupying the precise position of the priest before whom the couple stand, humble yet wonderfully dignified in their composure, for the celebration of their marriage, and moreover in a place in which it will apparently at once be consummated, for the bed stands ready...

In fact this painting radiates a profound secrecy, a mysterious silence, such as I have never yet found in any other. For a picture is generally the personal interpretation of an event sufficiently well known, if not quite commonplace to the spectator. But here a secret is preserved in the souls of those portrayed and of the portrayer, whom we see, minutely small, in a concave mirror. The secret is there, eluding explanation, although articles, the symbolic character of which is obvious, are distributed about the room. A mute scene has been captured here which one does not forget, which indeed affects the beholder permanently as a human mystery."

Marbot did not visit Blake this time but went with Crabb Robinson for several long walks on Hampstead Heath. It would be interesting to know what they talked about, for in matters of art Andrew had no confidence in the judgment of his older, indeed by now almost elderly friend. Presumably Robinson was a kind of father-substitute for him, a confidant to whom he could naturally not confide his deepest secret, however much he might have liked someone both sympathetic and dispassionate to be privy to it.

At the opening of the Royal Academy exhibition he again met Turner, who that year was exhibiting his recently completed painting of *Dieppe Harbour*. This work aroused violent and in today's view almost incomprehensible arguments between the supporters of strict naturalism, led by William Etty, who accused the artist of a crime against nature, and the growing body of Turner's supporters. It was probably not so much this painting as Turner's art in general which fired Andrew's eloquence; it was as if his polemic talent had been waiting, and finally found its object here. The article in the *Literary Gazette*, his first, and one of the few in which he directly addressed the public, aroused considerable attention, not only as a defence of the painting and its painter, but above all because of its revolutionary views and the sharp tone in which he expressed them.

"Mr Etty says: 'If Turner abandons nature I must abandon him.' This means that for the rest of his life, and may it be a long one, Mr Turner will have to bear the harsh lot of one abandoned by Mr Etty, for it is improbable that he will return to what Mr Etty and his friends call 'nature'...The true artist does not portray nature but his own image of her essence: not nature itself, but his own nature."

Nowadays this may sound like a commonplace, but at that time nothing of the kind had ever been said about painting. Marbot went still further. The terms "right" and "wrong" must be eradicated once for all from the vocabulary of art appreciation, for—and this applied to all the arts—they could be used at most to define the technique, never the object.

"Whatever succeeds is permissible. A thing succeeds if it strengthens our imagination and broadens our view of nature; it need not reproduce it, for the artist neither should nor can be a match for nature."

This article undoubtedly made him many enemies of whom we know nothing, but above all it made him friends, not only Turner himself but men from other, unexpected camps, in particular Delacroix. He and the young painter Richard Parkes Bonington, who lived in France, were staying in London and he got in touch with Marbot.

There is no mention of this meeting in Marbot's notebooks; he generally mentioned painters in connection with their work, apart from which they meant as little to him as any other chance acquaintance. Bonington and Delacroix were no doubt travelling with sketchbooks and other materials but there is no reason to assume that they had any paintings with them, so Marbot had no immediate proof of the value and significance of his two new friends.

Marbot never again saw the young and highly-talented Bonington, who died two years later, before he was twenty-six years old: one of the great hopes of English painting of the early nineteenth century.

Andrew invited the two artists to dine several times in the family's town house and there arose between the three of them one of those friendships swiftly created when life situations coincide and views are similar. Delacroix asked Marbot to visit him in his new studio in Paris. In a letter of 30 July 1825, to his friend Félix Guillemardot, Delacroix speaks of Andrew's acute judgment and an analytical ability seldom found in the young. (He himself was only three years older.) Delacroix had no idea that he himself was to become a victim of this judgment, when Andrew followed up his invitation two years later and called on him in the rue d'Arras.

Like Marbot, Delacroix was an admirer and connoisseur of Shakespeare, who was being performed in several London theatres in the season of that year. Together they saw *The Tempest* and *Richard III*. *Hamlet* they saw three times, and these visits were not to be their last together, though Bonington's place was subsequently taken by Berlioz.

As one can imagine, *Hamlet* had its own, deeper significance for Andrew. He wrote in great detail to his mother about the performance and the players, closing the account with one of his significant comments, which illumines not only the play but also the Prince of Denmark in him:

"This struck me once again: Hamlet, sitting on the
queen's bed and appealing to her conscience, talks of
the 'incestuous sheets', which they are not, since

Gertrude is not related to Claudius, and so I assume that in the very depths of his heart Hamlet is moved by the desire that the sheets should so become. When he says: 'And—would it were not so—you are my mother', he believes he is speaking the truth, but what is spoken within him is different: 'And—would you were more than that—you are my mother'."

The parting from his mother and beloved was more than a mere parting; it was the definitive object-loss, all the more difficult because it was deferred. Andrew had to overcome this now, all hope of a reunion, then or ever, gone. Of course he also had to admit to himself that he had expected nothing else, and he then began to prepare for his final departure. On one of his last days in London the letter he had awaited and feared arrived—we will return at the appropriate point to the lucky accident of the preservation of two documents from Lady Catherine's hand. It came from Redmond Manor and was therefore, as Andrew may have observed, and certainly not without disquiet, written before the confession.

"Your letter was a luminous ray of fulfilment in the deep sea of frustration. It both moved and calmed me, and that which was previously silent in its arousal is now aroused in its silence. A terrible and hopeless struggle is taking place within me, and whatever the outcome, I must lose. Sometimes the feeling of loss predominates and I am all emptiness, I am desolate as the snow-clad statue of Ceres in the park, which you showed me on that winter morning, do you remember? 'Demeter dejected,' you said. Then once again I experience this all-pervading fulfilment, enwrapped in a warm wave of remembrance so overwhelming that I seem to swoon away, that I begin to tremble, and suddenly I am all expectancy as if you were coming to me."

Before the final "to", two letters have been fiercely deleted and made illegible. It is surely safe to assume that the word "into" "on to" or "unto" had been abbreviated to a more moderate, though no less unmistakable form.

"Sometimes I think that it is only my love that keeps me alive, like the wind that does not exist when it does not blow. I think that such words were never written by a mother to her son before, and in truth I do not know what it is that seduces me into such immodesty. Perhaps it is the Devil, whom we have conjured up and who in his triumph over me, suggests these words to me. I know I should be filled with deep repentance, yet it refuses to manifest itself, its way is barred by the feeling that I should be very poor if what has happened to us had not happened. None the less, the recognition of my sin prevents me from abandoning myself utterly to my dreams. So I hope and trust that I may have the strength to overcome the renunciation in my inmost heart and to mortify my passion and thus my grief. For my sin is greater than yours.

I know that you deny the sin. Therefore it is easier for you to taste the memory to the full. Perhaps you are right, perhaps God has already forgiven us. I put my trust in Fr G. as a just and compassionate mediator, yet he too will have to overcome himself. For the experience that our happiness has meant must be as unknown to him as the corporeal experience of God to us.

Lucky Andrew—you have the gift of being diverted by pictures, whereas the pictures that look on me here remind me still more painfully of you, the more so as they no longer mean very much to you. They are therefore worth less to me too, for I can no longer separate my views from yours. Nevertheless I linger often before that painting by which your curiosity was once inflamed. How little we could then suspect that your desire would be fulfilled and that I should be the one to satisfy it. You have conquered the unknown territory.

This is not to be a long letter, and what there is in it of complaint I withdraw, for it would not be justified. Whom should I accuse? Ourselves, or the destiny which made us sinners? Nevertheless my heart is lonely and empty. In the small hours of the night I often lie wakeful, then memory overwhelms me and I embrace it in extreme abandonment. So I am living a second life and at the same time praying for release from it, praying like the sinner which, alas! I am.

I can write this, if only once, and for the last time, for this letter will not fall into improper hands. Nevertheless, destroy it! Write to me soon, but remember that a letter to me here passes through many hands.

Farewell, dearest, God bless you!"

There is no signature, and probably never was on any of Lady Catherine's letters to her son. What could she have written? "Your mother" would have been as misplaced as "Your Catherine", if we can regard such forms as having any validity at all. Unfortunately we have no evidence of how she or Andrew regarded such peripheral matters, which would after all have been only a symptom of the underlying anomaly of their case. For as we have constantly to observe, with some partiality and just a trace of reluctance, this is a "case", the pathological aspect of which must be considered if we are to do it full justice. It is given to few people to dissociate themselves altogether from the "cultural demands of society", which would certainly preserve most of them by an instinctive inhibition from immanent incest, if such a stage were ever reached. The historic law—or is it more of a mythical taboo?—is anchored in our unconscious, its object bursts out of the framework of our experience and hence—in general—of the conceivable. I say that, in general, anyone who thinks and feels the case right through to the end will be able to liberate himself from a number of inherited prejudices.

For in the case of Marbot and his mother some of us may feel inexplicably involved, in a way which is probably anchored in the unconscious. It is as if we were asked for an opinion which we cannot give because that part of both partners' psyche which gave the decisive and definitive turn to their lives and governed them from then on remains incomprehensible. We look at Andrew Marbot and his mother, with a sense of shock which has to be mastered, and yet with deep compassion, and observe that they are marked for ever by their transgression, which was their carefully guarded secret, for as long as they lived.

Our research is handicapped by the fact that this secret did not survive them. Such an extreme and unique entanglement challenges our curiosity: we should be learning something from the case, if nothing more binding than tolerance. We become late witnesses, against the will of the two participants, to a love which was doubly tragic, in the subjective experience of the lovers and in the after-effects of their story, arising from the apparently amoral element in the relationship, which inevitably gave it a false stamp of disreputability; false, because in reality no element of depravity or wantonness attaches to it. On the contrary, we can scarcely help admiring the high degree of deliberate assimilation of "sinfulness" and the acceptance of its spiritual consequences: perpetual dismay, an excoriating estrangement from their unsuspecting contemporaries, a palpitatingly unquiet heart, a life in turmoil, an early death.

So we must take Andrew Marbot as he was, a complete man with all his contradictions, which are of course only apparent; in reality they made him into the man who has entered into cultural history: a towering intellect, guided and inspired by a mysterious power which for once was not, as in most cases, locked away or silenced—and not a few would be appalled at the revelation of their hero's secret life!—but the mechanism of which could largely be deduced. It is not the anomalous libido that is strange but its eruption from latency to action, which then encouraged rather than impeded the sublimation. It is not the Oedipus complex that is anomalous, but the fact that it matured into action and its resulting consummation with the willing partner: the conduct of two highly differentiated characters who were anything but infantile or primitive or dissolute.

The passage in Lady Catherine's letter about the painting—the Tintoretto of course—gives us an unexpected and significant clue. The comment leaves scarcely any doubt that this is her first reference to the picture; so Andrew and his mother had never spoken together about the fateful role of that painting. We therefore surmise that these two were never able to enjoy their union at leisure, like those who in the intoxication of fulfilment lovingly recall the steps which led to it. So this relationship was not destined to unfold in relaxed tranquillity; on the contrary, the expiatory omen of taboo was ever-present, they were weighed down by the burden of proscription, with the added strains and stresses of secrecy. These two partners actually never received the gift of peace enjoyed by the less guilt-laden; no rest in the other's arms, but hasty recourse to stolen hours, whispered words, sighs suppressed. We have said it before: this relationship could scarcely have borne the load imposed on it for any length of time, and who knows whether complaints about unpropitious circumstances might not gradually have turned to bitterness and blame against the other partner. Admittedly, the fact that the liaison

131

stood up to two years of irksome stratagems, gainsays this supposition.

Lady Catherine's unambiguous farewell reaffirms this finality, and with it the element which one might call "romantic renunciation", "nevermore". Andrew took it in, probably in an upsurge of grief, but in the depths of his unconscious mind the unalterable verdict was probably what he really wanted. He left London on 23 June 1825, took ship at Dover a day later and on the 26th reached Hamburg, where he stayed for two days before travelling on to Brunswick. We do not know who suggested that he might visit the art collection founded by Duke Anton Ulrich; probably some connoisseur of his grandfather's acquaintance, but it could have been Crabb Robinson, who knew the area and presumably its paintings.

Marbot's letter to his mother from Brunswick has not survived in its entirety. The intimate part of it was destroyed in accordance with the arrangement between him and his mother, an agreement which neither of them seems to have observed quite consistently. Having made the tell-tale transitional text illegible, she left the pertinent pages to Father Gerard for assessment. Once again the biographer has to entreat the posthumous forgiveness of his heroine, since—with the help of quartz lamps—this passage is now legible and has been read. It runs:

"...in the silence of the night, or should happen again now, and will happen again tonight. If, as your letter seems to tell me, you have the same experience, then let us take it as a sign of the fate which has been simultaneously bestowed and imposed upon us, to be neither allowed nor able to forget anything. Let us be courageous and face that part of our past which you have called our sin and which was, in fact, a rapture of sweetness and bliss. Let us never again think of our sinfulness like petty penitents, as if we

132

were other than we are and were. We have unmasked sin as a phantom, a mean rumour, to which
the noble spirit closes its ears."

Hamlet of course - "a noble spirit". Hamlet as seducer,
here openly desiring his mother; who speaks to her conscience,
not in order to call her belatedly to order, but to seduce her into
his audacious denial of sin. Hamlet as anti-Hamlet, not
demanding repentance but rejecting it with scorn as the
invention of hawkers of indulgences. Sir Andrew Marbot,
picking a fight with the implacable authority that sets up
ethical laws and has the audacity to demand obedience even of
him; the elitist rebel, who arrogates to himself the right to
ignore the rules of the social game, and indeed, as we see it,
with some justice. For in my view, anyone who is not
condemned to experience in himself the enormity of such an
involvement has no right to insist on or defend a commandment which society gains nothing by observing.

For lack of a proper museum at that time, the Brunswick collection was housed in the Duke's armoury. Here
again, Marbot must have made a few notes on the spot, as raw
material for his notebooks. He writes in 1828 on Rembrandt's
Stormy Landscape:

"The viewer experiences this idealized natural
drama so intensely because there is no intermediary
between him and the tumultuous space; no human,
biblical or mythical event is taking place, for the few
human figures are so far off as to form part of the
landscape. The spectator is alone with the
elements...The landscape here is hero, not background, so that the painting is an intimate portrait of
a storm. No model with a secret stands before us
here, but the secret itself, the portrayal of which stirs
the soul more deeply than could the representation
of a human being."

His letter to his mother, however, goes on to discuss the portrait of Giorgione, then not fully authenticated. It impressed him deeply, in fact it stirred him to the heart, as one of those objects of attempted identification in the light of which he sought to penetrate the artist's psyche.

"In the picture gallery here I saw a wonderful portrait of Giorgione da Castelfranco. It is so perfect that I hope it may accompany my dreams. A gaze of positively piercing vagueness, of tormented, passionate and yet doubting self-love. It must be a self-portrait; Rembrandt apart, no painter penetrates so deeply into the soul of another. Moreover, I believe that I can always recognize a self-portrait, not only from the gaze directed at the beholder, but also from the nature of that gaze, which as the artist wishes, is supposed to divulge only what his consciousness and hence his self-estimation allow or command it to divulge. Whatever else it betrays is his hidden possession, which we steal from him where we can. Seldom, however, do the eyes speak as candidly as here. They say: 'This is I, whose work you are admiring, and you are right to admire it. For I am your superior.'

The true artist loves only himself, and of himself only the creative part, while he neglects the human part or fails to consider it or ruins it with earthly pleasures, as, if we read Vasari rightly and believe him, Giorgione did. It is not that he egotistically desires the best for himself, but the creative self occupies the whole of his will and constantly demands self-expression. The true artist is—without knowing it—an enigma to himself, which he seeks to solve afresh in every work and never, subjectively speaking, succeeds in solving. Other men are to him merely servants, who must support him in his

134

self-realization or actively help him in it. His happiness and unhappiness are self-made, he requires no external causes for them. He parts easily from things for which he has no further use, not throwing them away but dropping them. Then, as I looked long at the painting I remarked in that gaze a barely disguised cast of contempt, as if the artist would say: 'In reality you will learn nothing about me, you cannot'. "

Whether Marbot was over-loading the painting psychologically will not be discussed here, yet no one to whom Giorgione's painting means anything is likely to ignore his interpretation, which steals into the receptive processes of the viewer, whether he will or no.

The attribution to Giorgione was not fully confirmed until 1908, when Ludwig Justi recognized the work as one of the Master's three self-portraits mentioned by Vasari. Justi's conclusion was based on an engraving of 1650 by Wenzel Hollar for which the painting was the model, though of course in its original state, showing the artist as David with the severed head of Goliath—playing a dramatic role, in fact, rather than in free, spontaneous confrontation. Thus, though Marbot did not know it, the work which he saw was truncated and alienated.

In Hollar's engraving, David's fingers are still clutching Goliath's head by the hair, as if they had just placed it on the scales but were not yet prepared to release the precious trophy. It is not easy for the viewer to recognize the figure as David, there seems to be no connection between it and the grisly object. Today we still see the cut-down picture as a self-portrait, in spite of the armour indicated by the metal clasp on the left shoulder. Marbot does not mention it here because he is writing a letter, not analysing a picture. However, the painting recurs in his later notes, when he interprets the armour as a symbol of psychological self-defence, a "noli me tangere". This does in fact sound a little far-fetched, and yet

135

here too, as always, the false deduction is retrieved: he interprets the two vertical lines above the root of the nose as a sign that "the pose of proud distance is not adhered to without a certain effort and not without a subtle touch of coquetry, spreading a filmy layer of serenity not over the artist himself but over the painting. He was, after all, a Venetian." As far as we know, no other critic at that time had ever made such comments on a work of art.

The rest of the page shifts back to intimacy. Lady Catherine did not make it illegible, evidently feeling that the nature of the personal allusions did not call for concealment. But she may possibly have forgotten to delete this passage. At all events, van Rossum, obviously with an instinct for ambiguity, did not include this passage in the book.

"The true artist parts easily from people and things; attachments mean little to him. For that he is to be envied. But we ordinary mortals [as we have already noted, this was not yet a cliché] have no point of escape to help us get over our losses. How much better it would be to be able to reduce the ardent and agonizing losses to a space of two dimensions than to have them embodied before one's eyes in dreams by night and day and yet nevermore to attain them, so that the desire remains for ever unfulfilled. For that is what..."

Here the surviving part of the letter breaks off, at the end of the fifth page. We can easily complete the sentence: "For that is what it does, and will do, as long as I live." The longing for his mother was indeed to stay with him for the remaining five years of his life, if not to dominate him to the same extent. Preoccupation with research, which he regarded as his task in life, increasingly convinced of its necessity; his unstinting, passionate absorption in it and the human contacts connected with it, probably from time to time at least caused him to forget

136

the fruitlessness of his antisocial desires. They may even have been completely sublimated, we do not know, since he generally omits personal references from his notes. The replacement of libidinous consummation by theoretical penetration into the art of its portrayal in the broadest sense, and over and above this into the world of creativity in general, is in many respects a typical object-transference. But it was this, in turn, which led him beyond the intellectual heights of pure selfless cognition; it led him down again on the other side, into the emotional abyss of the death-wish. The decision to end his own life originated partly in the realization that if he could have had his wish, he himself should have been the creator of the works which, as the creations of others, had passed by him as sublime evidence of a life whose deepest mystery his words were incapable of reaching. What we do not learn from his writings is that his admiration was never quite unmixed, that he was always influenced by the feeling of his own inadequacy.

V

The typical biographer not only selects his hero, but—as Freud observes—has a peculiar kind of fixation on him, in other words—my interpolation—he becomes increasingly convinced that his hero has selected him. And even if he adheres to the truth to the best of his knowledge and belief, making a clear and strict distinction between proved and unproved, fact and conjecture—he still cannot help celebrating the heroic in his hero, while deploring the unheroic; applauding actions that he himself would have committed, and feeling a slight shock of amazement or uncongeniality when he would have done the opposite.

Marbot's visit to Weimar added valuable material to his

documentation, for which the present biographer must be grateful. And yet I cannot help regarding his decision to seek out Goethe as not altogether worthy of him. I would have preferred him not to belong to that eager swarm of Englishmen smitten with the desire for culture or perhaps merely accumulating it, who used to beat a pathway to Goethe's door. They were the ones who turned the "venerable bard" into an attraction to be viewed and listened to, the crowning item on their programme, the pride of their family albums and, if the ladies among them were in luck, their poetry albums too. And scarcely one of them seems to have been aware that for the poet, as for the Pope, these audiences meant simply doing his job; if not exactly a necessary evil—he was fully prepared to pay the price of his fame—they were at least an exercise he had to perform, by popular request. A man who rightly saw himself as great, he doubtless regarded it as his duty to let his visitors descend on him, so to speak, and expose himself to the uninitiated in this way. And there is no evidence that he did it grudgingly. There was certainly no vanity involved, either; his unflagging interest in people was one reason which impelled him to go on holding these receptions almost until the end of his life, though it ultimately cost him a great effort to adjust to each of his visitors and say something "fitting and appropriate" to them. That he was bound to repeat himself in so doing is self-evident and was unavoidable.

We can only explain Marbot's wish to know Goethe as another instance of what he had described in his letter to van Rossum in 1820; once again he wanted to study the way in which "greatness" reveals itself outwardly in an individual, whether it is communicated as an unconscious aura or as a conscious demeanour, and how it influences his "humanity". Accordingly this visit was probably made less to the poet than to the "great man" whom the whole world recognized as such.

We do not know whether Marbot was introduced; it is

probable that Goethe was at least notified of his coming. But by whom? Boisserée is not a possibility, since their meeting in Paris had passed off coolly. Possibly Crabb Robinson, who revered Goethe but did not yet know him—he first visited him in 1828—had suggested to Marbot that he might seize the opportunity of a meeting with the great man of the century, and found someone to arrange it for him.

The first visit, as we have seen, is partially documented; the rest are not. The fact that, as Marbot recorded, Goethe encouraged him to spend a few days in Weimar—he liked to dispose in an authoritarian way of the arrangements of any visitors whose presence he enjoyed and who in any case were probably not in a hurry—seems to indicate that Marbot paid several more calls on him. He was certainly invited to a meal once or twice, with a number of other people, among whom he also met Goethe's son August and of course August's wife Ottilie, who predictably fell in love with him and would have liked to keep him in Weimar longer, if not actually for ever.

Ottilie von Goethe, as we know, confided to her diaries, and later in her letters to Adele Schopenhauer and Sibylle Mertens, her feelings, ranging from tender to tempestuous, for many of the young Englishmen who came to Weimar to call on her father-in-law. While August was alive there were naturally some impediments to the development of these inclinations, especially the importation of adultery, though this would have been excused by the more understanding witnesses and contemporaries, since her marriage with August had become an endless succession of misunderstandings and quarrels. But after August's tragic death in Rome in 1830, fate, while making the fulfilment of love easier for her in some ways, nevertheless denied her any happinesses which might have sprung from one of these relationships and which she had expected with a hopefulness that never abated, though it soon took on the quality of desperation.

Ottilie was a romantic, the slave of her emotions, and in a state of constant exaltation. Her inner life was chaotic—it was no accident that the journal she published for a time, condescendingly subsidized by Goethe, was called *Chaos*. Extreme in everything, for ever excited, she squandered what she had—herself—and what she had not—money. She had an independent and generous mind, honest towards herself and others, devoid of envy and hypocrisy. In her capacity for love and her will to love, which was detrimental to her own best interests, she was prepared for any sacrifice, indeed sometimes she seems to have sought self-sacrifice in order to test her own limits. She was not a nymphomaniac, but she needed to expend herself and take what she was offered in return, and in both respects she was governed by surges of intense passion and the need to suffer; suffering was her normal state. Every unhappy love, every parting or renunciation, every letter she wrote or received afforded her an opportunity, for evidently none of her lovers ever chose to link his life with hers.

Andrew was no exception. He was probably one of the first of her extra-marital lovers and she never forgot him, though physically he was replaced by many successors, above all the Anglo-Irishman Charles Stirling, whom she had met in 1822 and did not finally lose until 1834, and who in Ottilie's judgement so much resembled Andrew: her last great love again frustrated. He had declared that the life he had mapped out for himself—he intended to be a missionary—would be unacceptable to her as his wife, thereby involuntarily hinting that it was she—eight years older than himself—who would be unacceptable as his partner in life. Ottilie certainly did not put this interpretation on it, however: cool pragmatism was beyond her imaginative grasp.

Ottilie was five years older than Andrew, but deviation

from the usual was her norm, she did not feel at home in an ordinary, well-regulated life. Later, in 1830, the twenty-one-year-old Felix Mendelssohn appealed to her, but they never became lovers; she then transferred her possessiveness, always at most slumbering, never extinguished, to a twenty-two-year-old English student, Samuel Naylor by name, who fell seriously in love with her and wanted to marry her after August's death, but this too came to nothing. As this unhappy woman had sensed at an early stage, her life was not destined for fulfilment. We would have wished it otherwise, for she was not only in need of love but extremely lovable.

There is every reason to think that Ottilie was the prime mover in this hasty affair with Marbot—it lasted only four days—for he was certainly not prepared to find here, so soon after the parting from his true love, an occasion for the severance which no doubt he mentally desired but which he must also have feared as a major psychological upheaval, a deliberate infidelity committed for his own salvation and that of the far beloved. Such a radical object-transference is beyond the powers of the will alone. Of course there can be no question of his having merely succumbed passively to a woman bent on seduction, for after all the affair must have been thought out and planned. Once again a prohibition stood in the way, compelling secrecy, and even if he was to some extent looking for a cure, he seems successfully to have overcome the act of violence inherent in such a decision; he was not simply the object of the conspiracy, but an accomplice. So for the second time we see him as a partner in adultery, though in less exceptional circumstances; one imagines that it was arranged in a rapid, whispered aside in Goethe's house and that the deed in all probability took place in Andrew's room or rooms in the hostelry known as the Elephant. But however much he may have wanted it, it can certainly not have been easy for him, and I think that in the moments of ultimate abandon-

141

ment his longing and his desire were for his true love, Lady Catherine.

We learn nothing from Andrew himself about this relationship. Our secondary evidence comes from a couple of lines addressed to Crabb Robinson, which naturally mention nothing except the meeting with "Goethe's daughter-in-law, a strangely attractive woman of independent mind". Robinson himself, when he met Ottilie in Weimar in August 1829, found her "attractive and intelligent, exceedingly brilliant and lively". This was more or less the general verdict of those who met her at Goethe's house. Councillor Schultz found her "intelligent and exceedingly full of ideas", Chancellor von Müller called her "capricious and bizarre, but also witty and charming".

Our knowledge of the relationship is based on a letter of August 1825 from Ottilie to Andrew in Rome, probably the only one she ever wrote him. It was found among van Rossum's papers, and we must be grateful to the Father for preserving this precious document, if only perhaps through oversight.

> "Weimar, Aug. 11th 1825
> Would that God had made me so that I might take everything as lightly as others do! But I cannot. All that one may dream and feel in moments of Happiness can only be set in order and felt anew when those moments are past and the feeling of Love is captive in the breast, no longer shared with the Beloved whose head one feels upon one's bosom. I would gladly be alone now, in some place where no one knew anything of my sufferings and my joys. My heartstrings quiver when I think of you, and yet—I know that I have loved sinfully, forgetful of my duty—my soul was forfeit and forgot the law. Nevertheless it was a drop of Balsam for me, for I have gathered strength to live on and the Memory is

142

still mine, concealed within the 'picturesque apparel of my soul', which so pleas'd you. Now I am calm and unabashed when I think of our secret hours together (and at the brief fright when there was a knock at the bolted door and we held our breath, and it was only a note from Goethe!).

I know that I have lost my way on the road to Paradise and to Heaven, for I have deserved neither. My life will be difficult now that I have made it my resolve to act in accordance with my Inner Laws, heedless of the appearance it gives me, and whether it may perhaps be wrongly understood. It may be that I shall be accused of wanting womanly pride, but I shall bear it, for I am conscious of higher motives, I am no false coquette, I am in need of Love. I will bestow it with devotion and accept it with ardour if it is offered to me. In the fragmentary life I lead, in a few years' time it will no longer lie in my power to make a man happy. And my smile, which you said was borrowed from the Angel with the long finger in the painting of the Annunciation, will be extinguished. The cup of my Sorrow is bottomless—when I think I have drained it to the dregs, still it is not empty for me—just as in the old mythology Thor could not empty the horn because its tip was in the ocean, and it was this he had been trying to drain. Farewell, my dear—forget me not as I shall not forget you, and suffer less than

Your Ottilie."

The confession in this letter shows Ottilie's clear, unvarnished assessment of herself, her analysis of her own ecstatically troubled soul. The excessive agitation of that heart of hers was never able completely to suppress her intellect and reason, and she retained the capacity to see herself, if not objectively, then at least as an object. In the relationship with Andrew we see her more distinctly than him; he ultimately eludes us in his intimate associations. He too failed to bring her happiness, for he did not—or so we fear, if one can fear in retrospect—allow himself to become too deeply involved, not only because his true love could not be displaced from his heart by any other partner, but no doubt also because Ottilie's exaltation, her impetuosity and the solemn intensity with which she expressed her emotions were alien, if not actually disturbing, to his inmost being. On the other hand, he had the gift of empathy with others, especially those close to him, of feeling his way into their fate; indeed, he had the imagination to experience it in detail, if he wanted to. So he must also have recognized and appreciated Ottilie's human value. The fact that he enjoyed her "bizarre" attraction and assented to her moods is confirmed by the allusion in her letter to the *Angel of the Annunciation* by Van Eyck (then privately owned in England, now in the National Gallery, Washington), whose smile, pregnant with mystery, seems to be directed less at the Virgin looking back at him than at some purifying process within himself.

We do not know how Andrew responded to this moving letter. We can only hope—if one can hope in retrospect—that he replied to it, with the compassion that truly unhappy woman deserved.

Andrew's destination was, of course, Italy, but he was in no hurry to reach it; he knew that he was no longer on a journey from which one will return, but on a road on which one can linger, because the goal, the point of rest will be reached quite soon enough, and a decision awaits one there which is deferred as long as one is travelling. This is conjecture, to be sure, but we are encouraged in it by one of those entries in tiny script at the bottom of the page in which, though Andrew

144

tries to objectivize himself as "he", we are constantly aware of the traces of his deepest, as it were half-conscious feeling, as if he were scattering alms to satisfy our eagerness for discovery. Once again, then, a flash of lightning illumination of his inmost heart, coming immediately below the note concerning Goethe's questionable understanding of art, with which it has no connection whatever. Here it is:

"Sometimes he was moved by a longing for
'The undiscovered country, from whose bourn
No traveller returns...' "

The words of Hamlet's debate between being and not being, when he has decided long ago in his soul in favour of the latter. One might call these strange entries "thinking aloud" if they were not the very ones which are inaudible. It is a "visible thinking" in which the diarist does not really want to indulge, and yet he clings to it, disguised as another person, in a brief moment of acknowledged weakness.

Marbot, then, did not set off at once for the south from Weimar, but first travelled west, to Kassel, to see the paintings in the gallery at Wilhelmshöhe Castle, which, like the Brunswick gallery, was a model instance of a collection which had been open to everyone, not only to the privileged, since the late eighteenth century, even before the French Revolution— and contained art treasures which in both cases had been in the hands of intelligent princely agents. The Kassel collection alone included twenty Rembrandts, sixteen of them genuine, which could be said of few collections then or now. Marbot noted, probably while still at Kassel:

"Rembrandt's paintings have a metaphysical quality, for the soul of the model seems to be enriched by that of the artist and so inseparably united with it that we are incapable of mentally re-establishing the model in his reality, and therefore in our own.

145

The model has become a work of art because the artist has inspired him with the breath of life ...

If we look closely at the portrait of Nicolaes Bruyningh, we see in this young man the object of both affection and sympathy. His smile is melancholy, as if he were contemplating a missed opportunity, something below and diagonally in front of him which is vanishing from sight, and will never present itself again. The mouth, with its full lips, is slightly open as if for a half-timorous but half-suppressed cry. The golden-brown hair is long and curling, painted as if the artist would have liked to stroke it consolingly. For this man is not posing, rather he has forgotten that he is sitting for an artist, he is alone with himself. A decisive moment in someone's life has been captured here by a painter to whom such moments were familiar from his own life. He would have been incapable of portraying any emotion which he himself had not experienced."

Marbot's other notes on Rembrandt were written later, probably in 1828, in the quiet of Urbino and in a state of inspired retrospection. They are full of information, not only about his view of Rembrandt but also about his criteria for general art appreciation, betraying here and there the (presumably unconscious) desire to objectivize and arrive at generally valid theories.

"Just as the painter is not always in a state to give his best, so we are not always in a state to accept the best when it is offered. The true art-lover experiences moments of enlightenment in which a work of art seems to reveal itself fully to him, after he has tried in vain to solve its mystery in unreceptive moments. In the case of mythical, historical or biblical scenes the

146

desire for receptivity can sometimes be created by means of the event portrayed, in so far as it is one to which we respond affirmatively. The content leads us to the form, and loses its importance in so far as we are impassioned by the form. We enjoy looking at the most preposterous allegory if it was painted by a Master such as Tiepolo. But to make the countenance of an unknown man so familiar to us that we become participants in his destiny—for that we need a Rembrandt and we need too the right moment, in which his greatness can work upon us...

One wonders how Rembrandt succeeds with every brush-stroke in penetrating more deeply into the soul of the model, for he paints *alla prima*, wet on wet, not like Titian in his later portraits, who applied up to thirty glazes one on top of another and in this way penetrated the depths, so to speak, layer by layer...With Rembrandt it seems as if the model's soul were the light-source of the painting. In order to paint that soul he uses the corporeal form that belongs to it, drawing the body forth from the obscurity into which, once painted, it will fall back again. But it is the illumination of the soul, not the details of the body which abide in the memory of the beholder. With Rembrandt, no one will remember details of appearance, only the whole, the countenance as the mirror of the soul...

Rembrandt's attitude to the world was negative. The darkness behind his figures testifies to the silent rejection of all glitter. It is the darkness of loneliness, from which he snatches the figures—I mean the poor, not those he was commissioned to paint—for a brief time, to make them his companions in suffering, fellow travellers in a tragic world which is topographically beyond our grasp. Here this world is the closest at hand, the streets of the poor folk of Amsterdam. More distant goals did not concern him, Italy did not exist for him, his sombre world was within, not without, his riches were not those of the material world. 'When I would distract my spirit,' he said, 'I seek not honour but freedom.'...

The artist's impulse to paint a portrait which is not a commission appears to me as a dual phenomenon, namely projection and identification with the model, which first arouses the desire to capture it, whose life the artist makes his own for the duration of the painting process, even to the most superficial details such as posture and mimicry. In Gérard's painting-class I saw five students with gloomily wry expressions painting a gloomily wry-looking sergeant: the act of painting caused them to become that sergeant...

Rembrandt is the greatest artist at interpreting the soul, yet he would never have been able to express his insights in words. His visual interpretation contains a part of himself, just as a great actor plays Hamlet and through the power of his mental transference becomes Hamlet while remaining himself. The great actor becomes Hamlet; Rembrandt becomes the bearded man in a cap or his own son Titus. We have here a third way between reality and imagination, uniting both into a synthesis which can be re-experienced. What we see in the picture is an artifice created by a great artist with the intention of touching or even stirring up our souls by means of a chance object..."

Some detailed interpretations of other Rembrandt portraits follow, shedding light here and there on details which

148

escape our attention. For instance, he thinks that Rembrandt introduced mystical chiaroscuro effects, not in order to confuse the viewer but simply in the pursuit of painterly perfection, thus deliberately ignoring the thematic logic of his representation. "The golden chain which Rembrandt hangs round the neck of a poor old man"—Marbot is speaking of the 1632 portrait at Kassel—

> "serves as an almost hidden additional source of light in the lower half of the picture, which is otherwise dark; but whence it draws the light that it reflects is known only to the God who made the artist paint the picture."

In the case of the ponderous *Juno* of 1664 or 1665 (then in private ownership in London, now in a New York collection), he even has the temerity to doubt the attribution. Not only are face and stature quite untypical of a Rembrandt model, but the texture and modelling of the flesh parts are closer to Rubens. Moreover, Rembrandt never painted three-quarter length portraits in a frontal view. Hadley-Chase, who admittedly was sometimes too inclined to believe in the infallibility of his hero, endorsed his scepticism. As far as I know Rembrandt's authorship has not since been called in question. The painting is unsigned and undated, but this in itself has no particular significance. Personally, however, I share Marbot's misgivings; after all, he recognized two other "Rembrandt" portraits as unauthentic, and so they are.

On his first Italian journey Marbot had already noted the idea of "commissioned art" as a keyword, placing it in brackets after the name Benozzo. From the notes on the Florentines which he probably made at Marbot Hall between 1822 and 1825 it appears that he was moved to speculate on the significance of this concept, as he understood it, by the self-portrait which Benozzo Gozzoli slipped in among the portraits of other people in the frescoes of the Medici-Riccardi

Palace. The portrait is unmistakable, for the words OPUS BENOTII appear in large capitals on the cap—Marbot observes that the angry gaze which meets the viewer must in reality have been directed at Cosimo di Medici, who commissioned the frescoes: far from smiling obsequiously, the painter wished to express his indignation at a patron who not only dictated the subject-matter but took it upon himself to dictate the arrangement of the persons portrayed, in other words the whole composition; indeed, Marbot claims— I could not find any sources for this—that he is alleged even to have selected the colours he preferred. So what we see is the angry face of the humiliated artist, apparently robbed of his freedom. In Marbot's notes this is the starting point for an excursion or essay which became one of his main themes for a time, until he revised his opinion: the primacy of the "internal commission"—another glimpse of the Romantic—vis à vis the "external commission", which must necessarily give rise to a lesser art, since instead of deploying his own talents to the full, the artist must make the best of the often arbitrary ideas of others. "The supplier", he notes, "is always the servant of the one supplied, who disposes of the commodity and fixes its value." Yet the note was almost overtaken by the doubt: "On the other hand, in their time even the greatest and most highly esteemed suppliers, Titian or Tiepolo for instance, were dependent on commissions, it was all they had, and they would not have had it otherwise." In London a friend of his grandfather had told him that he had once asked Haydn why he had never written string quintets. Haydn had stared at him in astonishment and said that no one had ever commissioned him to do so. Marbot does in fact mention this reply in order to query and ultimately to modify his own theory: he realized that the commission, which many—if not actually all—artists were free to refuse, had not necessarily restricted a freedom which existed a priori but had been the necessary condition for

150

the artist's existence and the cornerstone of his fame and fortune.

The real stimulus for this modification came from his visit to the Tiepolo frescoes in Würzburg, to which he travelled from Kassel. "A world of absolute and unbroken beauty," he wrote to van Rossum,

"and nothing could prevent me from lying down on my back on the floor and on the steps of the stairway in order to range with my telescope across the vastness of that splendid sky under which curious figures float in consummate grace and radiant naturalness, and in truly boundless freedom."

The notes he made on the spot here too—and there must have been many of them —were probably destroyed, after he had worked them into his notebooks on his return to Urbino from his stay in Rome in 1827, which means that they also have inevitably lost the immediacy of his experience. And yet he has a clear picture of the subject.

"Allegory works, if at all, exclusively through its pictorial quality, never through the evidence of its meaning. None of these visual parables has ever imparted an insight which transcended the visual, or caused anyone at all to reflect on qualities and attributes that he sees depicted here in symbolic form. Even with as great an artist and as great a spirit as Tiepolo, the allegorical character withdraws behind the lively diversity of his portrayal of people. Allegory was to him the pretext and the occasion for his sublime enchantment...Nowadays allegory has degenerated into the handicraft of simple moralists and religious fanatics, lacking in all sensuality and therefore in all creative power."

This was undoubtedly a dig at the Nazarenes, whose paintings he had seen in various collections and whose frescoes he saw in the Palazzo Zuccari and probably in the Villa Massimo.

"Tiepolo's allegories are therefore illuminating, even when their meaning is obscure. He succeeded as no other Master in animating the gestures and poses of his figures with such truth and dignity that we forget to retranslate from the language of the paintings into that of the abstract concepts from which the idea sprang. Every figure, even the smallest angel, justifies its existence simply by its position in the composition, allotted to it between the graduated strata of Heaven, where it embodies its role, of which we never know precisely whether it originated in the Bible or history, in myth or the artist's imagination. But that is in any case a matter of indifference, for each part is played as perfectly and naturally, without the slightest histrionical mannerism, as if this were the daily life of Heaven, to the contemplation of which the firmament lifts us, that we may hover and participate therein, indeed we even feel ourselves becoming celestial bodies, drawn into this moved and moving eternity of the Divine...

This tremendous panorama in the Würzburg Residency, the largest ceiling fresco in the history of art, was created by one man, who between his fifty-fifth and fifty-eighth years lay on his back, high up on a wooden scaffolding, day after day except in the extreme cold of winter, covering square yard by square yard of gigantic white surface with the creations of his imagination, without ever being able to step back a single yard to give himself distance, whereas I have not sufficient imagination even to envisage such a process..."

Nowadays we endorse Marbot's paean without reservation but in his day the recent, as yet unclassified eras of baroque and rococo were not rated very highly. Tiepolo had been completely forgotten and no artist or connoisseur knew the Wüzburg ceiling fresco. And yet, as Marbot clearly recognized, the fresco is in the true sense of the word a world picture, immortalizing a man who possessed a conception of the ideal, of the perfect harmony of all creation and reproduced it in an imperial range of visions. "What, I wonder", Marbot writes,

"would these solemn German painters have said, faced with the illusionistic pleasantries in which Tiepolo indulged? And what—ye pious brethren— when faced with the portrait of a prince of the church borne through the air t'wards Heaven by naked nymphs, or dryads or goddesses, or whatever they may be?"

We do not know where Marbot spent that September. He must have paid a brief visit to Nuremburg, because he mentions the *Annunciation* by Konrad Witz in his notes, otherwise nothing, not even a painting, from this town. He probably left Wüzrburg at the end of August and certainly arrived in Chur on 5 October. The intervening period, including Nuremburg, is obscure. Hadley-Chase's guess that he crossed the Brenner and on van Rossum's advice stayed in Innsbruck and its environs can be explained only by the fact that Hadley lacked two key documents: Marbot's letter to his mother from Splügen and evidently the one to van Rossum from Cremona as well. The "extravaganzas of nature", by which Marbot meant the Via Mala, was taken by Hadley to mean the upper Eisack valley, which indicates either that he knew only the less tremendous mountains of the Alps or that he credited his hero with more modest sources of experience,

153

and accordingly failed to do him justice in this area. His great astonishment at not finding anything about the paintings of the public Munich collections in Marbot's notes—for he must have passed through that city on his journey—can be countered by the observation that little was known about these galleries until King Ludwig I acquired the collection of the brothers Boisserée in 1827.

More than four weeks, then, on a journey which could easily have been accomplished at that time in four days. That stirs the passive imagination of any biographer, including mine. And yet it refuses to settle on any of the stopping places on the direct route of that journey, and any serious supposition by the reader would be worth as much as mine.

There is another, rather deeper question here, however, which we wish to explore, because of the time of the journey and prompted by his own curious apparent reticence: how did Andrew work through his brief affair with Ottilie von Goethe, that breach of faith which, however much it was justified by reason, still violated a secret emotion? Was his silence during those five weeks only apparent after all—did he perhaps spend some difficult hours in composing a letter to his mother in which he confessed that which he may have thought he must confess, and explained what did not need explanation? Such a letter would certainly not have contained any passages about art or any other subject, so Lady Catherine would have destroyed the whole of it. And how would she have received this confession? Although she must have been aware that some substitute would have to be found sooner or later, the account of the event which had now taken place, sooner rather than later, must have hit her hard, confirming the loss of what was already lost, but now making the emptiness of her soul complete and casting a deep shadow on the memory as well.

But all this is speculation, for nothing but a strict, not

even intelligent logical consistency, which Andrew would probably have rejected, points to such a letter actually having been written. All the indications are to the contrary, in fact, especially the tone of perpetual longing in the subsequent letters, whose truthfulness it would be absurd to doubt.

Where his mother's second—surviving—letter reached him is uncertain. This too would point to the improbability of a confession by Andrew, had it not been sent off at about the same time, in September 1825—it is unfortunately undated. That the letters, had Andrew really written his, might have crossed is a nasty thought which every reader will no doubt try, as I do, to banish.

"My love,
Just as my happiness now lies behind me, so also the
heavy burthen that it occasioned lies behind me, or
at least part of it which even God cannot remove
from me and which I now have to bear to the end.
My hope in Father Gerard did not deceive me. I will
keep silence to you about his anger and his sternness,
for it would be a breach of confidence between two
souls united in the supreme faith which you deny.
Yet since that hard day of confession his dear
compassion comforts, quietens and refreshes me,
directed as it is, not at my loss but at the aberration
of my poor heart, which I too recognize more
clearly with every day and yet which haunts me
afresh every night as an infliction of temptation.
Longing which will not be appeased cannot, I think,
be a sin, for neither will nor courage is sufficient to
oppose it. It is true that I have been released from the
dreadful—as you said, 'irrational'—feeling of guilt
for your father's death, but mistress of my secret
desires I am not, and so now I long for age, when all
passions will be spent, all recollection of sin faded

155

and only from the far distance will those few happy moments still shine out, in which we were able to forget our guilt. Yet do I fear to have forfeited the right to earthly peace and death therefore begins to lose its terror for me. Had I still the right to have one single wish fulfilled, it would be that you might be happy.

God bless you, my love"

Poor, unhappy Lady Catherine! She seems to have forfeited the right to that last wish too, for neither then nor later was Andrew happy.

On 5 October 1825 Marbot arrived in Chur; we know this from the entry in the visitors' book of the Gasthof Stern (then an inn, now the Hotel Stern), which, in contrast to many another Grisons hostelry at that time, enjoyed (and enjoys) a good reputation.[5] We do not know how long he stayed there, but he would scarcely have formed any closer connections with this town, the qualities and virtues of which are not immediately apparent to the stranger. He then took the scheduled coach service, newly established on the Splügen Road, which had been extended only a few years before, along the Via Mala, and represented a fearful ordeal at that time for many travellers who felt they were being exposed to goblin powers; how many fervent prayers must have risen to Heaven from that place! Marbot writes of it to his mother:

"...a precipitous crack in the globe, marked by a splintered rock, like a gigantic wound on its mon-

5. In his book *Reminiscences of the Lake Poets* De Quincey explains why Wordsworth took a relatively unintellectual travelling companion on his Swiss journey of 1788: "...I have heard Wordsworth speak of the ruffian landlords who played upon his youth in the Grisons; and, however well qualified to fight his own battles, he might find, amongst such savage mountaineers, two combatants better than one." This journey admittedly took place thirty-seven years earlier.

strous vertical edges, the upper half of which is adorned here and there by some errant, straggling tree growing on a narrow ledge or even out of the stone while the lower half is never touched by sunshine, on the one hand at a reckless height but on the other at a perilous depth, alongside the road. A fall from the coach window and one would be at the centre of the earth, though its glowing core is not betrayed by this narrow cleft, for through it rages the water which, although one does not see it from the coach, one can hear roaring and thundering with ever-changing strength and varying pitch, now soft as the hissing whisper of water sprites, and now, multiplied by the echo from the rock walls, so loud that it drowns the terrified cries of the travellers. Opposite me sat a German baroness, or perhaps a confidence trickster, who flew into a dreadful agitation because she believed we were making straight for Hell. I endeavoured to explain to her that this could not be; that, on the contrary, a coach like ours travelled along here in both directions every day, the inmates of which, so far as one can verify, had reached their destination. But she was not amenable to reason and resorted to swooning, which was the best thing she could have done in the circumstances."

And in Marbot's notebooks we find:
"In view of this extraordinary spectacle I have asked myself once again whether such extravaganzas of nature are 'beautiful', but I am at a loss for an answer, since the word is not applicable to the phenomena of nature. In nature we have the primordial state, hence the beginning of all contemplation of the visible; the absolute reference point which refuses our aesthetic judgment. The

absolute remains forever absolute and its manifestations elude both description and assessment. Only objects of human volition and knowledge are 'beautiful', the word lives by its relativity. Nature is the subject of beauty, but not its embodiment."

Here too, apparently, faced with the direct spectacle of nature, Marbot is working with cool detachment on the modulations of his aesthetics and testing their usefulness. The Via Mala, the subject of so many travellers' amazement and panic fear in his day, elicits no exclamation from him, no emotional utterance, but becomes the object by which he tests himself and his theory, indeed, at such moments he becomes almost identical with his theory. At all events, he denies himself the admiration felt by the majority of his romantic contemporaries; on the other hand, of course, he does not support the condemnation of nature by a minority, to whom the high mountains meant nothing but dread, like Stendhal, who considered them a source of horror, "...precisely as the mountains of Cumberland in north England, when one compounds them with the chasms". And Stendhal was not the only one to see the Swiss mountains as a barbaric whim of the divinity, which instead of making men awestruck makes them hostile to superfluous trumperies of nature.

In Splügen, barely a day's journey from Chur, Marbot became very ill, having probably, like so many travellers in those days, contracted pneumonia following a protracted cold. We see from the letter he wrote to Lady Catherine on 2 November 1825 that he was unable to travel for almost a month, at first confined to his bed and then convalescent, dragging himself painfully about, nursed by an old-established and respected family called Simmen in their own house. He was not the first Englishman to be smitten here. At that time the Splügen Pass was one of the most frequented frontier points between north and south, and Splügen the place where, especially at inhospitable seasons, people prepared themselves for the rigours of a crossing, hazardous in our eyes, more like an expedition, or where they recovered from it and stayed to get over the consequences—or not, in the case of some more susceptible travellers. Quite a few travelled no further and lie buried there in Splügen cemetery. Marbot writes to his mother:

"So here I lie, still so weak that before every movement I pause to wonder if it is really necessary, in a friendly wooden room, which is yet so strange that it denies me its sympathetic interest for good or ill, for it regards me, rightly, as an object of accident— tended by a family of good spirits, whose helpfulness and compassion are naturally for the sick man in me, who might just as well be any other. And so I am alone in a state of idleness far too luxurious—blurring the present and conjuring up the past over and over again —to face the question whether I am still the person I was a little time ago. The answer is naturally yes, I am still he, with all my heart. Sometimes it seems to me as if we were at times the happiest of people. Or were we not, is my state leading me to believe in a dream? Perhaps one is never happy, because the experience of happiness excludes reflection on its nature and every feeling of happiness falls victim to the past at the moment when one is reflecting."

The next section has been crossed out by Lady Catherine (and restored to legibility):

"I dream that you are beside me—in my feverish imaginings you were always round me, enveloping me like a cloud, so that I lay in deep abandonment and drank in your heavenly presence. I am better now, since I am on earth once more, but I am also worse, since I cannot decide whether I want to be on an earth which robs me of the vision of your nearness. Will this longing ever end? And should I hope or fear the end? Shall I ever..."

The page ends here, the remainder of the letter is missing. We do not need it in order to see how deep the feeling of loss was, and how lightly the affair with Ottilie must have weighed; indeed, this letter seems sufficient proof that Andrew did not tell his mother about it.

One may wonder at this extremity of emotion, so seldom revealed by Marbot, this indulgence in the sense of "nevermore"; no doubt it was largely brought about by the fragility of a man undermined by illness. This kind of "negative euphoria" never recurred as far as we know, irreplaceable as his mother remained even to the self-controlled Marbot.

If not fully recovered, by mid-November Marbot was at least in his own estimation ready to travel. The November of that year was mild, the mountain roads still free from snow. His host did indeed urgently try to dissuade him from crossing the Pass in view of the uncertain weather, but Marbot could wait no longer, he yearned for the south and, above all, for change. We can also assume that his growing fatalism made him reckless: the idea of exposing himself to the irrational blows of elementary forces, so typical of the Romantics, also appealed to the Romantic in him. But he had also ascribed a kind of symbolic significance to the great step across the heights from north to south: he thought of it as a step out of the darkness of personal involvement into a new freedom, enabling him to stand in an objective relationship to all that was past, and leaving his soul completely free and open to experience and perception. This is quite clear from the notes, or, if you like, from the non-notes, the obviously deliberate omission: we find a blank white page in this journal, on which the only words are squeezed in at the very bottom of the page, as always when an unconnected comment appears among the interpretative texts: "This whiteness is the snow, which, though it never allows his soul to forget that which serves cognition, would cleanse it of all that does *not* serve it." A grand resolve, no doubt, though its categorical rigour is slightly alleviated when we see how, ultimately, all that he did and left undone was to serve cognition, even if it did not concern his real area of research.

Andrew describes how he crossed the Pass, seen as the consummation of his purification, as both link and dividing line between two sections of his life, in a letter to Father van Rossum from Cremona, which he reached after three more days of travel:

"Shortly before the departure a general state of chaos still prevailed, for the weather was visibly worsening and the people said it was too late for the coach and too early for the sledges. The word of power 'We're off!' was spoken by the coachman, a bearded giant who bestrode the box as a king his throne, and we left. It was uphill at once and beginning to snow lightly, as if the sky had been holding back its offering for the undivided attention of the traveller. Up and up we went, the snow falling more and more thickly, as if to efface all traces of more friendly seasons before one of us decided to return to them. The forest became straggling, then sparse, until it petered out, leaving only a withered stump here and there, and we drove into a basin ringed by gigantic, inimical heights offering no means of escape. I confess that I became a little fearful—I thought perhaps Hell was not beneath the earth but in the clouds. But the coachman, that

161

stronghold of confidence, knew better, he sent the coach zigzagging ever upwards at shorter and shorter intervals into sheer nothingness, for by now it was not only snowing but blowing too, so that the coach seemed to be riding now on the left-hand, now on the right-hand wheels, but this troubled the coachman little, to him it was a gamble without risk and to me too it was now a matter of indifference, I felt too weak for fear and was only half in the world, which was by now a brilliant white, broken here and there by patches of darker white that raced over us, and upward and onward we rolled, past a house before which stood two men in uniform, to whom the coachman called something incomprehensible, and on again, swaying and lurching, until we breasted a summit and began to zigzag downhill again, how long I know not, since my feeling for time had been obliterated, and with it all expectation. Suddenly we came to a halt, I thought it was already dusk, but it was nothing more than the grey sky, and a pair of armed bandits opened the carriage on both sides, so that between one door and the other the snow drifted and swirled across us. But they did not run us through—that too, in the circumstances, I would have accepted—but wished to see our passes, although I could have sworn they could not read. Their language was incomprehensible to me, perhaps it was Tyrolean, at all events they were Austrians, as a passanger, a Protestant parson, remarked. They inspected all the stamps, then closed the doors again, and we drove on, towards unknown depths in which the darkness now engulfed us. Our course seemed to me like a spiral leading through a wide hole into the underworld, but it led only to this world, a homeless world, in which I had no desire to be. All was black, for there was no more snow here, but there was nothing else that was recognizable either. Somewhere, sometime, we made a stop, somewhere too I slept, but I no longer know where, the journey seems to me as if it had never been, I had but dreamed it."

The place must have been Chiavenna, from which he probably travelled the next day to Colico and from there by ship through the fog across the motionless Lake Como—"the surface of the water almost invisible, but as still as a pond and as noiseless as the realm of the dead"—to Lecco and on again, into the Brianza, along straight roads between bare willows and poplars—"which stepped out of the fog like silent freezing phantoms only to vanish into it again at once"—and out into the Po Valley, no longer as it had been when he had sat on the reedy stretches of the river bank, but dripping wet, dismissive. Shivering and weakened by delayed convalescence, he took in the change in the images, a cold reception to his Italy, not threatening, but unrelenting—"breathing the damp, the fog and the foul air of swamp. I am not well but safe."

"Not well but safe." He must have had a robust constitution and have been one of the many travellers of his time and earlier, whose resistance now seems to us almost inconceivable, suggesting that the body of those days, however sensitive the psychological constitution may have been, had a more robust substrate than today. In reality Marbot was probably one of those asthenics, whose soul was both vulnerable to injury and injured, yet who can order the conduct of their bodies according to their own imperturbable plan.

Marbot had intended to spend a few days in Cremona, recovering from the journey and completing his recuperation, but it turned out otherwise. On the second evening, when

163

eating at the inn, he met an elderly Austrian officer, whose name is not mentioned, with whom he began to talk of painting. The Austrian proved to be a connoisseur and offered to take Andrew with him the next day to Mantua, where he was stationed, and to which he was travelling, and to show him the Mantegna frescoes in the Castel San Giorgio, in which he himself was lodged with his family. They reached Mantua, then an Austrian garrison town, by the next evening. The day after, the officer, who turned out to be the commandant of the garrison, took him to the Camera degli sposi, so that Marbot was probably the first, and certainly for some decades the last art traveller of the nineteenth century to see the frescoes. They had been restored in 1790 by Martin Knoller, who had fortunately done no more than cover up the scratches and scribbles, a legacy of various billetings. For the rest, the condition of the walls in particular must have been more "authentic" than it is now, since notorious restorers have made small "improvements".

Andrew recorded his immediate notes and kept them in the quarto volume, presumably because the date of his suicide pre-empted more detailed study of Mantegna. Here then we have the marks of immediacy, the spontaneous reactions which are unfortunately wanting in the case of other major impressions. "A strange and powerful assembly", he calls the monumental work,

"...a meeting of the Gonzaga family, apparently at full strength, and their court, put on the stage by Andrea Mantegna. I walk into the room and am surrounded by solemn figures, I do not venture to speak, for every word disturbs this deep and perfect silence, to which they all yield almost actively—I have no wish to disturb them. But then I observe that none of these figures is looking at me, not even the glum artist himself, standing among some others

164

and gazing, like them, helplessly into the distance, as if something had just occurred which should not have occurred. What are the figures doing? They are doing nothing, they are engrossed in their silence, their lips firmly closed, they gaze out in various directions, not in expectation but in submission: come what may, they are composed and ready. The one man in motion is the secretary, hastening forward as the Duke beckons, *um ihm etwas ins Ohr zu schweigen* [to be silent in his ear]."

The last phrase is written in German, and at the bottom of the page, as an aside, comes the rhetorical question: "Why do we not have a word for the verb 'schweigen'?"

"A toneless silence reigns. Everyone is completely at a loss, because no one seems to have told them what they are supposed to be doing here, except perhaps the painter, whose demeanour compels them to model for him. And there they stand as if petrified, people, horses, and dogs too, of a strange, indefinable but ugly breed, seemingly awaiting some kind of release from the obligation to remain, which they all so uncheerfully fulfil...

No blame attaches to the painter, compelled as he was to portray a family of notorious ugliness, as of course he must have suspected when he obeyed the summons to the Court of Mantua. His business was to capture the image of this court, as it were an emblem for all eternity, and he knew that for the perpetuation of contemporary reality and existing people, the state of animation will not serve, because no one motion is capable of reflecting the image of the whole man and only an untroubled stillness can transform the idea of him into reality. So it is no accident that they stand as they do. Not only must

165

the dictates of court etiquette coincide with those of the composition, but the artist's intention was to create a microcosm, which was to bring nothing less than his own world into the picture, just as every artist, in every painting and at all times desires to give all he has on his palette."

"To have something on one's palette" is not an English idiom, but it has taken root in Germany; though it says exactly what Marbot means here, the phrase probably did not originate with him.

"This world was to be one of classical harmony, and he would use its representatives to convey his concept of the dignity and reality of art as an everlasting example and precept. So there they stand, each one a sculptured monument, yet true to life, for ideal figures are more beautiful than these. And the imagination the artist had to forgo in them he put into his boldly designed landscapes instead. In them the ingenuity of the man triumphs indeed, creating an architecture which would constitute a contemporary match for the artist's antique ideal, if only perspective had been mastered, which it could not be at that time. Yet if we take the twofold meaning of the word perspective we may say that although it could not be effective as a pictorial stratagem, in the figurative sense of the word, signifying breadth of thought, it erects a monument to the great painter such as he might have wished for himself."

I have avoided making a list of the sights, especially the works of art, which Marbot did not see. It would be long, of course, but considerably shorter than in the case of the others of his time who travelled in search of art, or of those numerous artists and connoisseurs—including Carl von Rumohr—who were hoping above all to find in body what they thought they had already found in spirit, or were travelling in order to have their ideal images confirmed on the spot. Goethe, whose Italian journey had of course taken place some forty years earlier, spent two hours in Florence out of his twenty months in Italy and even those seem to have irritated him. He saw the Mantegna frescoes in the Eremitani Chapel in Padua and never tired of the façade of the Temple of Minerva in Assisi, but although they were open to the public he did not see the Giotto frescoes which were two hundred paces (and in Padua twenty paces) from the objects of his admiration. Most travellers failed to notice what they were not expecting to see, or noticed it only fortuitously. Vasari, more of a false luminary than illuminating in his views, could at least have provided approximate locations, but there was scarcely a single non-Italian who had read him.

There would be some justice in accusing me of negligence because I have not tried to find out if the paintings which Marbot probably did not see, or at least has not mentioned, would have been open to the public—or, if you like, to the privileged traveller who might have been given an introduction. But my purpose was less to convict my hero of desultoriness than to present him in the light of his actual achievements. It would also be fascinating to know how he would have reacted to this or that work of art, to Giulio Romano's frescoes, still in Mantua, or—to concentrate on the stopping places on his journey from there to Urbino—to the frescoes in the Palazzo Schifanoia at Ferrara, though these were probably not accessible at that time. If I am right about him, the mosaics at Ravenna would not have meant very much to him, because he had made up his mind, in some cases much too hastily, to avoid looking at anonymous works which could tell him nothing about the psychology of the artist. There were limits even to his receptivity, but he was more aware of them than others.

Urbino belonged at that time to the Papal States and, like the other Marchesan towns, was extremely provincial; the landed nobility and gentry, mostly related by blood or marriage, lived in a world of their own and officials, if not actually minor members of the priesthood themselves, were in the service of the clergy, whose vassals and servants made up the rest of the population. Foreigners and travellers were rare here. The town lay then, as it lies today, on its windy summit, compact and yet expansive, as if a single architectural idea had conceived a building complex at once large and unified and shaped it of honey-coloured bricks. Its great past had dwindled long ago into an unpretentious present, but not to the detriment of the life there, which was peaceful and completely ordinary. Nowadays Urbino has become lively and populous again, but at that time it was sleepy and depopulated, fading into an unambitious life of its own.

Marbot was probably less in search of quiet—he needed no external buttresses for his intellectual studies, which were actually never strenuous or even forced—than the breadth of the surrounding countryside, the distant skyline, a place where one could range at ease without encountering chasms or cliffs, and yet with the constant promise of unexpected views, contours, intersections, art in Nature. He also needed the atmosphere, redolent of the past; not so much the historical background as the place where the arts had held sway, which they had chosen and immortalized. Nevertheless, his decision to come to rest here—in the true sense of the word—has almost a romantic air about it, inspired by melancholy if not by self-denial, a retreat from the world and the present which had nothing to offer him except diversion, and that he neither needed nor wanted.

He rented a spacious house, the Casa Baiardi on the via Santa Chiara—now the Palace of Justice—looking southward on to stepped ranks of hills, the panorama that creates the "longing for something undefinable". The owner, a nobleman of Urbino, had recently died, also—a strange coincidence—as the result of a hunting accident. His widow, thirty-two year-old Anna Maria Baiardi, also from an old and respected family, and her two small children were kept on by Andrew, who was not used to keeping house or controlling servants; he did not want a major-domo, and being pampered had never appealed to him. The house was large and extensive, with plenty of room for other people; it called for a chatelaine, not a professional housekeeper, whom he would probably not have tolerated, but a calm ruler, who knew how to give orders to those who supplied their daily needs and would take charge of what was hers in any case. Whether when he was negotiating the lease he already saw this chatelaine as the future lady of the house we do not know; at all events, at least after his return from Rome in November 1826, that is what she was: his companion and lover. She had neither disapproval nor indignation to fear from Urbino society; provincial as it was, it was not prudish, especially since Andrew, though detached and courteous rather than cordial, was a much sought-after guest in their houses. "Il milord Inglese", as they called him, not quite accurately, with his faint aura of mystery, probably detectable only by the discriminating, brought an element of worldliness and enlightenment into the drawing-rooms of Urbino.

Anna Maria Baiardi, née Catani-Ligi, born in Urbino in 1795 and educated at the Santa Chiara Convent at Faenza (where Countess Teresa Gamba, later Guiccioli, was also educated), married in 1816 and had three children, the first of which died soon after birth. It is not easy to reconstruct a picture of her. Reliable testimonies from descendants are generally available only if the person to be remembered promises in his or her lifetime to become a worthwhile object of remembrance, so that any remarkable features or events are recorded. Although Marbot was quite well known among art-lovers in Italy, in Urbino he was simply the "milord Inglese", and hence clearly, if by no means unaffectionately, defined as an idler, and naturally unknown as an art theorist until in 1980, his memorial year, a detailed appreciation by Livio Sichirollo in the *Studi urbinati* connected him with the town. Consequently no one had ever asked the woman who had, after all, shared the last three years of his life anything about that life, and she had said nothing about it of her own accord. Her son Gianfrancesco, born in 1817, began attending the Cadet School at Modena in 1827—so he left the house soon after Marbot's arrival—and fell in the Battle of Solferino in 1859, as a Piedmontese brigadier. Her daughter Bianca, born in 1820 and also educated at Faenza, married in 1842 the Milanese doctor and surgeon Carlo Perone, later Professor at the Universities of Milan and Pavia. Around the turn of the century her house was frequented by the intellectual elite of Milan, including Manzoni and Verdi, and here in 1861 Herman Grimm arrived with an introduction. I shall return to him later in this connection.

A portrait of Anna Maria, of inferior artistic quality, engraved in 1827 at Milan whither she had accompanied Marbot on his journey to France, shows her in a portrait pose in the contemporary fashion, with severely parted and smoothed hair, a little pale, grave and slightly melancholy, her expression enigmatic; yet this, as well as the drawn-down corners of the mouth and the varnished-looking hair style, are the fault of the artist, who had evidently contracted some pedestrian, Biedermeier habits of portraiture. In their daily life in Urbino the fact that she was six years older than Andrew may have imposed certain restraints on her and caused her some inward insecurity, for she never knew how much of her relationship with Andrew was known to any visitor, or how he might be expected to take it. Nevertheless she maintained her position with extreme discretion and with dignity. August von Platen, who seldom writes about women in his diaries, notes:

"...a woman no longer young but very beautiful and charming, quiet, yet witty and sympathetic. One is glad to linger in her presence, indeed she almost soothes one."

Anna Maria's cousin, Giancarlo Catani-Ligi, born in 1789, owner of great brickworks in Urbino, a sensitive and cultivated man, gave an account when he was seventy to his visitor, Herman Grimm, of life in the Casa Baiardi, which he claimed to remember in precise detail. His cousin Anna Maria, he said, had been very quiet, imbued with an affection for Sir Andrew Marbot, which, though contained, was passionate, he being probably the first and only man she had ever loved, for her husband, though not loveless, had been rather sober and narrow-minded. She was moderately well educated but played the piano very well and often, and was well versed in the *"musica tedesca"*. French was her only foreign language. She had been not only the lady of the house but also its mistress, externally assured in her demeanour and control of her position in it. She had never made any secret of her relationship with Marbot and yet probably no one suspected it who did not know it already. She had no sense of being accountable to anyone, even to God, apparently, in whom she believed, and certainly not to His deputies in this world, in whom she believed less, for the people of Urbino have never had much use for priests.

We owe to Herman Grimm some valuable information, in the form of notes which he made for himself on his Italian journey in 1861, and a few letters which he wrote on this journey to his wife Gisela (the daughter of Achim and Bettina von Arnim). They show that for some time he toyed with the idea of writing an essay about Marbot. He had read *Art and Life* in English and been "impressed and surprised by the illuminating, sometimes even compelling vision of this solitary worker in the theory of art, or rather of artists". He had subsequently abandoned this project, however, because he sensed "a secret behind this personality" which he rightly feared he would be unable to plumb. Presumably, he too found himself faced with the great double problem of writing about someone who has written about others. Grimm was a conscientious and honest man, disinclined to venture on a subject which contained an obvious and yet unfathomable enigma.

He stayed on in Urbino principally to continue with his Raphael studies, but through Catani-Ligi, who was the honorary administrator of the Casa Raffaello—the house where Raphael was born and Raphael Museum—he was also able to pursue his study of Marbot. The old man was happy to talk; the memory of the days when the town had been enlivened by an unusual phenomenon enlivened him in retrospect. "Andrea"—he could never get used to the "oo" sound at the end of the English name—had been rather silent and reserved, he had no doubt lived in a world of his own, known to no one other than Anna Maria, but he knew nothing of that. At dinner, on the other hand, with a few guests whom he reserved the right to select himself, he had been at ease and talked of his background and his youth, of his father and his grandfather and other relations, though no one had ever been quite certain if he was in earnest or if all these characters were the object of deliberate, if not really malicious irony. He had often made his companions laugh, though no one was ever sure if he had intended to do so, for he himself remained serious.

And then, while emphasizing that such topics were frowned on in England, he had talked of food, of the origin or history of this or that dish, now and then minting delicious words to convey their flavour vicariously. One ate and drank well at his table, he had a cook from the Emilia Romagna, whose salary was the subject of surmise in the alleyways of Urbino. He had loved animals, especially cats, with whom he would converse in an undertone, perhaps more readily than with most people. There had been signs of the melancholic component in the Englishmen's personality but he, Catani, had not recognized them as such until after his suicide. It had been easy to forget that he was only in his twenties. It was not that he looked older, but that from time to time a kind of wisdom had emanated from him, as if from some immeasurable depth.

Grimm found these accounts confirmed and supplemented by the comments of Anna Maria's daughter, Bianca Perone, whose house in Milan he later visited several times. Bianca had known Andrew when she was still a child, and only in the holidays, but they lasted for three months in the summer. He had laughed seldom, and had even told funny stories perfectly seriously. He had told many stories, sometimes eerie ones about ghosts in castles, but also stories of dwarfs and giants, who had so much in common but were unable to communicate because the distance between high and low was unbridgeable—and of gods (Jupiter and Juno?) and Greek heroes (Oedipus?). She and her brother Gianfrancesco had always been made welcome, indeed he had positively ordered them to disturb him at work whenever they felt like it. They had never felt neglected by their mother who had treated them with kindness and empathy (to use Marbot's word), although Bianca now thought that Andrea—whom their mother actually addressed formally as "Voi"—had come first in her thoughts and above all in her feelings.

This sounds like an astonishing confession to a stranger

and foreigner. It is also remarkable that Grimm should have recorded it so conscientiously, as if he were really wanting to plumb unknown depths.

I am sorry that I cannot give the reader a real and convincing picture of Anna Maria Baiardi: I have none myself. There is nothing written by her, except for one or two dinner invitations which Catani-Ligi kept. She presumably wrote some letters to Andrew in Paris in 1827, but he probably did not keep even these, or else Anna Maria destroyed them after his death. Nevertheless we should be grateful to her, because his memory would not have survived at all but for her thoughtful disposal of Andrew's notes and all the other material she could find. She probably never even glanced at Andrew's books, notebooks and papers, and when she sent the bundle off to Lady Catherine she did it blindly, so to speak, unless she came across some letters in her own hand, which she would probably, and rightly, have destroyed. She saw the mother of her beloved as the sole rightful heiress, obviously in the belief that she was no more than his mother. The true state of affairs would naturally never have occurred to her. She could scarcely have hoped to be Andrew's first love, but had she ever learned that her role was that of a substitute, however responsible in moral terms, her whole world of trust and belief in love would have collapsed.

Lady Catherine's last role before she died was to be the recipient of this bundle of papers. A moving role, which could no longer be mastered. Mother and lover of the dead man, abandoned sinner and penitent, who probably now felt she was guilty of her son's fatal destiny as well, she now had no support but her great friend and confessor. There is no need to ask if she looked for evidence of Andrew's personal life in his papers. Once again, only a superman would not have done so, and the

174

bereaved are seldom supermen; on the contrary, nothing reveals the humanity of man more clearly than the death of his or her beloved. We can therefore assume that Lady Catherine destroyed one or two documents, in addition to the really compromising material, and we would not deny her right to do so. The question which concerns us above all is whether, apart from Ottilie's letter, she found evidence of any of her three successors—if we can call them that. She would have been unable to read Ottilie's letter and she would naturally not have had it translated by Father Gerard. But she could have read a letter written by Teresa or Anna Maria. Did she do so, and destroy the letters? Or did she do so and not destroy the letters, but leave them in the packet for Father Gerard, to convince him that not even the memory of her sin and her son's existed now? It would have been untrue, of course, but she could forgive herself that, since it was nothing compared with the guilt that was in the past. In that case it would have been Father Gerard who destroyed the letters. Why should he have made an exception of Ottilie's?

My guess is that, of the three figures involved in the drama, it was on van Rossum that the mantle of superman fell. He certainly could not and would not have tolerated the continuance of the relationship; he had to insist on permanent separation. But he knew that the soul cannot be commanded; it obeys the will at times, but never definitively and is always being forced to win its battles over again. He had exercised his office on earth, these sinners had to settle their account with Heaven themselves. He did not presume to mediate in an affair which he could not understand. No good could come of this evil, two immortal souls would have to atone. But he did not want to add the few years remaining to the two sinners on earth to their penance in purgatory. He would also have regarded Andrew's sin of incest as no less terrible than his estrangement from God, and his suicide would have weighed down the scale to breaking point. Yet van Rossum never allowed the fact of the suicide to penetrate his consciousness. In the depths of his heart he knew it, just as Lady Catherine knew it, but like her he suppressed it, with all the strength of feeling inspired by defensive despair.

A single passage, all too short and taken from Andrew's letter to him from Cremona in November 1825, indicates that forgiveness had been granted and accepted with deep and heartfelt thankfulness:

"My soul therefore now lies open before you once and for all, for it is beyond my power to change it. Otherwise, believe me, I would have mortified it. I can, however, command my thoughts, which I do all the more gladly since I shall be able to disclose them to you henceforth."

From the fact that Andrew had been in communication with him until shortly before his death we can assume that to Father Gerard he was not a godless and incestuous person but a sinful human being who seemed to elude succour and with it all possibility of salvation, and for whom one must therefore feel compassion. We can also be certain that Father Gerard was able "to some extent"—to use a jesuitical expression—to imagine what had been in those parts of the letters which Lady Catherine had rendered illegible.

Unfortunately we have not a single line from van Rossum's hand, apart from those very messages to his nephew which disclose that his love for the two sinners and penitents had conquered the harshness of condemnation. In this conquest lies his greatness.

Andrew himself naturally never shared his secret with anyone. There was no one at that time who was fit to hear his confession, had he intended to make one, and few would be fit to do it even now. Indeed the only person who would have

176

accepted the true position with sympathy was Byron. He would probably have envied Andrew this supreme achievement of apparent amorality, especially as he had hated his own mother. But he would have been one of the last people in whom in whom Andrew would have confided.

During his first months in Urbino, before his journey to Rome, Marbot read Goethe's *Maximen und Reflexionen* and the *Schriften zur Kunst*, which he annotated, partly with approval and partly with vehement criticism. One of his most important objections, that Goethe all too often did not know his subjects in the original and interpreted them in the light of engravings, is difficult to invalidate. But he was irritated above all by Goethe's apodictic guidelines, which he recommended to artists as mandatory instructions:

"Goethe says: 'Of art one demands distinct, clear, definite depictions'. It is necessary first of all to define who 'one' is. In all probability it is Goethe himself, making himself the representative of the demanding party and therefore quite obviously the one who is to decide what is 'distinct, clear and definite'. But this can be decided only by the artist himself, whose quality cannot be judged by whether he achieves objective distinctness, clarity and definition, but only by whether his subjective view illumines the object in such a way that its viewer also sees it in a new light. What we demand of the artist—I mean of course the great artist—is therefore a view of his subject, which expands our former image of this subject by one dimension, by revealing its metaphysical aspect."

No more and no less. We wonder what Goethe would have said to this dictum. And Marbot may have wondered what Goethe would have said about Turner's paintings. For "distinct, clear and definite" in Goethe's sense they are not.

A further bone of contention for Marbot was Goethe's proposition:

"The noblest demand which can be made of the artist is this: that he should adhere to Nature, study it, copy it, and produce something resembling its phenomena."

Marbot's reply:

"When Germans of our time speak of 'Nature' I never know exactly what they mean. But no matter what they mean, the artist must study it, because he must study all the phenomena of life, since Nature, whatever else it may be, is the sum of them. That he should adhere to it may also hold good, for whatever he creates stands in a precise relationship, even if it is a contrary one to Nature and its laws; in other words, the artist must be fully aware of the degree of his deviations and accountable for them. So from time to time an Angel of the Annunciation in an Italian Renaissance painting—or a work by Konrad Witz, the only German who could paint a mystery without distorting those who are taking part in it—derives its enigmatic and supernatural quality from the fact that it is beyond Nature, and in physical respects its most other-worldly point lies between the shoulderblades, where its wings have grown. But that the artist whould copy Nature and produce something resembling its phenomena—and here the concept of Nature is restricted to the visual—is a claim, however we may interpret the concept, that could be made only by one who is a stranger to its phenomena. It has never been the function of art to compete with Nature. Nature, whatever else it may be, is the starting point for

178

man's creations and achievements. But that which he creates leads away from her and that which he has achieved is not a copy of Nature, nor anything resembling it, but her likeness. The secret of the great artist is that he understands Nature better than others, that he begins at a depth and stops at a height beyond the powers of the mere beholder."

In April 1826 Marbot is in Rome at last, apparently devoid of the euphoria of expectation and therefore of, as would soon be evident, cool in recording its charms, and hence probably the only traveller of his time who did not see the city as the absolute centre and crown of Italy—it could not yet be called a capital city at that time—and therefore, as was his wont, he regarded its mythical greatness with scepticism. To van Rossum, he writes:

"Everyone I meet is building a city for himself here out of ruins and living in the age of his choice. I too enjoy the sight of ruins, but I see them for what they are—elements which, though they call history and hence the present into question, do not make the value of the past absolute, far less ideal. For me the present is not an extension of the past but a state of consciousness which I would sometimes gladly shrug off, if only it were possible."

It is not quite clear what he meant by the last remark. Would even he have preferred to have lived in the past, which he mistrusted and which, as he once said, becomes "the more mysterious, the more imagination one invests in conjuring it up"? Or—more probably—did he mean his own past, in which he would rather live than the present? But would he have said this to Father Gerard? At all events, four years later he did shrug off the "state of consciousness"—and not that alone.

To his mother he writes: ·

179

"Rome lives on its past, inasmuch as it attracts hordes of foreigners who want to enjoy that past and make it all present ... The artists here seem to be busy adding their own myths to that of the holy and eternal city and by this extension finding admission for themselves into eternity, and into holiness too."

The notes make it clear who these artists were: the post-Napoleonic classicists on the one hand and the German late Romantics on the other, particularly the Nazarenes, "who mistake priggery for saintliness and mission for message ... The German painters in Rome affect a kind of solemn conviviality, they feel themselves to be so much brothers in experience that the experience is ultimately the same for all of them, and each one expresses it according to his ability. The experience is not sensual, however, but moral, intended to purify the soul of the beholder. Their pictures are stages on which historical or biblical dramas are performed or ideas personified, and all these characters address the public like bad actors. These paintings contain no mystery, all the figures and all the objects have the same sharpness of contour, whether they are near or far, revealing all the more distinctly the unclearness of the thoughts which gave them birth. For those thoughts revolve about a naive ideal of irrevocability which can be neither portrayed nor realized in art."

He met some of these painters in the house of the Prussian minister to the Vatican, Karl Josias von Bunsen, but he does not name names; it is as if he wanted to play his part in allowing all these artists to be forgotten. He must have been quite serious about this curious aversion; such obdurate tendentiousness is quite untypical of him. He explains his verdict in the notebooks:

180

"Symbolism or allegory, that is, the encodement or personification of doctrines or ideals, of qualities such as vice or virtue, of destinies such as happiness or unhappiness, all these derive from times when thought was still younger, its history not generally known, and pictorial examples could convey an idea. This will no longer answer now; the ingenuousness of the transmutation of abstract into concrete is no longer met by ingenuousness in the beholder ... It is not the function of the painting to make its beholder ponder on its subject-matter. A picture does of course interpret certain events from the Bible or from mythology, by bestowing individuality and character upon the actors in the event, but where painting invents, that is, where the idea must first be explained before its illustration can be understood, it becomes superfluous as a medium. A double portrait of two evidently chaste maidens, of whom one is called Italia, the other Germania, is laying claim to a kind of interpretation which far exceeds that of art, if indeed it is possible at all, without knowing the soul of the artist, its discord or its harmony."

It is not difficult to recognize the painting in question as Overbeck's allegory—if one can call it that—but Marbot makes no mention of its considerable, though hardly truly great artistic quality, almost as if under some strange emotional stress, the source of which is obscure, especially as we have gained the impression that from time to time he actually enjoyed giving vent to feelings of rejection, or even aversion.

Marbot saw the frescoes by the Nazarenes in the Palazzo Zuccari, whose owner, the Prussian Consul-General Jacob Salomon Bartholdy, had died in 1825, and since he frequently visited the Marchese Massimo he probably saw

Overbeck there, still working on the frescoes for *Gerusalemme Liberata*; he must have met him at Bunsen's house, but he does not record that either. It is obvious that the Nazarenes would not have figured in any final version of his notebooks, although they were the very people to supply copious material about work that was consciously of the soul, and its unconscious motives.

Bunsen was a scholar: philologist, theologian and connoisseur of the arts. Andrew felt at ease in his house and was soon treated as a relation, as Bunsen's wife Fanny was English and distantly related by marriage to the Clavertons. Bunsen's predecessor in the ministerial post, Barthold Georg Niebuhr, had never been able to come to terms with Italy and things Italian, and the only Italian he had respected was Leopardi. He had even tried to procure a chair of Italian literature for the poet at Bonn University. But Leopardi had not wanted to leave Italy, probably not only because of his fragile health but because he knew that his homeland would be a constant source of negative thematic inspiration for his poetry and he feared, probably quite rightly, the effects of being uprooted. Bunsen had as it were taken over Leopardi as an intermittent guest, he knew his work, which was still slight at that time, and was following the development of this poet who was so consistent in his grief. He it was who gave Marbot the *Canzoni* to read, ten poems published the year before and later included in the collection *Canti*. Andrew was at once strangely moved by these verses and assumed a constitutional affinity with their author—both rightly and wrongly, as time would show. In his notebooks he says:

"Poets are unhappy people. They draw on their own substance of memory, which is always painful. There are no poems of happiness ... A poet is great when he succeeds in seeing objectively the subjec-

182

tive aspect of his unhappiness: that is, when by the depiction of his personal inner world he is able to make his unhappiness so exemplary that the happy no longer understand him."

In May or June 1826 Marbot arranged an introduction to Marchesa Sacrati's salon, where he hoped to meet Leopardi. It was true that the Marchesa had called the latter "a fat little female with yellow hair, always spinning flax", but in spite of these unflattering remarks Leopardi had visited her when he was in Rome. Now, however, he was no longer in Rome but in Bologna. Instead, Marbot met the Marchesa's niece, Teresa Guiccioli, whom he had known in Pisa and who after Byron's tragic death (though he had left her before then in favour of the freedom of Greece) would console herself with this or that English aristocrat visiting Rome. But perhaps I am doing her an injustice and the purpose of her diversions was similar to Marbot's, if more actively pursued: a substitute for the unforgettable beloved, whom one hopes to find in every fresh partner and yet never finds, since memory increasingly transfigures him.

When Andrew met her again, now aged twenty-seven, in the Marchesa's salon, she was having a liaison with the twenty-two-year-old Lord Fitzharris, an enthusiastic water-colourer and Byron worshipper on his Grand Tour, whom she soon dropped in order to bestow all her devotion and intensity on Andrew, who would certainly not have invited her affection, but now it was given to him, he accepted it, if not with enthusiasm, then surely not without complaisance; for Teresa was beautiful and though grief for her Byron tinged her composure with melancholy, she radiated a certain disarming gallantry, a deliberate will to find comfort in active love, which its object would have found difficult to resist. In her book *The Lost Attachment*, her biographer, Iris Origo, who at that time did not and could not know of her brief affair with Marbot, writes that poor Teresa—and it was not only in this that she resembled the far poorer Ottilie von Goethe—had always run foul of cynical cads in her love affairs, and it is entirely possible that Andrew was the only man in her life to whom this observation does not apply. In any case, the brief attachment was certainly not without its peaks and troughs on her part. Her temperament, which even Byron had not always been able to curb—on the contrary, she seems at times to have curbed him—must have been exacerbated by Andrew's certainly not uncompliant, but reticent and ultimately detached attitude. His heart was elsewhere, though naturally none of his three substitute lovers could ever be allowed to suspect where. However, it seems to me that this was just what Teresa wanted to know—she called him "enimmatico Andrea", and later even "impenetrabile Andrea"—and that, fierce as Elsa in *Lohengrin*, she pestered him constantly, until he gradually tired of her importunity.

The affair began in June or July 1826 and lasted until Andrew left Rome early in November. They probably met in the place he had rented on the Piazza Navona. I think he was a considerate lover, with more empathy and more tenderness than the egocentric Byron, though he probably could not compete with the active virility which made Byron so irrestible.[6] Andrew would certainly have been less passionate and more detached, for he had no need to prove his masculinity and would even have been prepared to accept self-denial in this direction. He gave himself as he was, with as much devotion as he was able and willing to give. Unlike Byron he was not in the

6. "His sexual organ showed quite abnormal development." (From the report on the opening of Lord Byron's grave on 15 June 1938 by A.E. Houlsworth, People's Warden 1938-1942, Hucknall Parish Church, as an Appendix to *Byron*, the biography by Elizabeth Longford, London, 1976.)

habit of recording his conquests, and naturally he never spoke of them. He did not talk about "the women" and avoided men who did, like Byron, with whom he had scarcely anything in common and least of all the tendency to ostentatious dissipation. He always tried to be clear in his mind about the qualities of his few partners and his relationship to them, just as he accounted to himself for all experiences, and not only for his ideas; indeed his life sometimes looks to us like a deliberate act of didacticism, calculated to prove that the "sin" in which hehad lived and would have continued to live, had he had his way, had strengthened rather than damaged his soul. Only—to whom should he, or would he have proved it, and why?

There was no doubt that Teresa was a strain and Andrew, who was not used to adapting his arrangements, would scarcely have endured four months with her had he not granted himself four weeks' leave, from Teresa and from Rome, by crossing Latium and the Campagna, mostly on foot, which he enjoyed: this must have been the only penchant he shared with the German painters in Rome. Again we begin to suspect that his health must have been indestructible, for in those regions, and above all in the swamps which were never far away, malaria and various infectious diseases were rife, spreading rapidly in the summer and claiming many a foreign traveller as their victim. Marbot was perfectly aware of these dangers but his fatalistic attitude had grown in proportion to his greater experience of life and without calling for active risk-taking, it imbued him with passive equanimity. He writes to van Rossum from Frascati:

"Here I am totally exposed to Nature and enjoying the exposure. Here all is Nature, the senses absorb nothing else, it speaks to me through the people who belong to it, who are indeed a part of it. The wine here is rich and heavy, it fatigues the limbs but

185

refreshes the spirit and keeps the body in a state of inward invulnerability, which I almost believe I sense in the form of a perpetual slight drunkenness, seeming rather to clarify my understanding so that nothing escapes me. All is become experience, the flavour of a fig and the wind in the olive trees..."

In the light of this manifestation of his vegetative side we observe that perhaps for the first time he is happy—or to be more cautious, content—has forgotten the past and is looking his future and its goal in the eye with a kind of restrained intoxication.

In the neighbourhood of Frascati Marbot came across a young French painter, of whom he writes to Rumohr: "...a simple, agreeable, quiet man of about my own age, fascinated by light and, as far as I could judge from the almost finished picture which he was painting in the open, fascinating in his ability to paint it. He paints with calm self-confidence what he perceives, and he perceives much, but he restricts himself to the essential, not losing himself in details, he translates what he sees without deliberating on it, for he relies on an internal mechanism. His three-dimensional effects are astonishing and all is quite natural to him, as if he had sketched it out in advance. There were also one or two charcoal drawings lying about, but as far as I know he made no use of them. I fell into converstion with him. He said that he had no desire to paint philosophy or religion, but only what was perceived by his eyes, with which he could not only see but also sense, feel and hear. That, I own, sounds very simple, but he convinced me. I shall try to keep in touch with him, for I think it possible that his art will outlast our

186

time. His name is Corot ..."

This letter was among Marbot's papers in van Rossum's possession. Either he had not sent if off because he did not know Rumohr's address, or else the letter was returned because Rumohr was not in Italy at the time.

What would Rumohr have thought of Corot, how would Goethe, who might have seen his early work, in which the pure, simplified and atmospherically-charged landscape appears, have assessed him? An amusing game of question and answer, with no winners or losers. How, for instance, would the Nazarenes have reacted to Turner, whose conversion from objective reality to its dissolution in light and atmosphere coincided almost exactly with their era? Negatively, no doubt, since they held that the subject-matter might depart from reality, but not the form from its traditional pattern. They would never have understood or approved the transmutation of what they meant by Nature into pure phenomenon, the victory of the visual over the intellectual, for none of them had eyes to see the landscape in the strictly individual manner of a great artist: they did not recognize the great in the art of their time.

One might almost see Marbot's unexpected meeting with Corot as a symbolic stroke, a compensation for the disappointment in Rome, an accident designed by fortune and therefore only apparently an accident.

In early November 1826 Marbot left Rome without regret, and Teresa too, probably also without regret. In a farewell letter from Perugia, which came to light in the archives of the Gamba family only in 1976 (now in the possession of Sir John Murray, the publisher), he says:

"...You complained to me that I found you foolish. That I have never said. Yet I do find most people foolish, including myself, even if I am not quite foolish enough to overlook the foolishness of others. Would that I were—just as I would so gladly be another. Who, dear Teresina, would dare to think himself wise, but for those few who have proved their wisdom in their work! You at all events were wise enough to expect no protestations that exceeded the sentiment of the moment. I honour you all the more for it. No tears at parting! You made it easy for me thus, and I thank you. Farewell! We shall not meet again, yet I shall not forget you. May your God bless and protect you.

Andrea."

A little sidelight is shed on this affair by a letter from Lamartine, who soon after this parting became Andrew's successor in Teresa's favour, to his friend Charles Vacher:

"...They say here that la contessa loves men for their resemblance to Byron, therefore making her choice principally among Englishmen, and has only recently been parted from a young English idler of rank and wit who wore a gold bracelet. Whether this was his sole claim to individuality, originality or even superiority I do not know..."

Towards the middle of November 1826 Marbot was back in Urbino, where he now installed himself, for the first time since his youth, in a "residence", a place to which he would "return" from journeys, knowing its advantages and peculiarities, its climatic and meteorological tricks, and prepared to adapt his life and habits to it. "There is always a wind here," he wrote to Lady Catherine,

"it seems to come from several directions at once, it is as if Zephyr and Boreas and all the winds of the compass rose and met together here to do battle ...

At this very moment two opposing winds are blowing round my house, bringing all its movable parts into motion. My cats stare restlessly and greedily at the birds which are blown hither and thither outside, but I am calm and in so far as I can tell, in equilibrium. I have no wish to complain, I am well."

Calm and equilibrium then, no complaints. Was this the unobtrusive manifestation of something more deep-seated? At all events, the words have a mysterious and equivocal sound, as if equilibrium had been won by the decision to strip everything away and never again to expose himself to any change of circumstance, or any form of turbulence, until the end.

So for the first and last time we see Marbot in a home of his own, chosen and acquired by himself. Characteristically, this home contained nothing that belonged to him, except for one wardrobe full of clothes—perhaps there was more than one, he was selective in such matters and preferred the exquisite—and two or three fine brass-bound mahogany chests—still in the possession of the Catani-Ligi family—containing linen, his papers and notebooks and the books he read in his final years, or in which he referred to things already read: Goethe, Schopenhauer, both Schlegles, Hegel's *Enzyklopaedie der Wissenschaft*—who could have recommended that? Certainly not Schopenhauer!—Winckelmann ("this inspired investigator into Beauty"), Leopardi, Vasari, Alberti, Montaigne's *Essays* in English ("this wonderful work by an enlightened pupil writing his own textbook"), between whose pages 88 and 89, in Volume 2, Professor Livio Sichirollo discovered in 1977 those two letters from Lady Catherine which we have quoted. Folded twice, they had been slipped in at the beginning of the chapter "On Repentance", which begins there:

"Others form man, I only report him, and represent a particular one, ill-fashion'd enough; and whom, if I had to model anew, I should certainly make him something else than what he is; but that's past recalling."

I shall spare myself and the reader any speculations as to the connection between the letters and the chapter. One could of course call this find a lucky accident—it is the key to everything that was to be described here, and also the one real and wonderful sign of life from Lady Catherine—but for that very reason it makes us painfully aware of what has probably been lost for ever: letters, not only from Marbot's mother, the crucial reference figure, but also documents of secondary importance, letters from De Quincey, Crabb Robinson, von Platen and Rumohr, perhaps from Delacroix or Turner.

There were other books: Edmund Burke, Byron, Shelley, Keats, Coleridge, Burton's *Anatomy of Melancholy*—which he regarded as a joke sustained by the author throughout his life in order to overcome his own melancholy—and, of course, Shakespeare, whom he probably knew by heart. Also De Quincey's translation of Lessing's *Laokoon*, which the translator had sent him shortly after it was published in *Blackwood's Magazine* and which Marbot found wretched, whether rightly or wrongly I do not know—there is an exaggerated brand of biographical meticulousness that goes in for his kind of checking-up.

Marbot had no other possessions and no doubt desired none. He once wrote to De Quincey from Marbot Hall, when he was eighteen:

"...once again the house is full of noisy guests—who they are I know not, I cannot recall the names—but certainly each in his own way is a smug possessor, owner or proprietor ..."

Hadley-Chase, who incidentally owned this letter,

thinks that here, under the influence of the rising tide of socialism as propagated by Coleridge himself, the young Marbot was expressing an ideological attitude. His unconcealed contempt for the type of house-guests mentioned at Marbot Hall may in fact point to this, but there is no other indication of anything of the sort, no subsequent words on the subject, no sign of any social commitment, whereas there are many indications of his genuine personal rejection of property, though he never tried to make a doctrine of it, since he truthfully never saw himself as an example, as someone from whom people might learn.

So here he was living in the quiet of the Casa Baiardi, beloved of Anna Maria, respected by the people of Urbino, attended by a devoted factotum, Raffaello by name, a peasant boy from Fermignano, cooked for by a cook from the Emilia and engrossed in his theme, to the development of which he now addressed himself, but which was never to achieve its final form. What else engrossed him and never truly left his soul in peace, we know.

A new, critical edition, with commentaries, of his works and the letters which must be regarded as integral to them, is forthcoming. I do not want to anticipate it more than necessary here, since in Marbot's case one should not, strictly speaking, take anything out of context: it is difficult in a quotation to strike the note of continuity to which the reader can attune and which accompanies the reading like a counterpoint. Moreover, the author's intellectual development and the corresponding clarity of his deductive process is revealed—at least in rough outline—only by reading the whole of his work. Nevertheless I think it is important to expose the main lines of his thinking here; there are, after all, accounts of experience, closely interwoven with his life and as inseparable from it as that life is from his reflections on art.

191

Marbot's liveliest experiences and emotions were generally stimulated by specific works of art, and were therefore linked to them; it was on this basis that he then adduced the evidence of other examples of thesis. He distinguishes between the independent and the commissioned work and between "descriptive" and "reflective" painting and among the former he emphasizes in turn the "soul-inspired choice of subject", which he turns into a phychological hypothesis. His distinctions are sharp and methodical—a fact insufficiently appreciated by either Hadley-Chase or Renshaw, who regarded them as typically romantic—and yet inspired by that passionate subjectivity of vision which is argued over to this day, whether as proclamation or provocation. As we know, the first to question it was Ruskin, but this was before the discovery of the psyche as an analysable component of the human being, and many others found it hard to swallow. As in psychoanalysis, so here: its bitterest enemies are always those who have a suspicion that it applies to their own psyche, but are unwilling to admit it. So Marbot was not only the instigator but was himself the subject of scholarship, when he became the object of inter-disciplinary research; in other words, scholars had to study him as a personality as well as his theories.

His thinking transcends art in so far as he is trying to arrive at the source of creativity itself, yet he personally never emphasized this claim; perhaps he himself was not aware of it:

"...for objectively speaking, what we call reality can be neither experienced nor portrayed. Each man feels it differently in his soul and expresses it accordingly, in keeping with his spiritual and technical abilities. Each man is alone with his reality, his faith and his myth, his past and his present, and although they are not communicable he tries to communicate with them because he does not know

192

or will not admit or is unaware of the resistance, the impediments, the barriers and the barricades in the other, who has a reality of his own."

Thus he sees the great artist as the man with the ability to break down these resistances in "the other", that is in the beholder, because he has the expressive power to impose his reality on him visually. Unless the subject was dictated by his patron, to anyone who knows how to get to the heart of a work of art, to "read" it, the artist reveals his inmost soul, where the choice of subject took place, the chosen subject took shape, the roles to illustrate it were allotted and their positions decided. So much for "descriptive" painting, where the impulse arises from the artist's desire, retained from childhood and established in the unconscious as he grows up, to reproduce what is strange and wonderful: the thing that may have appeared to him in early childhood as a dream or wish-dream, a source of terror or mystery, and now having assumed its final shape, demands expression; he can now, by virtue of his acquired skills, transform it into two dimensions to effect his release from them and see them pictured before him as the result of the workings of his psychology.

Viewed subjectively, the impulse for this painting is of course the inner urge for self-expression, but objectively it is painterly only via the indirect route of dramatic illustration; not primarily, since it is "story-telling in pictures"; this may have been aimed at a—no doubt more acceptable—variant of Overbeck's insistence on his absurd claim about "preaching in pictures". He does acknowledge that this painting has the function of creating myth and history for all those who require pictorial visualization to activate their imagination; nevertheless it pre-empts the latent imaginative powers of the beholder by the implied statement: it was thus, because I see it thus. Of course the nature of the great artist's subjective conviction is such that it inspires conviction in others as well and it is possible that our concepts of mythological or historical events come from these same pictures by the great painters. Yet this true conviction is rare because it calls for a mastery which few possess:

"For every poorly painted detail, every weak point of composition, every trifling makeshift, such as an unnatural colour transition, causes the carefully constructed world of the picture to collapse and all is in ruins: the beholder's illusion of being the immediate witness of the event depicted fails to materialize. In Tintoretto's *Origin of the Milky Way* (!) we see Jupiter, the all-regnant, only from behind, but the inadequate painting of the back of his head is enough to dismiss the event, not exactly convincing at best, as slapstick comedy. To breathe the spirit of greatness into a figure painted from behind calls for a greater artist than Tintoretto was."

Is this emotion, speaking out against the ostensible catalyst of the first manifestation of his anomaly? The aggressiveness of the assertion would lead one to think so. On the other hand, there is no denying that Marbot is right: the back of Jupiter's head in the centre of the picture is the weakest detail of this—truncated—painting, which no one would in any case describe as one of Tintoretto's masterpieces.

"Reflective painting", on the other hand, he described as a primarily pictorial process, not infrequently a subjective compulsion—"...many painters live only to paint, only as painters do they feel themselves to be men, under the device 'pingo, ergo sum'"—in other words "reflective painting" works through the artistic transference of what everyone sees into a metaphysical image that no one has yet seen, that the painter—and only the great painter, at that—first makes visible, but still only for those who are capable of reliving the act of making visible in their own, potentially creative inner

194

being. Reflective painting, he says, discloses the depths of the inner life of its subject, where descriptive painting interprets an event by offering new versions.

"Jupiter and Juno (!) are a part of us, they live in the air we breathe and every one of us gives them a different shape in his own heart. But an unknown old man, or a woman reading a letter, or the play of sunshine in a room or of passing shadows on a field, all this exists as an inexpressible mystery only through the sublime invention of a great artist."

An effusive statement, to be sure, but we must remember that it was made in the Romantic period, when scarcely a single artist proceeded from the form rather than from history and stories.

"...of the narrative painters it was given only to the supremely great to bring a real world into being, whose characters, instead of courting the beholder's favour, experience or endure or fulfil their destiny with no regard for us as observers. For the most part, however, these characters are acting for a public. In Leonardo's *Last Supper* twelve men are sitting on the far side of the table so that the near side is left open to view; we are as it were invited to supper on a stage. Giotto, on the other hand, has them sitting round the table, and the haloes float in the faces of the five men whose backs are turned to us, but what we sacrifice by this impairment of our deeper penetration into the event we gain through the empathy of the artistic will, in the face of which any inconsistency arising from the failure to portray things as they are becomes insignificant."

In his book on Giotto, Martin Gosebruch says of Winckelmann:

"Let no one think that his great successes in the elucidation of the history of ancient art owed everything to his superior intelligence alone. They are based on the enormous explosive force of a labile and sensitive spirit, on his violent urge to create everything afresh. There was in him something of the darkness of the fallen angel."

An outstanding assessment, which could equally, with modifications, be applied to Marbot. True, his "labile and sensitive spirit" had no "enormous explosive force", but rather the ability to extract an individual from his age and illuminate him from within. But Marbot's urge to create everything afresh was violent too, and the inner source of his search betrays the "darkness of the fallen angel", only his fall was different from Winckelmann's, he was a different person and the child of a different time.

In the autumn of 1827 Marbot set out on his last lengthy journey. His destination was Paris. Anna Maria accompanied him as far as Milan, where she stayed with a widowed aunt until his return; apparently a routine visit, repeated every two years. Her portrait must have been made at this time, no doubt at Marbot's request. Whether he was satisfied with the result we may perhaps doubt.

Marbot stayed in Paris for two months. The main reason for the visit was supposed to be his interest in Delacroix, through whom he must have hoped to extend his picture of contemporary artistic creation. Delacroix was probably expecting him and it can therefore be assumed that some correspondence took place between them, but if so, it has not survived.

Delacroix had just finished his great painting *The Death of Sardanapalus*, the paint was still virtually wet when Marbot saw it—and reacted against it—in his studio. The painting became the source of crucial elements of his aesthetic philosophy.

"Delacroix has a mighty visual imagination which enables him to make a precise disposition even of the largest formats, without causing the beholder to feel that the canvas has been filled up with irrelevancies, for every object seems at first to be part of the immediate event ... In addition, however, he possesses the gift of transmuting an idea into a dramatic scene effortlessly and with the force of true inspiration. But with each gift the longing to put it to use grows, he is also the victim of his own insatiability and indulges in allegory and symbolism ... Only shout words such as 'Liberty! Equality! Fraternity!' at him, and he is at once visited by the idea of a triptych, his one remaining problem being to decide which of these virtues deserves the central panel. Admirable as the ability to paint all this is, the desire to paint all this is strange, and one would have to dig deep into the soul of the artist to find the wellsprings of that desire. He himself does not know them: he knows little about himself. Thus, as he allows the thought to harden into substance, transforming the idea into a play, so the idea as such is extinguished, for the characters portrayed become its vehicles; they solidify and rigidify in the pose of realization, of incarnation, and thus become collaborators in a tableau, who receive their wages from the artist, after it is painted. In return for their wages they do their best for the work, with justifiable confidence in the art of their arranger, for if they did not know he was a good painter, they would hire themselves out as models to better artists. Not the people alone, but the animals too do their best. The

197

lions in Delacroix's paintings know that they have to represent not only lions but also the idea of Lion, and that their rapacious appetites must not make them forget the grandeur of the king of beasts: they know Schopenhauer's idea of the 'principium individuationis'.

The painting of all this is masterly down to the last detail, here a beautiful expanse of silky female back, which Rubens helped to paint, there the glitter of gold harness in which Rembrandt took a hand, flash of dagger, gleam of velvet—precious materials indeed. Hats off to your skill, M. Delacroix!

But what lies beneath that delicate skin, beneath the gold and silk and velvet, behind the drawn daggers which will pierce the silken skin a moment later! Is there perhaps some stratum of the artist hidden there which he conceals in life? An unacknowledged yearning, which he would prefer to assuage in life instead of reducing it to two dimensions? A secret, unconscious desire, for which painting is a mere substitute? Are forbidden fantasies hidden here, which the artist, in order to be free of them, banishes on to the canvas?"

Psychological research has confirmed these suppositions, but Marbot was the first to voice them. As we know, there are sketches extant of bloodthirsty details, on one of which the slave girl, the central female figure in the painting, is actually beheaded, but it is probable that Delacroix did not show these to Marbot.

"The Assyrian King Sardanapalus, so the story goes, aware of the hopeless situation in his palace, which had been under siege for many weeks, had caused his deathbed to be set upon a funeral pyre and ordered the death of all that had been dear to him in life. The favourite wives were therefore stabbed before his eyes by his favourite slaves and the slaves afterwards took their own lives. Favourite horses were slaughtered and Ayesha the Bakhtiari hanged herself in a last spasm of free will. All this inevitably generates a mighty confusion and much surface is needed to reduce the event to a single picture. Delacroix has done it, he has created a petrified chaos. The unlikelihood of the proceedings has been converted by him into theatrical pantomime, which is intended to give us artistic enjoyment by removing us from life and setting us down in an exotic—not even mythical—world of fairy-tale.

Each individual actor in this tableau is well aware that he is assisting in the account of a grisly occurrence, even the horse that has been dragged into this picture, yes, even the mutilated elephant heads, the significance of which escaped me. But as I said: the scene never really comes to life. An orgy seems to have been captured and immortalized here in the studio, one breathes the dust on the velvet portières and other set pieces. Everything seems to be taking place soundlessly, not a shout, not a groan, not a cry, not a whinny, not a chink of fallen harness, the picture is dumb.

It could naturally be argued that every picture is dumb. That is true, of course, And yet there are pictures which set our imagination so vigorously in motion that they appeal even to those senses which do not serve the direct reception of the painting. In a Botticelli *Annunciation*, for instance, we seem to be hearing still the last beat of the angelic harbinger's wings; in Tiepolo's heavens, unless we are deaf, we hear the echo of celestial calls.

But this picture remains mute, an arranged tableau in the studio, crowned by a comfortable divan on which the model mimes a king who, though he scowls, is relatively uninvolved. He seems to be listening to a distant ballad-singer, singing him his own story, or perhaps it is the story of the real King Sardanapalus, or Byron's version, which is better than the one depicted here. But whatever the singer distantly sings, we do not hear it. The fact that a wounded slave is about to light the fire under the king with the last of his strength leaves him cold, his destiny is behind him, and before him is his share in the immortality of the painter to whom he owes his being. Or is it the artist himself whose fears are at one with his desires and who is here enjoying a long-harboured nightmare of destructive love and lustful death? It would be pointless to ask him, for he would not know, and the question would dismay him deeply."

I personally find it difficult to disagree with Marbot's verdict, though most people would probably think otherwise. What is astonishing is that he is following the trail of a theme peculiar to black Romanticism—death and sexuality as counterparts—and recognizes it as a hidden and probably unconscious driving force.

In a letter written to Rumohr in English, Marbot makes a terse and derogatory comment on the painting, only to pass on with a frankness unusual in him to his relationship with the artist:

"I esteem M. Delacroix as a man of human greatness, of dignity, humour, culture and taste. I esteem his profound and yet reasonable desire to convince, the subject of which is of course generally the pre-eminence of painting over other arts, and which,

200

therefore, does not really touch the heart of the matter. For I myself incline, with Schopenhauer, to the view that this place is reserved for music, since music is the expression of the will alone. True or not, confronted by such a man I am prepared not only for reservations, but—and I leave it to you, my friend, to set a value on this principle—also for prevarication. For I know, and you know, that even among the great there are some who are not endowed with the ability to endure criticism. I do not know the man well enough to judge whether with all his virtues he also possesses this rare and priceless one. In brief: I praised the picture, the overwhelming conception, the masterly distribution of light values. I did not tell him my real feelings, for an artist does not learn from others, to try to change his soul is pointless. He must paint as he does, he is succumbing to a compulsion, perhaps even to a thirst for fame, of which he himself is not even aware."

The painting of *The Death of Sardanapalus* was in fact absolutely contrary to all the positive criteria that Marbot applied to painting and he continued to regard it as a negative textbook case, no doubt with regret, since he obviously valued Delacroix the man. We may even be surprised that his urge for truth, usually so absolute, paused before Delacroix the man—a conflict he never otherwise encountered as far as we know. It looks as if in this case his conscience must have moved him to confess to another friend and explain why he had strayed from the truth.

There may also have been a purely utilitarian reason: Marbot did not want to forgo the company of the agreeable and stimulating Delacroix for the rest of his stay in Paris. There really was an affinity between them, a mutual recognition that the other nursed an unconfessed and never to be confessed secret. We know Marbot's secret, Delacroix's we do not know. He too was reticent and controlled; not a man to pour out his heart. To his mother Marbot writes:

"M. Delacroix is suffering from something. I do not know what it is, and yet I believe I understand him. But he suffers nobly and discreetly, with manly dignity, whereas that young Berlioz's suffering compels every one to participate, whether he knows the cause or no. Probably he suffers from himself—but who does not!..."

Marbot had met "young Berlioz"—he was two years younger than Marbot—with Delacroix, who was a friend of his. He had given up his medical studies a year before to take up music professionally and some of his minor works had already been performed in a modest way. He was a passionate self-tormentor, fostering his emotions, an eternal lover, always changing the objects of his love. Although by no means spurned by women, for his appearance was striking and he was witty and cultivated as well, he succeeded in turning each of his affairs into an "unhappy love", which allowed him to lament his fate and to live it out accordingly. He needed this fate as a source of inspiration. In a letter to his mother, Marbot calls him:

"...a strange, difficult person, who is quite incapable of seeing the smallest thing independently of himself and its relationship to him. Every one of his words is an attack or a defence, a cry of enthusiasm or indignation. He wanted to talk to me about Beethoven, who died a month or two ago. I told him that I do not speak of music, because the experience of it cannot be captured in objectively appropriate words. Although he assented, he spoke for the

202

remainder of the evening of nothing but music, or rather, of himself in relation to music. Yet I listened to him with pleasure for the sake of his mastery of words; he is an out-and-out phantasist, to be sure, but a captivating companion."

In his memoirs Berlioz describes Marbot as a sensitive but cool interlocuter, who spoke French as slowly as if he feared to be punished for each mistake. Yet he had made no mistakes. This sounds plausible; Marbot sought perfection in all outward forms of communication because he could not hope for inward perfection as he envisaged it. And yet none of his colleagues seems to have noticed how he was working on himself, except for Berlioz. "The Englishman did not want to speak of music," he says in his memoirs,

"for it was, so he said, an untranslatable language, whose grammar could indeed be discussed, but whose significance each would understand differently. These were his words: 'Should you, Monsieur, and I understand the same thing, it would say less about music than about our spiritual affinity. There is a sense in which it is the purest of the arts, because it has no theme that can be expressed outside itself. It does not describe, therefore it cannot be described'. 'You are a thousand million times wrong!' I cried. 'Music can describe the whole world, in a mighty tongue. One day you shall hear my refutation'. The gentleman bowed politely and said he would look forward to it with eager expectation and that I should not delay it too long."

Berlioz did not say what "answer" he meant, but it could be surmised from much of his music, and expecially the *Symphonie Fantastique*, which, if it does not describe "the whole world", does describe the troubled inner world of its composer. But this was the very work which was probably not

203

in progress, for the source of the disturbance had only just been disclosed: the Irish actress Harriet Smithson who was making a guest appearance in Paris that autumn with the actor Richard Kemble and his English theatre group, and whom Berlioz worshipped fervently, from a distance until now, but coming closer all the time, so close that she sent him packing and he was once again able to relish the "unhappy love", which was soon to be transmuted into the *Symphonie Fantastique* itself. Later, of course, happiness could no longer be avoided; as we know, she listened to him in the end, married him, and that was the end of love, happy or unhappy.

Once again we see Marbot with Delacroix and a third man, this time an equally ardent admirer of Shakespeare, spending almost every evening at the theatre, three times at *Hamlet*, twice at *Romeo and Juliet*, and once again Shakespeare was discussed after the performance as a matter of the utmost topicality, though without Berlioz, whose habit it was to pace the streets of Paris at night, profoundly stirred, both by the poet and by his fascinating interpreter, of whom he wrote, or rather exclaimed in writing: "She opens the gates to the divine art with perfect majesty", while Marbot wrote to his mother:

"...Miss Smithson does her job quite well, in so far as an actress can do her job well or ever transcend the superficial imitation of prescribed emotions. It is still best to read Shakespeare and perform him on the stage of one's own soul."

It is true that Marbot very seldom spoke about music; he never commented on concerts or operas which he had heard in Milan, Paris or Rome, and yet, as we believe we have established, music must have moved him strangely and strongly, for the sole entry on the subject that we find in his notebooks, probably written in 1826, is in the first person singular, which of course reveals yet again his deliberate and acknowledged subjectivity, but also the significance of the subject to his psyche:

"...its transitory character means that when I am listening to it I become aware of the transitoriness of all Beauty in life in a special way, not otherwise to be attained, and therefore it is to some extend a fluid and vanishing image ... So its effect is deep and tragic, it is an excitation of the soul, matched by though, for the soul has no language and can communicate through art only when it can pass indirectly through the object treated by art. But music has no object ... I feel myself drawn into an event to which, like a barbarian, I could give expression only with an exclamation which, but a moment later, would no longer serve, or would be a different one—as if one could not react to art other than by exclaiming 'Potztausend!' ['Upon my soul!'], as Herr von Schlegel says."[7]

Apart from his social dealings with Delacroix and a few people in his circle, we know little of Marbot's stay in Paris. He may well have tried to track down Corot, but the painter was still in Italy. We know that he visited the Louvre, from his notes on Vermeer's *Lacemaker*—"the only painting by Vermeer that I know in which the light comes from the right...a poetic study of prosaic work..."—which in 1820 had not yet been hung. We know nothing of the return journey either: did he take his ease for the last time "sitting in the shadow of a pine" or "on the broad banks of a mighty stream", in order to regain his innocence?

7. "If many a mystical art lover who regards every criticism as dismemberment and every dismemberment as destruction of his enjoyment were to think consistently, then *Potztausend* would be the best verdict on the worthiest work of art. And there are critics who say no more than that, though far more verbosely" (Friedrich Schlegel, *Kritische Fragmente*).

VI

We are approaching the end: the last two years of Marbot's life, which as we look back on it over the distance of time, always in the awareness of his death, suggest a certain pathos. For to us—to me—his fate can claim to be called tragic. We do not know what his own feelings were about this last span of time. There is much to indicate that though he was constantly aware of the "ultima linea rerum"—we shall be coming back to this sombre entry in his notebooks—he put off the appointed time; but that he was as little conscious of Pathos as he was of self-pity. If he had only called himself to order, earning our gratitude, and settled down to writing his "work", the programme would have been in keeping; but there is nothing to indicate that his method of work was directed towards a final goal. He certainly edited, clarified, amplified; he eliminated—unfortunately not always profitably for us—the traces of spontaneous impressions in favour of a definitive version, but he did all this with a composure more suggestive of having sufficient leisure to look it over than of time running out. At the same time he was writing long, informative letters—almost as if he had wanted to scatter his self-documentation a little more widely—but above all he was reading intensively, and clearly with a view to critical assessment, giving the impression that perhaps under Schopenhauer's influence, and ultimately ranging more widely still, he might have been trying to arrive at a comparative appreciation of the arts. But the impression is probably deceptive; he would presumably not have wished to delay his death until the outcome of such a project, particularly as he would have had far too much work to do in other areas, especially that of absolute music, and his knowledge of literature was patchy too, although as we know, he had very decided views on it from an early age.

Marbot's curious hostility to literature—or to be more precise, his antipathy to the narrative prose of his century and the century before—was probably the result of his suspicion of the written word when it is trying to reflect the subtle movements of the soul. All his comments on narrative literature show that it did not satisfy his feeling for the potential and manifestation of psychology. Here, strangely enough—inasmuch as he is concerned with literature as a discipline and is not simply using it for purposes of comparison with the other arts—he applies the yardstick of strict realism. For instance, he not only wants to know how the body reflects the mind but also how the mind experiences the body. Hadley-Chase rightly interpreted this tendency, though not until 1888:

"...for here he is demanding of literature an objective nearness to reality which he does not demand of visual art. Naturally we understand him to the extent that for him the great visual work of art is always *true*, in the sense of the subjective vision and conviction of its creator, whereas narrative literature, besides the truthfulness of the author, must deal also with the subjective truthfulness of his characters, which, as he asserts, is unattainable or at least never attained."

Thus Hadley-Chase. I would add: Marbot felt—and this is quite clear from his notebooks—that psychological consistency is usually sacrificed to the idea it is intended to serve. As he writes: "In literature the mind is being adapted to the part of the character it has to play, whereas it should be vice versa." [8] We may wonder how Marbot would have reacted to

8. We do not know, because he never put it in writing, whether Marbot was aware of the most striking example of this view: Goethe's *Wahlverwandtschaften* ("Elective Affinities"). In the letter from the headmistress's assistant about the enigmatic Ottilie—the same Ottilie, in

Moritz's *Anton Reiser*! He is quite unlikely to have wanted to see a case like his own described in literature, yet he felt, probably rightly, that the soul is always unexplained and the body, not only as a reverberative base and seismograph of the soul but also as its generator and instigator, is left out, in other words the physical body is neglected.

"...literature is too well-mannered, too discreet to busy itself with the body. It knows, to be sure, of the gout which ties a Mr Pennythorpe[9] to his armchair and his footstool, but not of the sudden savage toothache which befalls a young lover, making him forget love and causing unaccustomed, evil images to pass before him ... What happens beneath the garments is deemed almost as offensive as that for which one is obliged to undo or remove them. The lover may of course disclose his heart to the beloved, but actually to open the appropriate place in his shirt would call for that shamefaced assent into which our literature seldom ventures, and then with the most delicate circumlocution, because a further advance into lower regions of the body must be feared and nothing would then seem to stand in the way of reproduction. The heart indeed has properties beyond its function of maintaining life; a noble or ignoble life of its own, which no other organ can

fact, who reveals overwhelming cognitions here and there in her diaries—the author is offending against all psychological probability and insight in such a way that the character pales to a blurred outline. It is no good saying: "And so it should"; its etheral unreality is drawn from another source.

9. Neither I nor anyone I have asked has been able to identify Mr Pennythorpe. Most people guessed Dickens, but that is a chronogical impossibility. Marbot quite probably invented the name to typify a character in a novel.

boast. In both good and ill it turns towards the world, recording the mind and soul of its possessor, whereas the stomach, lying only a little below it, reacts to nothing that seems worthy of literature. It concerns only the doctor, who has already committed himself in his choice of profession to encountering words such as belly and backside with understanding. These words are unknown to literature, although our body would like its well-being or its unwell-being to be articulated, for it is the part that maintains the soul in motion."

It touches us strangely that if we were to attempt to transpose his negative observations into a corresponding positive, the result would in fact be a plea, if only in part, for a realistic literature. It is difficult to imagine that this was his intention. Did he really want literature to break its silence about bodily functions, or did he merely want to demonstrate that literature, by suppressing what is common to humanity as a whole and creating its own ideal figures, sets itself apart from life and therefore lacks the cathartic effect inherent in all true art? Or is it only the prudery he objects to, the omissions or the bashful circumlocutions which attract this irony?

Scarcely. It was attracted most of all by the element that he regarded as untruthfulness, the omission of the living at the expense of ostentatious detail in the description of superficialities.

"...for just as in the painting of certain eras there is a kind of mime and gesture which interprets to the beholder the condition of the soul of him who performs them: the eyes raised heavenward, the outstretched arms suggesting profound suffering or despair ... so too in literature there is a manner which illustrates the violence of the sufferer's reaction to the blows of fate. No doubt a German visited by ill

209

fortune conducts himself differently from an Englishman ... but would he really, unmanned by grief, press his palm to his brow and cry: 'Oh, ich Unglückseliger!' ['Woe is me!']? Who would hear him, other than the residents of the same house, perhaps, who hasten in to ask what has befallen him? Would he beat his brow and murmur: 'Du Nichts-würdiger!' ['Thou good-for- nothing!'] and dash from the room only to recover himself somewhere else and wonder what he does there? I have tried it, I have apostrophized myself: 'Thou contemptible wretch!' without hearing any inward echo— well, perhaps I am a happy man ... One wonders—did the models for these characters, the living people, that is, really behave so? Did they require the performance of this voluntary act of, as it were, corporeal formulation, of gesture or of mime, in order to make their suffering comprehensible to themselves and demonstrate it figuratively? Does not such an act presume a partner, to whom the sufferer displays himself in his extreme behaviour? Or would he not rather wish to preserve his composure because the other was present? ... Anyone can shed tears, no act of volition is required. But to force the body deliberately to express emotion is, as I see it, an act more histrionic and artificial than true."

Here too, as always when he views the subject with distaste, he names no names. He knew *Werther*, which he greatly underestimated—as his biographer, I regret this for I would have liked to record his response to brilliant, breathtaking spontaneity and sovereign skill—he knew *Wilheim Meister*, or at least the *Lehrjahre*; what other narrative literature he had read we do not know. Had his comments on literature been intended for publication, which

210

they were not, we could scarcely have avoided charging him with dismissing it in far too summary and flippant a fashion in some curious access of emotion—otherwise, as we know, so foreign to him. We should then of course have fallen into the all too familiar biographical error of reproaching our hero for something.

Once again in his last two years Marbot left Urbino for a week. In December 1828 he heard, probably from Bunsen in Rome, that Leopardi was visiting his parents' house. After a brief correspondence to fix the dates, Marbot travelled to Recanati, which lies about sixty miles south of Urbino.

In 1826 an expanded edition of Leopardi's poems had appeared in Bologna under the title of *Versi*, which the admiring Marbot had—one might almost say—taken to himself. They were followed in 1827 by an edition of the first twenty dialogues (*operette morali*) in Milan. These too were read and commented on at once by Marbot, his criticism being naturally reserved not for the form or the language, which even he thought perfect, but for the content: the theme of negation of life was presented so entertainingly in language and form and so picturesquely in its variations that it made one forget the monotonous treatment of the subject of those variations; the facets of negation—thus Marbot—very elaborately concealed the fact that their argument was always the same, if it could be called an argument at all. "In Leopardi's dialogues there is much feeling and foreboding, sentiment and despondency, but not a single real thought," he wrote to Bunsen. A harsh, but not totally unwarranted judgment.

Marbot naturally did not intend to discuss the quality of the texts or the soundness of the arguments with Leopardi, but the motives themselves; he wanted to get to know the great poet, whose negation of life was inconsistent, in that he was alive. Marbot was alive too, of course, but at that time he had not yet concluded his stocktaking; he was still adding up the pros and cons, whereas Leopardi had decided early on his negative reply, as soon, in fact, as he had learned thinking and unlearned believing. Then, too, Marbot was born under a different star; he was the favoured son of life, and though Leopardi always insisted that his hostility to life had nothing to do with the wretchedness of his body, there is no doubt that his deformity was responsible for those expressions of resignation, many of them wonderfully poetic.

Unlike Leopardi, Marbot did not see the world as a snare and a delusion, and so he taxed Leopardi with confused thinking, also with some justice. For delusions and snares, Marbot would have said, presupposed an unsnared, undeluded state, which, positively speaking, set the standard of judgment, just as untruth would not be recognizable if one did not have truth as a touchstone. On the other hand, he agreed with Leopardi that the accumulation of life's experience should have led to some kind of culmination about which life had deluded us; a great goal, a state of having-achieved which our fate denies us; instead it presents us with the humiliation of death, which—and here Leopardi would not follow him—could be counteracted by "free death". In other words, Marbot never understood Loopardi's inconsistency in living on in spite of it all. "He does actually cling to life", he concluded, "but I wonder at it, for he can expect no more of it. Probably he has not the courage to take the last step. He is too cowardly."

He made such copious notes on the visit that one would almost suspect that he had looked forward to evaluating it in some way; a simple aide-mémoire at this late date would have been otiose had it not been addressed as a message to others—survivors—as the record of a meeting with a man who though fundamentally of like mind had to some extent chosen a different brand of pessimism. Whether the entry was intended as a corroboration of his own decision is uncertain and rather unlikely: it would never have occurred to him to justify himself. He found the poet

"... of sickly aspect, sunk deep in an armchair, almost cowering, obviously freezing—for the whole house was cold and poorly heated, one could actually smell the niggardliness—in neglected, slightly soiled clothing, huddled in a threadbare covering in the half-darkness of the library, all mind, scarcely any body. Instead of sparkling, he smouldered. Perhaps he is the only unhappy man I have ever met, for he has the greatness and therefore the right to be truly unhappy. We conversed for many hours, interrupted by a walk on which we continued to converse, so that I was not aware of our surroundings, but I do not think they offered much on which the eye would wish to dwell. I passed the night at the Casa Leopardi, a large, beautiful but marble-cold house full of echoes, in which human coldness, too, seems to prevail. I took supper with him, which was a privilege, for he is accustomed to eat alone, never with his family. He says he is a μονοφάγος [monophagos = one who eats alone], for which the Greeks and Romans would certainly have despised him, though that they would have done in any case, because of his stature. He is probably right, but I did not tell him so. He prefers to eat sweet things, pastries and a kind of pudding, of which I prudently did not partake, since neither substance nor colour appealed to me. The meal was spartan and luke-warm, the wine sour and too light. (What would Herr von Rumohr have said!) It was, all in all, a joyless meal in an equally joyless atmosphere."

The cue for a conversation, which ultimately led to both men's inmost hearts, was Leopardi's news that he was vaguely planning a book, to be entitled *The Art of Being Unhappy*. Marbot asked him whether it would be worthwhile writing such a book and hence learning the art, since there were surely more effective ways of contending with being unhappy, for instance putting an end to it by elected death. Leopardi said that he had toyed with this idea, to which Marbot retorted that one does not toy with an idea of this kind, it is too grave and its result too final. Leopardi: even Hamlet had played with the idea and rejected it, in fact he had tried to find an opportunity to put an end to his life, and found it in his duel with Laertes.

"I observed without surprise that this conversation was not to his liking and that he would have liked to change the subject, but I did not want to let it go, for it was to discover precisely this about him that I had come. I said that in reality he was clinging to life, that being unhappy also anchored man to earth, since it was felt as a permanent counterpoint to a possible state of happiness. Yet again and again this possibility would encounter a sudden turn, and though it might perhaps be disclosed as no more than a delusion yet it always reawakened a degree of hope that everything would now change for the better. Leopardi said that nothing could ever change for him, he had already advanced too far into the realm of delusion, so that, if he were now to look back, he would no longer see the boundaries which he had already crossed as a child. Was it not true, I said, that profound melancholy, to which indeed I was no stranger, was the very thing that often bestowed a kind of negative well-being, if not an intoxicating enjoyment of all that was transitory?

214

For it was this, the transitory, after all, that governed our lives and our experience and it was precisely the knowledge of irrevocability which produced a certain, albeit morbid feeling of happiness—his poems, for instance, revealed this clearly; in them he recalled what was lost and luxuriated in the loss. But Count Leopardi remained stiff-necked, indeed pig-headed, and this at a point where I too was offering him the chance of stepping back into the land of the lost; grief quickened him, he said, and was his vital spark, for he had unmasked all beauty as illusion. I: objectively it is a matter of indifference whether we experience something as illusion or reality, as long as we experience it. He then asked if I myself were contemplating suicide. I said that every thinking man did so at least once in his lifetime. To be sure, one did not contemplate such a deed without alarm, but in order to carry the thought through to the end one must also consider the before and the after. After: 'To sleep, perchance to dream!', although I thought that highly improbable, for 'after' one would surely be in a world in which there would be no more dreaming. And before? he asked. I: well, should our souls succeed in preserving their peace to the last, then until the very moment of 'laying hands on oneself', as it was sometimes called, we could lead a normal, active life—just as someone struck by lightning is abruptly torn from life."

Marbot must have exhibited extraordinary eloquence, for him, which would indicate that the subject had gradually moved into the forefront of his mind. He had apparently not succeeded in persuading Leopardi. He had been speaking to himself and of himself. And so we come to the end of the notes on his visit:

215

"Count Leopardi was undecided and evasive. Perhaps he feared this final moment, one could understand that, or perhaps damnation, which would be less understandable, for then he would be other in life than he is in his works. But perhaps in his heart of hearts he loves life after all. Why, I do not know. This misshapen minstrel is not loved by God!"

God accused, Leopardi rebuked.

In fact, it looks as if Marbot did live an externally normal life until a few days before his death. The one year he allowed himself after his visit to Leopardi was by no means exclusively devoted to his work but embraced an almost programmatic sociability, as an affable and apparently carefree participant, guest and host. Catani-Ligi gives an account of well-planned evening parties in the English style, at which there was also music, of culinarily-balanced dinners which won him great admiration among the local nobility and seem to have attracted a new circle of foreign guests; close and distant relations of Anna Maria arrived, including the widowed aunt from Milan, who had not left her house for years; a Marchese Antici from Ascoli Piceno, incidentally a cousin of Leopardi's mother (who had been so miserly that at his funeral the tenants spat on his coffin) and other guests whom Andrew probably tolerated about him less for the sake of their intellectual qualities than for their entertainment value. And he was certainly friendly to all of them in his detached way, not only because it was in his nature, but also for the sake of his mistress, who would be thrown back on this society, to which she would be returning after his death. In fact she did not do so. After Andrew's death she retreated into the Casa Baiardi, where she presumably lived first for her children and then for her grief, until her death

216

in 1848: one more life unintentionally destroyed by Marbot.

Shortly after Marbot's return from Recanati in the middle of January 1829, William Turner, making a detour via Urbino on the way home from Rome, came to visit Marbot, although he claimed to be in a hurry. This of course did not prevent him for complaining about various coachmen who had refused to stop when he wanted to sketch, so that he had missed one coach in Macerata in order to paint a sunrise. Turner, as Andrew wrote to his mother,

"was laden with big portfolios and small blocks full of watercolours, sketches for paintings and drawings, some of them showing nothing but a skyline, but conjuring up everything else to complete a landscape."

Turner stayed for only two nights. He was full of admiration for landscape and town, for the house, its view and its rooms, but was surprised that there were no pictures on the walls; a circumstance which may have surprised quite a few before him, but which is fully explained by Andrew's reply to Turner:

"All the pictures which mean anything to me are in my memory. If I had some of them, or others, here on the walls as well, that would not only be an arbitrary preference, connected less with quality than with availability, but it would also be injurious to the collection in my soul and in my head, which two authorities divide the work of memory between them and which are always in action."

Not least, this statement too shows Marbot's lack of attachment to possessions and it explains the fact that after Lord Claverton's death he had not, as one might have expected, claimed his grandfather's collection for himself but left it to his younger brother, who probably saw little more in it than its material value and soon after his mother's death part sold, part gifted it to the National Galleries in London and Edinburgh in order to make a good name for himself in politics.

After Turner's visit Marbot entered in his notebooks: "Turner is on the way to dissolving the concrete objectivity of Nature into forms of manifestation. Gradually all firm outlines vanish, becoming atmosphere, air, mist, he is no longer painting creation, he is himself creating. Perhaps a time will come when people look at a sunset and say 'Is that not almost as beautiful and as real as a Turner?' He talks a lot, but only of what one should paint, what he has painted and not painted, he paints and draws all the time, even if he has no brush or pencil in his hand; what is not paintable does not exist for him. Fortunately he is moving away from mythology and hence from the heroic and noble, which he was always copying from Lorrain. He no longer dispatches Mercury to admonish Aeneas and no longer paints *The Decline of Carthage*, because he has no doubt perceived that Carthage did not decline on a single day on which the weather was suitable for painting, and that no mythical figures fit into landscapes like his, which themselves create a myth of Nature which is perceptible only to the senses. For after all they are not paradises, not the Elysian Fields, but extracts from Nature's own, perceptible life, calm or aroused, agitated or extended in unending panoramas... Happy is he who lives in his objects and thus himself becomes his object."

This final sentence is scribbled in the margin, a secret afterthought. It moves us because here again, and for the last time, his yearning to be an artist is revealed, the dream he never shared with anyone and yet which ran through his life like a descant part and a path of discontent.

One more painter came: Karl Blechen, on an excursion from Florence, and with an introduction from Bunsen, "was suddenly standing at the door with a couple of pictures, like a hawker"—it was the end of August 1829—

> "...an awkward and not very articulate German of insignificant appearance but extraordinary talent who had begun as a bank official and has never entirely outgrown the way of life of such a one. Yet his paintings show a great assurance, which he himself has not. His eyes have a strange unsteady flicker [the onset of mental derangement was probably beginning to manifest itself sporadically at this time], but he takes the landscape firmly in his grasp, it becomes for him a strictly personal likeness, into which he projects the figures of his dreams and wish-dreams, and yet his imagination does not lead him astray. He is an artist who lives on forces of which he himself is not aware. Pictures arise from a different side of the mind from words, and I think that most of us are guilty of an injustice when we set greater store by the artist who knows how to articulate the value of his work in words. Did Giotto ever talk about his works?"

Marbot assumed, no doubt rightly, that the fact that Blechen had brought some pictures with him constituted a tacit invitation to buy, and so he acquired the *Capuchin Monastery at Amalfi*; he gave it to Anna Maria's daughter Bianca, who evidently admired the painting. She later took it with her to

219

Milan and from there it came into the Reinhart Collection in Winterthur.

And the last visitor was August von Platen. He arrived in September 1829 with an introduction from Rumohr and stayed for several days. Marbot seems to have found his presence rather distressing. Marbot the Englishman, who bore his unsurmounted, insurmountable position as an outsider with incomparable composure, had no patience with the German Platen, who did not know how to bear his. Platen was tormented—it was probably his normal state—and in his need to communicate he seems to have spread out his inner life before Marbot with extraordinary indiscretion, but at the same time with the uncompromising, almost startling honesty he displays in his diaries. Marbot recognized in him a man "of noble mind, a stranger to all that is petty as long as one does not wound him." That is certainly true, only in fact we see him always wounded, and moreover in a state of exalted—and no doubt exhausting, for his host—and agitated longing for absolute beauty as a goal and form of life. Platen ranged restlessly through town and countryside, alone or with Marbot, "endlessly in search of himself". On one of these walks he wrote his couplet:

So that Sanzio the sooner should rise to the welcoming heavens,
Even his cradle was built for him high, looking down on the clouds.

Marbot's objections to this assertion can be found in Platen's diaries: he found the verse effusive rather than poetically expressive. The name Sanzio was the result of a scholarly misunderstanding; posterity should have the goodness to say Raphael, since that was his name. Moreover, Urbino never did lie above the clouds and the cradle in the Santi residence had stood in a dark chamber, as he, Platen, could find out for himself. And in any case, between his home in Urbino and Heaven, Raphael had been down below in Rome, where he had undoubtedly enjoyed a life which was not likely to be rewarded with an eternity in Heaven, nor had he made any secret of his excesses, in contrast to Michelangelo, who committed his in hole-and-corner fashion, which was why Raphael had said of him that he was 'lonely as an executioner'. Platen naturally took this personally and was injured, especially since he assumed, quite rightly, that Marbot too was harbouring a secret whose disclosure would have shocked the world. This, then, must be the explanation of the phrase "Sinful yourself, you seek the sin in others", which he wrote on a sheet of paper which, if our reconstruction is correct, he put on Marbot's table when he left.

But Platen was reconciled. It was in Marbot's house that he wrote his Ghazel 132:

My ropes I have shrugged off, my fetters cast away,
And from the trifling world I turned me fast away.
From frosty prosiness, from ruminative sense
How yearn I to begone, from tedium passed away!
If you speak ill of me, I'd spoken it before,
And of that fame I even took the last away:
I would have trod the path your virtue had prepared,
Yet did I ever stay, my soul downcast, away;
But he whose chosen goal, whose target is the sun,
He vainly shoots his darts thro' regions vast away.
Be silent, poet, now, and let the world run on,
And what you like not, let the cold winds blast away!

These verses, Marbot told him, gave voice to a noble resolution, the necessary condition for liberation, and this he should now attain in life as well. In his poetry (thus Marbot to Platen) complaint and resolve neutralized one another, whereas in life he was constantly succumbing to the object of

221

those complaints. He should therefore be inspired by his own poetry and finally release himself from the judgment of his disapproving fellows. A didactic criticism, in other words, which Platen seems to have taken quite well, but a certain discord smouldered throughout their time together, probably based on an unreasoning jealousy on Platen's part. Marbot writes to Rumohr:

"... in matters of art he is very receptive, he allows the works to work on him—for instance he has Carpaccio's *Coronation of Our Lady* in his memory—who else could say that of himself!—he praised the delicacy and liveliness of the Giotto frescoes in Padua—well, delicate is just what they are not, but lively—... but all in all he is an unhappy man, at odds with himself, and one cannot help him. I understand his sufferings well, better than he knows. On the other hand, he lives on them and I wonder what subject he would take for his poetry, were his state not as it is, and whether his sort of differentness which indeed is not infrequently the theme of art, may also be the motive that in certain circumstances impels a man to become an artist."

This seems to us to be an extremely astute question, which Rumohr of all men was eminently well fitted to answer. Unfortunately we do not know the answer, it probably never came. Andrew's question can be interpreted as an accusation against fate, in these terms: if so-called sexual deviation can be the driving force of art, why then have I been denied this power which I would have wished to possess above all others? We could of course have informed Andrew that the supposition is mistaken; that the explicitly creative in man is indeed abnormal, but sexuality alone cannot be the root of talent or genius. The artist's sublimation may very well be the source of great works, but the fact that he is an artist, his talent, his

genius, are already manifest, as immanent qualities independent of the awakening of his sexuality with its unconscious
drive—though whether those qualities are inherited or
acquired is still open to doubt. And August von Platen is a
perfect example of a man who did find sublimation as a source
of action, yet to whom true creativeness was nevertheless
denied, and whose great technical skills enabled him to
rummage among the fragments of his fate instead of reshaping
it objectively in metaphors of mastery. And so Marbot
continues:

> "The unhappy Platen has nothing to say, but he says
> it exceptionally beautifully. Out of suffering he
> models an artistic form that one can seize on and
> admire, but only as a form, not as a synthesis of
> mind and spirit. Leopardi, on the other hand,
> succeeds in his best moments—if only then!—in
> awakening within our souls some deeply hidden,
> even forgotten anguish, in bringing it into the light
> and thus making fellow-sufferers of us. He quarrels
> with God, Platen quarrels with himself. Why then
> does he continue to live?"

If we substitute "suppressed" for "forgotten" and
"consciousness" for "light", Marbot's statement anticipates a
process since defined by psychoanalysis.

"Why does he continue to live?" He was beginning to
ask this question in relation to each of his interlocutors.
Andrew was experimenting with identification models. The
decision to put an end to his own life instead of submitting to
the agonizing process of nature that he thought he had
observed in many others, had been a contrapuntal
accompaniment to his thoughts from an early stage and now
there are many signs that, far from deferring the date, he was
actually advancing it more and more. Twice we find Horace's

223

"Mors ultima linea rerum" written between the lines of his notes. We can date its first appearance with reasonable certainty during his first stay in Paris in 1820—although there are no recognizable points of reference—the second time it appears in the third notebook, less perhaps as a reminder than as a rejection of the almost tautological banality of the saying; for below it he adds caustically: "Indeed? Where did'st thou acquire such wisdom?" This jotting comes between aides-mémoire on Palladio and Venetian architecture. We are aware of the constant presence of death and sometimes it looms up, fittingly stern and soberly inexorable, and whispers: Here I am, at your service, to remind you of your goal and your own will. And there is no doubt that this goal drew nearer when Marbot returned from Recanati, still under the impression of Leopardi's weakness and irresolution. Only the decision was repressed from time to time, perhaps by social occasions and guests, until winter came again.

In the light of some quotations from letters and other thoughts recorded by Marbot the reader will have observed that Schopenhauer's *World as Will and Idea* had begun to play a considerable part in his thinking. He had probably started reading it when he took up residence in Urbino, and when he returned from Recanati in December 1828 he began to study it in detail, with sporadic commentaries. In a letter to van Rossum—written in German—he says:

"Schopenhauer's pessimism seems so genuine because it is not, as Leopardi's is, dependent on the personal, but on the absolutely objective. As I have learned from him, he knows very well how to profit from the good sides of life, he is in good health, travels much, lives according to his inclinations, and if besides this he also lives according to his disinclinations and duly nurtures them, he is by so doing pursuing something that seems vital to him,

224

for he does not like mankind, or at least not as it is, and he wants people to know it. And I think that were he ugly and deformed, and poor into the bargain, his negation of the world would not be believed at all, although it is firmly grounded in his philosophical system as 'negation of the will'. He describes optimism as 'an attitude of mind which is not only absurd but also truly nefarious, a bitter mockery of the nameless sufferings of mankind'. Who would deny that he is right? I will not."

The World as Will and Idea appealed greatly to Marbot, as a decided negator, only he did not consider its philosophy feasible in practice, since it called for an outlook foreign to the non-philosopher; the hard-won discovery that there is no deliverance from our sufferings other than the negation of the will to live, which would nullify the *principium individuationis*. Man, according to Marbot, is incapable of conceiving non-being.

But what can be conceived is that he had extreme objections, in particular, to Schopenhauer's rejection of suicide. In his notebooks, which now move increasingly into general matters—one might say from the aesthetic into the ethical—he writes:

"... what a horrible word is 'Selbstmord', which is 'self-murder'—whereas 'Freitod' is a wonderful word: 'free death', which would mean having the freedom to do with your life as you wish."

We know what he was talking about, and observe that his decision was taken.

"Were this free death not to have such a significant history, none would dare to commit it. As it is, each man takes his own negator of life as his pattern, and truly, there are so many of the great among them ...

To be sure, Schopenhauer does not think that suicide is the answer to the exactions of life but rather that we should live on, actively negating. But he forgets that the 'philosophical life' is other than the lived life—or perhaps he does not forget it, but he does not wish to admit it. One may not regard suicide as the expression of an attitude to the world, nor as a flight into non-being, but as a refusal of that which cruel Nature does, or plans to do, with us as individual beings. Suicide may not be the solution to any philosophical problems, but neither has any one ever committed it as such. Its motive has never been the expression of an attitude to existence in general, but only, and always, to the individual life of the self-murderer ... Schopenhauer treats this theme too dogmatically, he does not consider the soul. One must proceed from the human individual, his motives, his weariness, his despair. Life is not worth living out of obedience to the law of Nature. Self-murder is the ultimate freedom of the individual who takes seriously the choice between being and not being ... Otherwise, however, Schopenhauer is, as I see it, right in everything; his deductions, as he himself says, are 'excellent'. So the little man from the Boboli Gardens was right."

And in the same letter to Rumohr in which he tells him about Platen, Andrew recommends him to read Schopenhauer, which indicates that the conversations back there in Siena had not after all been exclusively about painting—or about eating:

"Schopenhauer regards suicide as the wrong answer to life. If he truly wishes to regard it only as the result of purely philosophical ideas he may be right, for then it amounts to nothing more than the demonstration of protest. But one may wonder: protest to whom? To God? Does He take note of it and realize that in His concept of creation there was one crucial error? No. One who is seriously planning a free death is not thinking of answering God, he is not considering theory or proof, he is thinking of himself. He does not want to punish the idea of life but to find a way out of it."

These words express the intense personal commitment he brought to the question, and behind them the determined answer looms. Like every thinking man—"thinking" here in contrast not only to believing but also to pragmatic—he never doubted his right to dispose of his own life.

"Life is a process which asks to be mastered—but who is the master? He who placidly accepts its adversities and injustices, or he who conquers his life by ending it?"

No thought was apparently spared here for a third possible way of mastering life, by assimilating all its heights and depths in an apparent flight into creativity—the artist's solution; he suppressed it because it was not available to him. Herein lies Marbot's tragedy, but herein too lies the limit of his self-knowledge, which he in fact never claimed, just as he disputed the possession of it by others.

"What an abyss would open up if we could know and understand ourselves and were at the same time unable to correct ourselves!... For he who claims to know himself is an impostor and he who never asks if he knows himself and never makes the attempt differs from the beasts only in his pretensions, his foolishness and his want of dignity ... Every self-portrait is untrue and since it feigns objectivity it is an imposition on him who is supposed to accept it from us. It is permitted only to the great artist, for by portraying himself he calls himself in question. His question assumes the form of a work of art."

We can fairly sense how much Andrew himself would

227

have liked to be one of those who portrayed themselves in the form of a work of art and thereby called themselves in question!

All the same, we should not see him as one of those young men whose life is ruled by *Weltschmerz* and whose vision is consequently distorted. Marbot's melancholy was profound and genuine, not, as many thought, the melancholy of the Romantic who delights in looking on the dark side of life because everything he tries to cling to is so painfully transitory. His negative feeling for life was motivated and thoroughly supported by precise observation of his experience and the experience of others.

"Every man is alone with himself and his world; only they who know it not can be happy. They are the meek victims of a system which they believe to be a full existence. They live in constant eager communication with the world about them, through which they appear to overcome their loneliness until their death, which they greatly fear, and which they hope will come as late as possible, so that they can while away their time till then."

In contrast to the earlier notes, the time of whose origin is difficult and the precise dates generally impossible to determine, the entries of the last few weeks and days are quite clearly recognizable as such. There is a growing intensity about them, a kind of *stretto* leading towards the end, quite without drama, confirming and disposing; no stocktaking and naturally no self-revelation; only the unconscious suggestion that the moment he had predetermined, marked on the calendar, so to speak, was now approaching. We cannot really even speak of "self-control", because the conditions for the popular understanding of the term are missing—Marbot had always been self-controlled. No resolve is implied: "Now it is serious!"—it had always been serious for him—but there seems to be a relaxed, underlying tenor, which means: "Now I shall be free!" Ideas about death are certainly to be found at many unexpected points in the *Notebooks*, and they multiply in the last year of his life, but we never find any clear reference to his own decision, only a kind of review of life and the various reasons for rejecting it:

"If one is willing to regard life as an experience which cannot be turned to account, in other words as an end in itself, one might call it liveable, at least for those privileged persons who do not have to work hard for every new day, and who, above all, are answerable to no one. But any one who expects more of it than a growing assembly of experiences, the quality of which is always the same, because it corresponds to the disposition of the experiencer, who cannot after all exceed his own capacity for experience—just as the view from a window is cut off at the top, lengthens a little as we approach it, but if we lean out, out we plunge—anyone who lives in the hope that something greater and more essential will be revealed to him than that which he already experiences, is deluding himself. But life is made easier by living in delusion."

This entry certainly betrays an, as it were, measured preparedness for the end; a purely intellectual approach, quite untouched by emotion, to the decision to leave this life. And it becomes equally clear that the eventual act was dictated neither by despair not by a feeling of hopelessness; that it was in fact the final item on a programme of life: if not perhaps included from the start, one which had become the necessary end of a protracted process. We see too that Marbot, when it came to the point, would not be killing somebody whom he despised or of whom he was weary, but someone whom he wished to spare

229

the routine of repetitive experience; who looked forward to nothing new and expected nothing better; who had borne his otherness with dignity, indeed with pride, and was now restoring it to its creator, with fitting thanks for earthly experience, yet with the incriminating accusation that this experience had produced no knowledge as to the sense and purpose of life: "signifying nothing". He knew that his life had been favoured by material circumstances, but nothing until his death could truly be said to have come to him on the wings of freedom. So this is something quite different from the ennui of the Romantic whom Hadley-Chase insisted on seeing in him, despite all the indications to the contrary. Marbot never projected himself as his own hero. He had been aware all his life that he would not, and had not, become the person he would have wished to be, and his death was the affirmation of this fact. Whether his feelings for life would have increased to this point of negation had it fallen to him to become what he wanted, it is impossible to say. It is clear and proven that he had never intended to linger until his life had run its biological course. For him the body was the servant of the mind, despite physical experience which he had been very well able to enjoy. A year before his death, having returned from Recanati stimulated by his talks with Leopardi, he had made the entry:

> "A man who can think should know when his time has run out. He will be punished for the unworthiness of outliving that point by becoming more unbearable to himself with every day that passes. Regard for his fellow-men must not impede him in the final act, for he cannot look into their souls, and therefore does not know whether they can still endure him or whether he has become a burden to them. He who cannot endure himself will not be endured by others."

Whether we should take this to mean that he could no longer endure himself we do not know. I think it possible, for there is no doubt that he saw himself ultimately as a failure in his work and hence in life. He had realized that he would penetrate no further into the essence of the subject to which he had dedicated his life only because he himself could never be one of those whom his research concerned: the artists. He certainly came closer than others to the heart of the enigma, but not to its solution. The task he had set himself had gradually proved incapable of fulfilment and he felt that his life no longer had any function or meaning. Marbot had grown tired.

But his self-control did not allow him to disclose this frame of mind. No one in his circle had ever seen him as a moody, or even unpredictable outsider. The little evidence we have from others of the last years of his life—mostly brief notes, messages to Giancarlo Catani-Ligi, invitations, enquiries—shows that there is no hint of his self-appointed end, which does not mean that, had his friends in Urbino suspected it, a few of them might not have looked for symptoms, and perhaps even found them. Andrew's entry about "unendurability", no doubt correct as such, might therefore have referred to Leopardi, his suspicious disposition, his withdrawn and in fact quite disagreeable egocentricity. But it certainly did refer— and earlier entries point to this, as we can see—to Platen, who found it difficult to endure himself and was therefore endured with difficulty by others; who was only too well aware of his unendurability and suffered painfully from it.

A single jotting, the last about his own state of mind, also, regrettably, undated, refers unmistakably to his own decision and both Lady Catherine and van Rossum could have interpreted it, had they not shrunk from the interpretation.

231

This entry, of which the handwriting and general impression in no way differ from the other late entries, reads:

"'... and I shall go to bed at noon'. Admittedly it is not yet noon, but why wait until the sun stands at its zenith? It is not *my* sun."

Shakespeare, for the last time. These are the last words of the fool in *King Lear*, his response to the king: "We'll go to supper i' th' morning." Andrew undoubtedly interpreted the fool's words as they are generally understood: "I shall put an early end to my life, and I shall do it now." It is true that the fool appears briefly once more in the next scene, but he is silent, perhaps preoccupied with his end.

The February of 1830 was mild and dry. It might very easily have tempted Andrew into those long walks or rides to which he was accustomed from childhood. He loved the Montefeltro mountains—"a weird and heavenly playground of all the winds there are". He probably knew every road and path in them and had often sent his house-guests hunting there, perhaps when he was sick of having them about. (He was probably even more sick of them when they returned with the spoils of the hunt, a wild pig, for instance!)

So one morning towards the end of the month he left the house for the last time. He was missed in the evening, but it was thought that he must be on one of his impromptu expeditions in the neighbourhood and would probably spend the night at the house of one of Anna Maria's relations. But when he did not return the next evening uneasiness turned to alarm. Giancarlo Catani-Ligi set out with Marbot's servant Raffaello to search for him—some of the tenants joined in the search. But that night came confirmation of the disaster, as if in a classical tragedy: Marbot's horse was standing outside the stable after midnight, "without a sound".

They had not given up all hope, however. Next day a

systematic search was organized, on foot and on horseback, but they found neither him, nor the smallest sign or trace of him. No one had seen him, no one could offer the slightest clue.

In fact, he was never found. After about a week his family in England was notified, as far as possible, though Andrew had never said very much about their present circumstances and distribution, so that they were rather shadowy figures to his Urbino circle. But as far as we know, nothing was done on the English side. Since it was understood that the body did not exist, so that there was no question of transport, they did not really know what there was to be done. Even Lady Catherine does not seem to have known. But we would surely not be mistaken in assuming that she realized at once that Andrew had chosen a final way out, perhaps she had even received a farewell letter, but on this, also, we have no information. We are sorely in need of some document here, not a proof exactly, but some human witness to let the curtain fall. After a month the missing man was presumed dead. It was at this point, too, that the sorrowful foreboding of Anna Maria and their Urbino circle turned into foreboding sorrow, even if they were not yet, and perhaps never would be, aware of the voluntary nature of his death.

So Andrew Marbot was presumed lost, and has remained so. We must understand this disappearance, literally without trace, in the sense that, with his aversion to dramatics, he had chosen the most inconspicuous way possible of leaving the world. He would certainly not have tried actively to efface all clues. He wanted to take his "step into freedom" without preparation, as it were incidentally. He had decided long ago between being and not-being, and he chose the time of not-being on the inspiration of the moment. He knew that few people would be stricken by his death: Lady Catherine, Anna

Maria and Father Gerard—he thought it would be unseemly to stage it and more dignified to vanish without trace in night and wind, than to burden survivors with a self-spoiled body. That he should never be found was part of the plan.

We know of no farewell words to his mother. We shall never know whether she, and she alone, learned of his purpose. If so, one wonders whether or not she would have confided in Father Gerard. On the one hand, she would certainly have wanted to conceal this undoubtedly deadly sin from him, but on the other hand, she must have been aware than van Rossum would not countenance any deceit and she probably needed her friend and confidant as never before. Her suffering must have been beyond measure.

Probably no such farewell words existed, and Andrew himself wanted his deed to be kept secret from his mother. Heedless of the fact that his last jottings would make his intentions clear to anyone, he left the world without a word, in order to make light of it to everyone, even to those dearest to him. Perhaps he did not sense that his conduct was itself an ostentatious, even a histrionic gesture; he was obliterating himself. It is even possible that he had intended to simulate an accident, a fatal fall or even murder with robbery, and his disappearance may in fact have been explained in this way at first. Then, several weeks later, probably in the course of an inevitable inventory-taking, Anna Maria discovered the unmistakable evidence: one of the two pistols was missing from its case, one of those little leather-bound wooden boxes—one might call it a duelling kit—lined with blue velvet, which Marbot must have bought on his trip to Paris, probably in Nancy, for the two weapons were the work of the gunmaker there, Charrières by name: finely-chiselled showpieces of their kind, which make one wonder whether the expenditure of

234

artistry was really worthwhile, since of the two buyers one would use such a pair only once, unless he acquired it as a collector's piece, which was not usual at that time. At all events: in this third inventory, one of the two pistols was missing from their case and it must have been an additional shock to the deeply-dismayed Anna Maria Baiardi to be confronted with a mystery which no one would ever be able to solve, and in which she perhaps fancied herself to be obscurely involved.

This ends the account of Andrew Marbot's life, or at least of all that we can know of it. Where his work is concerned I have had to restrict myself here to those sample passages and excerpts which throw light on his conscious and unconscious mind and, by interaction, are not only illuminated by the knowledge of this perfectly unique existence, but also lead in the directions which constitute his uniqueness and his originality. Readers may wonder why a biographical sketch—this book cannot claim to be any more than that—should appear before the new edition of the works and letters of its hero. The answer should be clear and understandable: this time it was absolutely essential to prevent the work and letters from being read on the basis of false premises. For although the copious supplements which it has been possible to add since the last edition relieve the material of the apodictic absoluteness mistakenly ascribed to it, if the acknowledged and sometimes passionate subjectivity of the text as it now appears had been insufficiently explained, the key to reading it would have been lacking. For there would have been no justification for presenting Marbot's writings in a form even similar to that of the first edition: notebooks and letters were once again kept strictly separate. The resulting duplication of many descriptions or interpretations of paintings has to be taken into account, which is all the easier since the formulations vary widely: in letters the wording is adapted to the addressee and Marbot's estimate of his receptivity, whereas in the notebooks, the choice of words has just that stamp of the categorical conclusions of a discoverer, which would inevitably have led to misunderstanding. The telltale marginal notes have been left out of the new edition since, as they apparently occur at random, they would have destroyed the rhythm of the deductive argument. This is the main reason for the publication of the biography before the works. For without these secret signals, sometimes of startling intimacy, Marbot the man would continue to be an even more enigmatic figure than he was.

What was extraordinary about him—the flight from life into art which was denied to him, the stigma and charisma of this tragic refugee—can no longer be exhaustively interpreted, since we lack the key to his human side, to the demand and need for human relationship. And yet his fragmentary work, supplemented by the letters and these almost infinitesimally small, yet extremely enlightening marginal notes, shed light on aspects of a unique personality: a deep, even vehement commitment to the investigation of relationships between the moving and the active force in the creative process; a sometimes agonizing tension between intense aesthetic experience and studied reserve towards living, emotional experience; the absolute desire for objectivity and the awareness of being captive to the subjective, which we would be glad to see in many an art-lover or historian today. In contrast to so many bunglers at failure, Marbot had mastered his.

He was the first, and for almost a century the only person to question the individual work of art as to its motivation in the unconscious, and hence its psychological origin. It was natural that he should choose painting for this, because the picture was not only what he lived for but

236

also his epitome of the integral, undisfigurable work of art.

"Looking at a painting forces us into a field to which no other art work can pretend. Nothing here is in motion, we see the work as if the artist had but a moment before laid down his brush. There it stands, open to an interpretation which, once it has been exhaustively made, will never change. The painting thus becomes a message, valid for all time. Because it requires no mediator, no singer, actor or performer, it enables us to relive the greatest hours of the artist. In so doing it expands our reality by the dimension of the ideal, of what might have been, had the artist ruled the world."

In painting Marbot tried to understand the artist as an individual, as object and subject, with his purpose and his failure, his pressures and suppressions. He became increasingly aware that his research would be denied a final outcome. He, who strove always for perfection and to whom all dilettantism was obnoxious, would never have considered publication in the 1832 form. His final entry reads:

"The answer of the work of art is addressed to the question of its beholder, and only he who questions it as to its essence will be answered by that essence. But to no one does it answer the question as to the greatest mystery, namely the spiritual necessity to which it owes its being. Therefore we shall not learn with certainty of anything that has taken place within the artist, other than his injunction as to what should take place in us. The artist plays on our soul, but who plays on the soul of the artist?"

With this question Marbot's notebooks end. He was the first to ask it. We are still waiting for the answer.

Index of Personal Names

Alberti, Leon Battista (1404-1472), Italian architect and scholar, 27, 190

Angelus Silesius (Johann Scheffler) (1624-1677), German mystical poet, Catholic convert and priest, 31

Arnim, Achim von (1781-1831), German writer of romances, 172 married to Bettina (q.v.)

Arnim, Bettina von (1785-1859), German writer of tales and essays, 172

Augustine, St (353-430), Bishop of Hippo and outstanding theological scholar, 30, 99f.

Bartholdy, Jacob Salomo (1779-1825), Prussian diplomat, uncle to Felix Mendelssohn-Bartholdy, 182

Beethoven, Ludwig van (1770-1827), German composer and incomparable musical innovator, 203

Bellini, Giovanni (1430-1516), Venetian painter, 26

Berlioz, Hector (1803-1869), French composer, married to Harriet Smithson (q.v.), 127, 202-205

Blake, William (1757-1827), English poet, painter and mystic, 5, 55-59, 73, 84, 124

Blechen, Karl (1798-1840), German painter, 219 f.

Boisserée, Melchior (1786-1851), art-collector, 154, brother of Sulpice (q.v.)

Boisserée, Sulpice (1783-1854), German art historian and collector, 78 f., 139, 154

Bonington, Richard Parkes (1802-1828), English painter, studied in Paris, friend of Delacroix (q.v.), 126 f.

Botticelli, Sandro (1444-1510), Florentine painter, renowned as much for his classical as for his devotional pictures, 99, 104, 200

Brewster, Sir David (1781-1868), Scottish physicist, inventor of the kaleidoscope, 24

Brummell, George Bryan (Beau), (1778-1840), Regency dandy, friend of the Prince Regent, 49

Büchner, Georg (1813-1837), German poet and revolutionary, 9

238

De Quincey, Thomas (1785-1859), English writer and opium addict, 22, 25 f., 31 f., 35 f., 44-48, 62 f., 64, 67, 88, 90 f., 157, 191
Dickens, Charles (1812-1870), English novelist and journalist, 209
Diderot, Denis (1713-1784), French novelist and critic, 42
Donne, John (1573-1631), English poet, Dean of St Paul's, 31
Duccio (di Buoninsegna) (c. 1260-c. 1320), Italian painter, founder of the Sienese school, 97
Dürer, Albrecht (1471-1528), German painter and engraver, 75

Eckermann, Johann Peter (1792-1854), German author, friend and assistant to Goethe (q.v.), 9
Etty, William (1787-1849), English painter, 125
Eyck, Jan van (c. 1389-1441), Flemish painter, unique in his dreamlike combination of reality and illusion, 53, 124, 145

Fitzharris, Lord (b.1806), English traveller, 184
Flemming, Hans Friedrich, Freiherr von (c. 1660-1725), German sporting writer, 4
Freud, Sigmund (1856-1939), Austrian founder of psychoanalysis, 61, 138
Friedrich, Caspar David (1774-1840), German painter, 18

Gainsborough, Thomas (1727-1788), English landscape and portrait-painter, 55
Gamba, Count Pietro (d.1827), brother of Teresa Guiccioli (q.v.), friend of Byron (q.v.), 87, 188
George IV (1762-1830), King of England, best known as Prince Regent from 1810-1820, 49, 52
Gérard, François Pascal Simon, Baron (1770-1837), French portrait-ist and historical painter, 77-79, 149
Géricault, Theodore (1791-1824), French painter, worked for some time in England, influenced Delacroix, 78
Giorgione, (Giorgio Barbarelli da Castelfranco) (c. 1478-1511), Italian painter, one of the earliest great Romantic artists, 134-136
Giotto di Bondone (c. 1267-1337), Florentine painter and architect, excelling as a master of the fresco, 80-84, 97, 168, 196, 220, 222
Giulio Romano (c. 1492-1546), Italian painter and architect, assistant

241

Horny, Franz (1798-1824), German painter, 95
Hunt, Leigh (1784-1859), English poet and essayist, 88

James I (1566-1625), King of England (James VI of Scotland), 1
Justi, Ludwig (1876-1957), German art historian, 136

Kant, Immanuel (1724-1804), major German philosopher of the
    idealist school, 106
Keats, John (1795-1821), English Romantic poet, 191
Kemble, Richard, English actor-manager of the 19th century, 204
Knoller, Martin (1725-1804), Austrian painter and restorer, 165

Lamartine, Alphonse Marie Louis de (1790-1869), French poet and
    politician, historian and biographer, 189
Lamb, Lady Caroline (1785-1828), novelist wife of 2nd Viscount
    Melbourne, Byron's mistress 1812-1813, 55, 112
Laube, Heinrich (1806-1884), German playwright, director of the
    Vienna Burgtheater, 96
Lawrence, Sir Thomas (1769-1830), popular English portrait-pain-
    ter, 55
Leigh, Augusta (b.1783), Byron's half-sister, 105 f.
Leonardo da Vinci (1452-1519), supreme Italian artist, painter,
    engineer and scientific explorer, 196
Leopardi, Count Giacomo (1798-1837), Italian poet, gifted lyricist,
    37, 44, 183, 190, 212-217, 224 f., 231 f.
Lessing, Gotthold Ephraim (1729-1781), German playwright and
    critic, 31, 191
Longford, Elizabeth, Countess of (b.1906), English biographer, 185
Lorrain (or Lorraine), Claude (1600-1682), French landscape-
    painter, 219
Ludwig I (1786-1868), King of Bavaria, 154

Mantegna, Andrea (1431-1506), Italian painter, architect and poet,
    outstanding for his technical excellence, 165, 168
Manzoni, Alessandro (1785-1873), Italian novelist and poet, 171
Massimo, Marchese, patron of the 19th–century Nazarene move-
    ment, 182
Medici, Cosimo de (1389-1464), Patriarch of Florence, patron of the

arts, 100 f., 150

Melbourne, Elizabeth, Lady, mother of Prime Minister, Lord
Melbourne (1779-1848), and mother-in-law of Caroline Lamb
(q.v.), 112

Memling, Hans (1440-1494), Flemish religious painter, 53

Mendelssohn-Bartholdy, Felix (1809-1847), German composer and
eminent pianist and organist, 141

Mertens, Sibylle (1797-1857), friend of Ottilie von Goethe (q.v), 140

Meyer, Johann Heinrich (1760-1832), art expert, friend and adviser
to Goethe (q.v.), 9

Michelangelo (Buonarotti), (1475-1564), most brilliant representative of the Italian Renaissance, sculptor, painter, poet, architect,
military engineer, 221

Milton, John (1608-1674), English epic and lyric poet, champion of
the Puritan cause, 32

Montaigne, Michel Eyquem de (1533-1592), French philosopher and
essayist, 190

Moritz, Karl Philipp (1756-1793), German writer and traveller,
precursor of the German Romantic movement, 208

Müller, Friedrich von (1774-1849), Chancellor, friend of Goethe, 142

Murray, John (1778-1843), English publisher of Byron (q.v.),
Crabbe, Mungo Park etc., 62

Murray, Sir John (b.1909), publisher, 188

Napoleon (Bonaparte) (1769-1821), general and subsequently
emperor of France, 75

Naylor, Samuel (b.1808), English man of letters, visitor to Goethe,
141

Niebuhr, Barthold Georg (1776-1831), German historian and diplomat, 183

Origo, Marchesa Iris (b.1902), Anglo-Italian biographer, 184

Osann, Friedrich Gotthilf, philologist, friend of Schopenhauer's
youth, 101

Overbeck, Johann Friedrich (1789-1869), German painter, member
of the Nazarene movement, 182, 194

Palladio, Andrea (1518-1580), Italian architect who modelled his style on ancient Rome, breaking away from early Renaissance architecture, 12, 25, 80

Pascal, Blaise (1623-1662), French mathematician, philosopher and theologian, 64

Pater, Walter (1839-1894), English scholar and critic, 68

Perugino (Pietro Vannucci), (c. 1450-1523), Italian painter, a bridge between the Early and High Renaissance, 82

Platen, August von, Count (1796-1835), German poet who strove for classical purity of style, 80, 171, 191, 220-224, 227, 232

Pope, Alexander (1688-1744), English poet and satirist, 32

Pratt, Sir Roger (1620-1684), English amateur architect, 12

Raeburn, Sir Henry (1756-1823), Scottish portrait-painter, 24

Raphael (Raffaello Santi) (1483-1520), venerated Italian painter whose genius is as apparent in large wall-paintings as in portraits and cartoons for tapestries, 82, 173, 221

Reinhart, Oskar (1885-1965), Swiss industrialist and art collector, 220

Rembrandt (Rembrandt Harmensz van Rijn) (1606-1669), greatest of Dutch painters, whose work was founded on the direct study of nature, both in his portraits and in his landscapes, 53, 55 f., 124, 134, 146-150, 198

Reynolds, Sir Joshua (1723-1792), leader of the English school of portrait-painting, first president of the Royal Academy, 55

Robinson, Henry Crabb (1775-1867), English diarist and lawyer who had close ties with the German literary world, 33, 42, 44, 56, 60, 62, 78 f., 84, 90 f., 124 f., 132, 139, 142, 191

Rossum, Frans van (b.1940), Dutch musicologist, 67

Rossum, Willem van (1854-1932), Dutch Curia cardinal, 29

Rubens, Peter Paul (1577-1648), Flemish painter and diplomat, celebrated as a landscape-painter and religious artist, but above all for his portraits, 39, 53, 56, 150, 198

Rumohr, Carl Friedrich, Freiherr von (1785-1843), German art expert and gastronome, 39, 63, 68, 91-93, 95 f., 98, 167, 187, 191, 201, 214, 220, 222 f., 227

Ruskin, John (1819-1900), English art critic and author, supporter of the pre-Raphaelite movement, 68, 193

Sacrati, Marchesa Orinzia, Roman society hostess in the early 19th century, 184

Schlegel, August Wilhelm (1767-1845), German poet and critic, famous for his translations of Shakespeare, 190

Schlegel, Friedrich (1772-1829), brother of above, major critic produced by the German Romantic movement, 190, 206

Schmeller, Johann Joseph (1794-1841), German draughtsman employed by Goethe, 17

Schopenhauer, Adèle (1797-1849), sister of Arthur S. (q.v.), friend of Ottilie von Goethe (q.v.), 140

Schopenhauer, Arthur (1788-1860), German pessimist philosopher, 5, 8, 10, 97, 101 f., 104, 190, 198, 201, 207, 225-227

Schultz, Christoph Ludwig Friedrich (1781-1834), Prussian Councillor, friend of Goethe, 1-4, 8, 38, 63, 142

Schulz, Heinrich Wilhelm, 19th-century German art historian, biographer of Rumohr (q.v.), 63

Shakespeare, William (1564-1616), England's greatest poet and dramatist, 32-34, 45, 127, 191, 205, 232

Shelley, Percy Bysshe (1792-1822), English lyric and dramatic poet, atheist and anarchist, 88 f., 191

Sichirollo, Livio (b.1929), Italian professor of philosophy in Milan and Urbino, 171, 190

Simmen, Christian (1790-1832), Splügen farmer, 159

Smithson, Harriet (1800-1854), Irish Shakespearian actress, married Berlioz in 1833, 204 f.

Somerville, Mary (1780-1872), Scottish mathematician and scientific writer, 25

Sophocles (c. 496-406 BC), Greek tragic dramatist, 31, 40

Staël, Mme Anne Louise de (1766-1817), French political writer, centre of a brilliant salon in Paris, 8

Stirling, Charles James (1804-1880), Anglo-Irish student, lover of Ottilie von Goethe (q.v.), 141

Tiepolo, Giambattista (1696-1770), last of the great Venetian painters, 27, 147, 151-154, 200

Tiepolo, Giandomenico, artist, brother of the above, 27

Tintoretto, Domenico (1562-1637), painter, son of the following, 59

Tintoretto (Jacopo Robusti) (1518-1594), greatest of the late Venetian painters, 27, 39, 41, 43, 132, 195

Titian (Tiziano Vercelli) (1477-1576), Venetian painter celebrated for his dramatic composition and use of brilliant colour, 26, 148, 151

Trelawny, Edward John (1792-1881), English author and adventurer, friend of Shelley and Byron, 88 f.

Turner, Joseph Mallord William (1775-1851), English landscape-painter and watercolourist, who foreshadowed Impressionism, 23, 26, 55, 62, 68, 125 f., 178, 191, 217-219

Vacher, Charles, friend of Lamartine, 189

Vasari, Giorgio (1511-1574), Italian art historian and architect, 27, 80, 82, 100, 135 f., 168, 190

Verdi, Giuseppe (1813-1901), Italian operatic composer, 9

Vermeer, Jan (1632-1675), Dutch painter, notable for his translucent interiors, 53, 124, 206

Watteau, Jean Antoine (1684-1721), French painter, pioneer in the study of nature and use of colour, 74

Westmorland, John Fane, Earl of (formerly Lord Burghersh) (1784-1859), English diplomat, dilettante in the arts, 23, 98, 100

Winckelmann, Johann Joachim (1717-1768), German archaeologist, 190, 196 f.

Witz, Konrad (c. 1400-c. 1445), major pre-Renaissance German painter, 154, 179

Wordsworth, Dorothy (1771-1855), sister of William W. (q.v.), 26

Wordsworth, William (1770-1850), English poet of nature and metaphysical experience, poet laureate from 1843, 5, 17, 26, 45